P9-DNY-418

THE
WIVES

THE WIVES

TARRYN FISHER

GRAYDON
HOUSE

If you purchased this book without a cover you should be aware
that this book is stolen property. It was reported as "unsold and
destroyed" to the publisher, and neither the author nor the
publisher has received any payment for this "stripped book."

**GRAYDON
HOUSE**

Recycling programs
for this product may
not exist in your area.

ISBN-13: 978-1-525-80978-1
ISBN-13: 978-1-525-80512-7 (Library Exclusive Edition)

The Wives

Copyright © 2019 by Tarryn Fisher

All rights reserved. Except for use in any review, the reproduction or utilization of this
work in whole or in part in any form by any electronic, mechanical or other means,
now known or hereafter invented, including xerography, photocopying and recording,
or in any information storage or retrieval system, is forbidden without the written
permission of the publisher, Graydon House Books, 22 Adelaide St. West, 40th Floor,
Toronto, Ontario M5H 4E3, Canada.

This is a work of fiction. Names, characters, places and incidents are either the
product of the author's imagination or are used fictitiously, and any resemblance to
actual persons, living or dead, business establishments, events or locales is entirely
coincidental.

® and TM are trademarks of Harlequin Enterprises Limited or its corporate affiliates.
Trademarks indicated with ® are registered in the United States Patent and Trademark
Office, the Canadian Intellectual Property Office and in other countries.

GraydonHouseBooks.com
BookClubbish.com

Printed in U.S.A.

For Colleen

THE
WIVES

ONE

He comes over on Thursday every week. That's my day, I'm Thursday. It's a hopeful day, lost in the middle of the more important days; not the beginning or the end, but a stop. An appetizer to the weekend. Sometimes I wonder about the other days and if they wonder about me. That's how women are, right? Always wondering about each other—curiosity and spite curdling together in little emotional puddles. Little good that does; if you wonder too hard, you'll get everything wrong.

I set the table for two. I'm a little buzzed as I lay out the silverware, pausing to consider the etiquette of what goes where. I run my tongue along my teeth and shake my head. I'm being silly; it's just me and Seth tonight—an at-home date. Not that there's anything else—we don't do regular dates very often at the risk of being seen. Imagine that... not wanting to be seen with your husband. Or your husband not wanting to be seen with you. The vodka I sipped earlier has warmed me, made my limbs loose and careless. I almost knock over the vase of flowers as I place a fork next to a plate: a bouquet of the palest pink roses. I chose them for their sexual innuendo because when you're in a position like mine, being on top of your sexual game is of the utmost importance. *Look at these delicate, pink petals. Do they make you think of my clit? Good!*

To the right of the vaginal flowers sit two white candles in silver candlestick holders. My mother once told me that under the flickering light of a candle flame, a woman can almost look ten years younger. My mother cared about those things. Every six weeks a doctor slid a needle into her forehead, pumping thirty cc's of Botox into her dermis. She had a subscription to every glossy fashion magazine you could name and collected books on how to keep your husband. No one tries that hard to keep their husband unless they've already lost him. I used to think her shallow, back when my ideals were untainted by reality. I had big plans to be anything but my mother: to be loved, to be successful, to make beautiful children. But the truth is that the heart's desire is a mere current against the tide of nurture and nature. You can spend your whole life swimming against it and eventually you'll get tired and the current of genes and upbringing will pull you under. I became a lot like her and a little bit like me.

I roll the wheel of the lighter with my thumb and hold the flame above the wick. The lighter is a Zippo, the worn remnants of a Union Jack flag on the casing. The flickering tongue reminds me of my brief stint with smoking. To look cool, mostly—I never inhaled, but I lived to see that glowing cherry at my fingertips. My parents bought the candleholders for me as a housewarming gift after I saw them in a Tiffany's catalog. I found them to be predictably classy. When you're newly married, you see a pair of candlestick holders and imagine a lifetime of roast dinners that will go along with them. Dinners much like the one we're having tonight. My life is almost perfect.

I glance out the bay window as I fold the napkins, the view of the park spread out beneath me. It's gray outside, typical of Seattle. The view of the park is why I chose this particular unit instead of the much larger, nicer unit overlooking Elliott Bay. While most people would have chosen the view of the water, I prefer a view of people's lives. A silver-haired couple sits on a bench, staring out at the pathway where cyclists and joggers pass every few minutes. They're not touching, though their heads move in unison whenever someone goes by. I wonder if that will be Seth and me one day, and then my cheeks warm as I think of the others. Imagining what the future holds proves difficult when factoring in two other women who share your husband.

I set out the bottle of pinot grigio that I chose from the market earlier today. The label is boring, not something that catches the eye, but the austere-looking man who sold it to me had described its taste in great detail, rubbing his fingers together as he spoke. I can't recall what he'd said, even though it was only a few hours ago. I'd been distracted, focused on the task of collecting ingredients. Cooking, my mother taught me, is the only good way to be a wife.

Standing back, I examine my work. Overall, it's an impressive table, but I am queen of presentation, after all. Everything is just right, the way he likes it, and thus, the way I like it. It's not that I don't have a personality; it's just that everything I am is reserved for him. As it should be.

At six o'clock sharp, I hear the key turn in the lock and then the whistle of the door opening. I hear the click as it closes, and his keys hitting the table in the entryway. Seth is never late, and when you live a life as complicated as his, order is important. I smooth down the hair I so painstakingly curled and step from the kitchen into the hallway to greet him. He's looking down at the mail in his hand, raindrops clinging to the tips of his hair.

"You got the mail! Thank you." I'm embarrassed by the enthusiasm in my voice. It's just the mail, for God's sake.

He sets the pile down on the little marble table in the entryway, next to his keys, and smiles. There is a tilt in my belly, heat and a flurry of excitement. I step into the breadth of him, inhaling his scent, and burying my face in his neck. It's a nice neck, tan and wide. It holds up a very good head of hair and a face that is traditionally handsome with the tiniest bit of roguish scruff. I nestle into him. Five days is a long time to go without the man you love. In my youth, I considered love a burden. How could you get anything done when you had to consider someone else every second of the day? When I met Seth, that all went out the window. I became my mother: doting, yielding, spread-eagle emotionally and sexually. It both thrilled and revolted me.

"I missed you," I tell him.

I kiss the underside of his chin, then the tender spot beneath his ear, and then stand on my tiptoes to reach his mouth. I am thirsty for his attention and my kiss is aggressive and deep. He moans from the back of his throat, and his briefcase drops to the floor with a thud. He wraps his arms around me.

"That was a nice hello," he says. Two of his fingers play the knobs of my spine like a saxophone. He massages them gently until I squirm closer.

"I'd give you a better one, but dinner is ready."

His eyes become smoky, and I silently thrill. I turned him on in under two minutes. I want to say, *Beat that*, but to whom? Something uncoils in my stomach, a ribbon unrolling, unrolling. I try to catch it before it goes too far. Why do I always have to think of them? The key to making this work is *not* thinking of them.

"What did you make?" He unravels the scarf from his neck and loops it around mine, pulling me close and kissing me once more. His voice is warm against my cold trance, and I push my feelings aside, determined not to ruin our night together.

"Smells good."

I smile and sashay into the dining room—a little hip to go with his dinner. I pause in the doorway to note his reaction to the table.

"You make everything beautiful." He reaches for me, his strong, tanned hands tracked with veins, but I dance away, teasing. Behind him, the window is rinsed with rain. I glance over his shoulder—the couple on the bench are gone. What did they go home to? Chinese takeout…canned soup…?

I move on to the kitchen, making sure Seth's eyes are on me. Experience has taught me that you can drag a man's eyes if you move the right way.

"A rack of lamb," I call over my shoulder. "Couscous…"

He plucks the bottle of wine from the table, holding it by the neck and tilting it down to study the label. "This is a good wine." Seth is not supposed to drink wine; he doesn't with the others. Religious reasons. He makes an exception for me and I chalk it up to another one of my small victories. I have lured him into deep red, merlots and crisp chardonnays. We've kissed, and laughed, and fucked drunk. Only with me; he hasn't done that with them.

Silly, I know. I chose this life and it's not about competing, it's about providing, but one can't help but keep a tally when other women are involved.

When I return from the kitchen with dinner clutched between two dishtowels, he has poured the wine and is staring out the window while he sips. Beneath the twelfth-floor window, the city hums her nightly rhythm. A busy street cuts a path in front of the park. To the right of the park and just out of view is the Sound, dotted with sail-boats and ferries in the summer, and masked with fog in the winter. From our bedroom window, you can see it—a wide expanse of standing and falling water. The perfect Seattle view.

"I don't care about dinner," he says. "I want you now." His voice is commanding; Seth leaves little room for questions. It's a trait that has served him well in all areas of his life.

I set the platters on the table, my appetite for one thing gone and replaced by another. I watch as he blows out the candles, never taking his eyes from me, and then I walk to the bedroom, reaching around and unzipping my dress as I go. I do it slowly so he can watch, peeling off the layer of silk. I feel him behind me: the large presence, the warmth, the anticipation of what's to come. My perfect dinner cools on the table, the fat of the lamb congealing around the edges of the serving dish in oranges and creams as I slip out of the dress and bend at the waist, letting my hands sink into the bed. I'm wrist-deep in the down comforter when his fingers graze my hips and hook in the elastic waist of my panties. He pulls them down, and when they flutter around my ankles, I kick free of them.

The *tink* of metal and then the *zzzweeep* of his belt. He doesn't undress—there's just the muted sound of his pants falling to his ankles.

After, I warm our dinner in the microwave, wrapped in my robe. There is a throbbing between my legs, a trickle of semen on my thigh; I am sore in the best possible way. I carry his plate to where he is lying shirtless on the couch, one arm thrown over his head—an image of exhaustion. I cannot remove the grin from my lips, though I try. It's a break in my usual facade, this grinning like a schoolgirl.

"You're beautiful," he says when he sees me. His voice is gruff like it always is postsex. "You felt so good." He reaches up to rub my thigh as he takes his plate. "Do you remember that vacation we talked about taking? Where do you want to go?" This is the essence of postcoital conversation with Seth: he likes to talk about the future after he comes.

Do I remember? Of course I remember. I rearrange my face so that it looks surprised.

He's been promising a vacation for a year. Just the two of us.

My heart beats faster. I've been waiting for this. I didn't want to push it since he's been so busy, but here it is—my year. I've imagined all the places we can go. I've narrowed it down to a beach. White sands and lapis lazuli water, long walks along the water's edge holding hands in public. *In public.*

"I was thinking somewhere warm," I say. I don't make eye contact—I don't want him to see how eager I am to have him to myself. I am needy, and jealous, and petty. I let my robe fall open as I bend to set his wine on the coffee table. He reaches inside and cups my breast like I knew he would. He is predictable in some ways.

"Turks and Caicos?" he suggests. "Trinidad?"

Yes and yes!

Lowering myself into the armchair that faces the sofa, I cross my legs so that my robe slips open and reveals my thigh.

"You choose," I say. "You've been more places than I have." I know he likes that, to make the decisions. And what do I care where we go? So long as I get him for a week, uninterrupted, unshared. For that week, he will be only mine. A fantasy. Now comes the time I both dread and live for.

"Seth, tell me about your week."

He sets his plate down and rubs the tips of his fingers together. They are glistening from the grease of the meat. I want to go over and put his fingers in my mouth, suck them clean.

"Monday is sick, the baby..."

"Oh, no," I say. "She's still in her first trimester, so it will be that way for a few more weeks."

He nods, a small smile playing on his lips. "She's very excited, despite the sickness. I bought her one of those baby name books. She highlights the names she likes and then we look through them when I see her."

I feel a spike of jealousy and push it aside immediately.

This is the highlight of my week, hearing about the others. I don't want to ruin it with petty feelings.

"That's so exciting," I say. "Does she want a boy or a girl?"

He laughs as he walks over to the kitchen to set his plate in the sink. I hear the water running and then the lid of the trash can as he throws his paper towel away.

"She wants a boy. With dark hair, like mine. But I think whatever we have will have blond hair, like hers."

I picture Monday in my mind—long, pin-straight blond hair, a surfer's tan. She's lean and muscular with perfect white teeth. She laughs a lot—mostly at the things he says—and is youthfully in love. He told me once that she is twenty-five but looks like a college girl. Normally, I'd judge a man for that, the cliché way men want younger women, but it isn't true of him. Seth likes the connection.

"You'll let me know as soon as you know what you're having?"

"It's a ways off, but yes." He smiles, the corner of his mouth moving up. "We have a doctor's appointment next week. I'll have to head straight over on Monday morning." He winks at me and I am not skilled enough to hide my flush. My legs are crossed and my foot bounces up and down as warmth fills my belly. He has the same effect on me now as he had on the first day we met.

"Can I make you a drink?" I ask, standing up.

I walk over to the bar and hit Play on the stereo. Of course he wants a drink, he always wants a drink on the evenings when we're together. He told me that he secretly keeps a bottle of scotch at the office now, and I mentally gloat at my bad influence. Tom Waits begins to sing and I reach for the decanter of vodka.

I used to ask about Tuesday, but Seth is more hesitant to talk about her. I've always chalked it up to her being in a position of authority as first wife. The first wife, the first woman he loved. It's daunting in a way to know I'm only his second choice. I've consoled myself with that fact that I am Seth's legal wife, that even though they're still together, he had to divorce her to marry me. I don't like Tuesday. She's selfish; her career takes the most dominant role in her life—the space I reserve for Seth. And while I disapprove, I can't entirely blame her, either. He's gone five days of the week. We have one rotating day that we take turns with, but it's our job to fill the week with things that aren't him: stupid things for me—pottery making, romance novels and Netflix; but for Tuesday, it's her career. I root around in the pocket of my robe, searching for my ChapStick. We have entire lives outside of our marriage. It's the only way to stay sane.

Pizza for dinner again? I used to ask. He'd admitted to me once that Tuesday was a takeout-ordering girl rather than a cooking girl.

Always so judgmental about other people's cooking skills, he'd tease.

I set up two glasses and fill them with ice. I can hear Seth moving behind me, getting up from the couch. The soda bottle hisses as I twist off the cap and top off the glasses. Before I'm finished making our drinks, he's behind me, kissing my neck. I dip my head to the side to give him better access. He takes his drink from me and walks over to the window while I sit.

I look over from my spot on the couch, my glass sweaty against my palm.

Seth lowers himself next to me on the couch, setting

18

his drink on the coffee table. He reaches to rub my neck while he laughs.

His eyes are dancing, flirtatious. I fell in love with those eyes and the way they always seemed to be laughing. I lift one corner of my mouth in a smile and lean back into him, enjoying the solid feel of his body against my back. His fingers trail up and down my arm.

What's left to discuss? I want to make sure I'm familiar with all areas of his life. "The business...?"

"Alex..." He pauses. I watch as he runs the pad of his thumb across his bottom lip, a habit I'm endeared to.

What has he done now?

"I caught him in another lie," he says.

Alex is Seth's business partner; they started the company together. For as long as I can remember, Alex has been the face of the business: meeting with clients and securing the jobs, while Seth is the one who manages the actual building of the homes, dealing with things like the contractors and inspections. Seth has told me that the very first time they butted heads was over the name of the company: Alex wanted his last name to be incorporated into the name of the business, while Seth wanted it to include the Pacific Northwest. They'd fought it out and settled on Emerald City Development. Over the last years their attention to detail and sheer beauty of the homes they build has secured them several high-profile clients. I have never met Alex; he doesn't know I exist. He thinks Seth's wife is Tuesday. When Seth and Tuesday were first married, they'd go on vacations with Alex and his wife—once to Hawaii and another time on a ski holiday to Banff. I've seen Alex in photos. He's an inch shorter than his wife, Barbara, who is a former Miss Utah. Squat and balding, he has a close-lipped smugness about him.

There are so many people I haven't met. Seth's parents, for example, and his childhood friends. As second wife, I may never have the chance.

"Oh?" I say. "What's up?"

My existence is exhausting, all of the games I play. This is a woman's curse. Be direct, but not too direct. Be strong, but not too strong. Ask questions, but not too many. I take a sip of my drink and sit on the couch next to him.

"Do you enjoy this?" he asks. "It's sort of strange, you asking about—"

"I enjoy you." I smile. "Knowing your world, what you feel and experience when you aren't with me." It's true, isn't it? I love my husband, but I'm not the only one. There are others. My only power is my knowledge. I can thwart, one-up, fuck his brains out and feign an aloof detached interest, all with a few well-timed questions.

Seth sighs, rubbing his eyes with the heels of his hands.

"Let's go to bed," he says.

I study his face. For tonight, he's done talking about them. He holds out a hand to help me up and I take it, letting him pull me to my feet.

We make love this time, kissing deeply as I wrap my legs around him. I shouldn't wonder, but I do. How does a man love so many women? A different woman almost every other day. And where do I fall in the category of favor?

He falls asleep quickly, but I do not. Thursday is the day I don't sleep.

TWO

On Friday morning, Seth leaves before I wake up. I tossed and turned until four and then must have fallen into a deep sleep, because I didn't hear him when he left. Sometimes I feel like a girl who wakes up alone in bed after a one-night stand, him sneaking out before she can ask his name. I always lie in bed longer on Fridays and stare at the dent in his pillow until the sun shines right through the window and into my eyes. But the sun has yet to curl her fingers over the horizon, and I stare at that dent like it's giving me life.

Mornings are hard. In a normal marriage, you wake up beside a person, validate your life with their sleep-soaked body. There are routines and schedules, and they get boring, but they are a comfort, as well. I do not have the comfort of normalcy: a snoring husband whom I kick during the night, or toothpaste glued to the sink that I scrub away in frustration. Seth can't be felt in the fibers of this home, and most days that makes my heart heavy. He's barely here and then he's gone, off to another woman's bed while mine grows cold.

I glance at my phone, apprehension making curlicues in my belly. I don't like to text him. I imagine he is flooded with texts every day from the others, but this morning I have the urge to reach for my phone and text him: I miss you. He knows, surely he knows. When you don't see your husband for five days out of the week he must know that you miss him. But I don't reach for my phone, and I don't text him. Resolutely, I throw my legs over the side of the bed and slide my feet into my slippers instead, my toes curling into the soft fleece inside. The slippers are part of my routine, my reach for normalcy. I walk to the kitchen, glancing out of the window at the city below. There is a snake of red brake lights down 99 as commuters wait their turn at the light. Wipers swish back and forth, clearing windshields of the mist-like rain. I wonder if Seth is among them, but no, he takes 5 away from here. Away from me.

I open the fridge and pull out a glass bottle of Coke, setting it on the counter. I dig around the silverware drawer for the bottle opener, cursing when a toothpick slides underneath my fingernail. I stick the finger in my mouth as I loosen the cap off the bottle with my free hand. I only keep one bottle of Coke in the fridge, and I hide the rest underneath the sink behind the watering can. Each time I drink the bottle, I replace it. That way, it looks like the same bottle of Coke has been sitting there forever. There is no one to fool but myself. And perhaps I don't want Seth to know that I drink Coke for breakfast. He would tease me and I don't mind his teasing, but soda for breakfast is not something you want people to know. When I was a little girl, I was the only one of my friends who liked to play with Barbie. At ten, they'd already moved on to makeup kits and MTV, asking their parents for clothes for Christmas instead of the new Barbie camper van. I was terribly ashamed of my love of Barbie dolls—especially after they made such a big deal out of it, calling me a baby. In one of the saddest moments of my young life, I packed away my Barbie dolls, retiring them to a box in my closet. I cried myself to sleep that night, not wanting to part with something I loved so much but knowing the teasing I'd take for it if I didn't. When my mother found the box a few weeks later while packing laundry away, she'd questioned me about it. I tearfully told her the truth. I was too old for Barbie and it was time to move on.

You can play with them in secret. No one has to know. You don't have to give up something you love just because other people disapprove, she said.

Secrets: I'm good at having them *and* keeping them.

I see that he made himself toast before he left. The remnants of bread crumbs litter the counter, and a knife lies in the sink, slick with butter. I chastise myself for not getting up early to make him something. *Next week*, I tell myself. Next week I'll be better, I'll feed my husband breakfast. I'll be one of those wives who delivers sex and sustenance three times a day. Anxiety grips my stomach and I wonder if Monday and Tuesday get up to make him breakfast. Have I been slacking all this time? Does he think of me as neglectful because I stayed in bed? I clean up the crumbs, swiping them into my hand and then angrily shaking them into the sink, and then I carry my Coke to the living room. The bottle is cold in my palm and I sip, thinking of all the ways I could be better.

When I wake up, some time has gone by, the light has changed. I sit up and see the bottle of Coke turned on its side, a brown stain seeping into the carpet around it.

"Shit," I say aloud, standing up. I must have dozed off holding the bottle. That's what I get for lying awake all night, staring at the ceiling. I rush to grab a rag and stain solution to clean the carpet and drop to my knees, scrubbing furiously. The Coke has dried into the knotted beige rug, a sticky caramel. I am angry about something, I realize as tears roll down my face. The drips join the stain on the carpet and I scrub harder. When the carpet is clean, I fall back on my haunches and close my eyes. What has happened to me? How have I become this docile person, living for Thursdays and the love of a man who divides himself so thinly among three women? If you'd told nineteen-year-old me that this would be my life, she'd have laughed in your face.

The day he found me was five years ago, next week. I was studying in a coffee shop, my final nursing exam looming ahead of me, a wall I didn't feel ready to climb. I'd not slept in two days, and I was at the point where I was drinking coffee like it was water just to stay awake. Half-delirious, I swayed in my armchair as Seth sat down next to me. I remember being irritated by his presence. There were five open armchairs to choose from; why take the one right next to me? He was handsome: glossy black hair and turquoise eyes, well-slept, well-groomed and well-spoken. He'd asked if I was studying to be a nurse and I'd snapped my answer, only to apologize a moment later for my rudeness. He'd waved away my apology and asked if he could quiz me.

A laugh burst from between my lips until I realized he was serious. "You want to spend your Friday night quizzing a half-dead nursing student?" I'd asked him.

"Sure," he'd said, eyes glowing with humor. "I figure if I get in your good graces, you won't say no when I ask you to have dinner with me."

I remember frowning at him, wondering if it was a joke. Like his buddies had sent him over to humiliate the sad girl in the corner. He was too handsome. His type never bothered with girls like me. While I certainly wasn't ugly, I was on the plain side. My mother always said I got the brains and my sister, Torrence, got the beauty.

"Are you being serious?" I'd asked. I suddenly felt self-conscious about my limp ponytail and lack of mascara.

"Only if you like Mexican," he'd said. "I can't fall for a girl who doesn't like Mexican."

"I don't like Mexican," I told him, and he'd grabbed at his heart like he was in pain. I'd laughed at the sight of him—a too-handsome man pretending to have a heart attack in a coffee shop.

"Just kidding. What sort of messed-up human doesn't like Mexican?"

Against my better judgment and despite my insanely busy schedule, I'd agreed to meet him for dinner the following week. A girl had to eat, after all. When I pulled up to the restaurant in my beat-up little Ford, I'd half expected him not to be there. But as soon as I stepped out of the car, I spotted him waiting by the entrance, just out of reach of the rain, droplets spotting the shoulders of his trench coat.

He'd been charming through the first course, asking me questions about school, my family and what I planned to do after. I'd dipped chips in salsa, trying to remember the last time a person had taken this much interest in me. Wholly taken with him, I'd answered every single one of his questions with enthusiasm, and by the time dinner was finished, I realized I knew nothing about him.

"We'll save that for dinner next week," he'd said when I brought it up.

"How do you know there will be a next week?" I asked him.

He just smiled at me, and I knew right then that I was in trouble.

I shower and dress for the day, only pausing to check my phone as I'm on my way out the door. Since Seth is gone for five days of the week, I volunteer to take the late shifts that no one else wants. It's unbearable to be sitting home all night alone, thinking about him being with the others. I prefer to keep my mind busy at all times, keep my focus. Fridays, I go to the gym and then the market. Sometimes I grab lunch with a girlfriend, but lately everyone seems to be too busy to meet up. Most of my friends are either newly married or newly mothered, our lives all having forked off into jobs and families.

My phone says that Seth has texted me. Miss you already. Can't wait for next week.

I smile stiffly as I hit the button for the elevator. It's so easy for him to express the missing when he always has someone by his side. I shouldn't think like that. I know he loves each of us, misses each of us when he's away.

Should we have pizza for dinner when I see you next? My attempt at a joke.

He texts back immediately, sending the laugh/cry emoji. What did people do before emojis? It seems like the only reasonable way to lighten a loaded sentence.

I tuck my phone back into my purse as I step into the elevator, a small smile on my lips. Even on my hardest days, a little text from Seth makes everything all right. And there are plenty of hard days, days where I feel inadequate or insecure about my role in his life.

I love you all differently but equally.

I wanted to know what that meant, the specifics. Was it sexual? Emotional? And if he had to choose, if he had a gun to his head, would he pick me?

When Seth first told me about his wife, we were at an Italian restaurant called La Spiga on Capitol Hill. It was our fourth date. The awkwardness of two people getting to know each other had rolled away, and a more comfortable phase had taken its place. We were holding hands by then…kissing. He'd said he had something to talk to me about and I'd planned for perhaps a conversation about where our relationship was going. As soon as the word *wife* was out of his mouth, I'd set my fork down, wiped any pasta sauce from my lips, picked up my purse and left. He'd chased me down the street just as I was hailing a taxi, and then our server had chased him down, demanding to be paid for our partially eaten meal. We'd all stood on the sidewalk awkwardly until Seth pleaded with me to come back inside. I'd done so hesitantly, but part of me wanted to hear what he had to say. And how *was* there anything to say? How could a man justify something like that?

"I know how it sounds, trust me." He'd taken an extra-long swig of wine before continuing. "It's not about sex. I don't have an addiction, if that's what you're thinking."

It was exactly what I was thinking actually. I'd folded my arms across my chest and waited. Out of the corner of my eye, I saw our server lingering nearby. I wondered if he was waiting for us to make another run out of the restaurant and abandon the check.

"My father..." he started. I rolled my eyes. Half the known world could start an excuse with "my father." Nevertheless, I waited for him to continue. I was a woman of my word.

The words glided over me: "My parents...polygamists... four mothers."

I stared at him in shock. At first I thought he was lying, making a bad joke, but I'd seen something in his eyes. He'd given me a tender spot of information and he was waiting to be judged. I didn't know what to say. What response was appropriate? You saw that sort of thing on television, but in real life...?

"I grew up in Utah," he continued. "I left as soon as I turned eighteen. I swore I was against everything they believed in."

"I don't understand," I said. And I didn't. I was tense, my hands clenched under the table, nails digging into my palms.

He'd run a hand across his face, suddenly looking ten years older.

"My wife doesn't want children," he told me. "I'm not that guy, the one who pressures a woman to be something she's not."

I'd seen him with a different set of eyes then—a dad with one kid on his shoulders and another at his feet. Ice cream sundaes and T-ball games. He had the same dreams that I did, that most of us did.

"So, where do I come in? You're looking for a breeder and I fit your type?" I was being antagonistic, but it was an easy stab. Why had he chosen me, and who said I even wanted children?

He looked stung by my accusation, but I didn't feel bad about saying it. Men like him made me sick. But I had come back to the table to hear him out, and I would. At the time, it was the most absurd thing I'd ever heard. He had a wife, but wanted a new one. To start a family. Who the hell did he think he was? It was sick and I told him so.

"I understand," he'd said, downtrodden. "I completely understand." After that, he paid the bill and we went our separate ways, me giving him a chilly goodbye. He told me later that he'd never expected to hear from me again, but I'd gone home and tossed and turned in bed all night, unable to sleep.

But I liked him. I really, really liked him. There was something about him—a charisma, maybe, or a perceptiveness. Either way, he never made me feel less when I was with him. Not like the boys I'd dated in college, who looked at their own reflection in your eyes, and considered you a "right now" relationship. When I was with Seth, I felt like the only one. I'd shoved all of those feelings aside to grieve the end of what I had thought was the promising start of a new relationship. I'd even gone on a few dates, one with a fireman from Bellevue and another with a small-business owner in Seattle. Both dates ended miserably for me, as I only compared the men to Seth. And then, about a month later, after grieving more deeply than

I should for a man I barely knew, I worked up the nerve to call him.

"I miss you," I said as soon as he picked up. "I don't want to miss you but I do."

And then I'd asked if his wife knew if he was looking for someone new to have his babies. There was a long pause on Seth's end, longer than I would have liked. I was about to tell him to forget I even asked when he replied with a breathy, "Yes."

"Wait," I said, pressing the phone closer to my ear. "Did you say yes?"

"We agreed on this together," he said with more confidence. "That I needed to be with someone who wanted the same things as I do."

"You told her?" I asked again.

"After our first date, I thought we had something and I told her that. I knew it was a risk, but we had something. A connection."

"And she was just okay with it?"

"No… Yes. I mean, it's hard. She said it was time to look at our options. That she loved me but understood."

I was quiet on my end of the phone, digesting everything he was saying.

"Can I see you?" he'd asked. "Just for a drink or a coffee. Something simple."

I wanted to say no, to be the type of strong, resolved woman who didn't budge. But instead, I found myself making plans to meet him at a local coffee shop the following week. When I hung up, I had to remind myself that I'd been the one to call him and he hadn't manipulated me into anything. *You're in control*, I told myself. *You'll be his legal wife.* I was so, so wrong.

THREE

I arrive home Saturday morning after my shift and immediately fall into bed. It had been a long night, the kind that stretches you into mental and emotional exhaustion. There was a ten-car pileup on 5 that brought a dozen people into the emergency room, and then a domestic disturbance sent a husband into the ER with three gunshot wounds in his abdomen. His wife had run in ten minutes later with a toddler on her hip, blood soaking through her yellow shirt. She was screaming that it was all a mistake. Every night in the ER was a horror movie: open wounds, crying, pain. By the end of the night, the floors were sticky with blood, slicked over with vomit. I wear black scrubs so the mess doesn't show.

I'm just dozing off when I hear the front door open and

close, followed by the sound of a train whistle. The whistle part of our security system notifies me every time the front door opens. I bolt upright in bed, my eyes wide. Did I dream that or did it just happen? Seth is in Portland; he texted me last night and never mentioned coming home. I wait, completely still, ears pricked—ready to shoot out of bed and—

My head swivels left and right as I look for a weapon, my heart pounding. The gun my father gave me for my twenty-first birthday is stashed somewhere in my closet. I try to recall where but I'm trembling from fear. Another weapon, then… My bedroom is a collection of soft, feminine things; there are no weapons on hand. I throw off blankets, struggling to my feet. I'm a stupid, defenseless girl who has a gun and doesn't know where it is or how to use it. Did I forget to lock the door? I'd been half-asleep when I got home, stumbling around, kicking off shoes… And then I hear my mother's voice from the foyer, calling my name. My panic recedes, but my heart is still pounding. I hold a hand over it, closing my eyes. A jingle—when my mother moves, she jingles. I relax, my shoulders slumping into a normal, relaxed position. That's right. She was coming over today to have lunch. How had I forgotten? *You're tired, you need to sleep*, I tell myself. I straighten my hair in the dresser mirror and scrub the sleep from my eyes before stepping out of the bedroom and into the hall. I arrange my face into something cheerful.

"Mom, hi," I say, stepping forward to give her a quick hug. "I just got home. Sorry, I haven't had time to shower."

My mother steps out of my embrace to look me over; her perfectly coiffed hair catches the light from the window and I see she has fresh highlights.

"You look fantastic," I say. It's what I'm supposed to say, but she really does.

"You look tired," she tsks. "Why don't you shower and I'll make lunch for us here instead of going out." Just like that, I'm dismissed in my own home. It's uncanny how she can still make me feel like a teenager.

I nod, feeling a rush of gratitude, despite her tone. After the night I had, the thought of getting dressed to go out is unbearable.

I take a quick shower, and when I come out wrapped in my robe, my mother has whipped up chicken salad on a croissant. A tall mimosa sits next to my plate. I slide into my chair, grateful. My freshly stocked fridge hadn't disappointed her. I learned to cook by watching her, and if there was one thing she emphasized, it was to always keep your fridge stocked for that surprise meal you'll have to cook.

"How's Seth?" is her first question as she takes her seat across from me. My mother: always to the point, always on time, always organized. She is the perfect homemaker and wife.

"He was tired on Thursday when he was here. We didn't have a chance to talk very much." The truth. I'm afraid my voice has betrayed more, but when I glance up at her face, she's preoccupied with her food.

"That poor man," she says, cutting into her croissant with determination. The undersides of her arms flap as she saws at the roll, her mouth pinched in disapproval. "All of that commuting back and forth. I know it was the right decision for both of you, but it's still very hard." The only reason she's saying it was the right decision is to not upset me. She'd told me in no uncertain terms that my duty was to be with Seth, and that I should give up my job to be wherever he was. She used to nag about marrying him, and now she's transitioned comfortably into the topic of a baby.

I nod. I have no desire to have this discussion with my mother. She always finds a way to make me feel like a failure at being Seth's wife. Mostly, it's about giving him a child. She's convinced he'll stop loving me if my uterus doesn't woman-up. I could silence her by telling her that he already has another wife, two actually, who fill the spaces where I fail. That one of them is growing his baby as we speak.

"You could always rent this place out and join him in Oregon," she offers. "It's not so bad. We lived there for a year when you were two, in Grandma's house. You've always loved that house so much." She says this like I don't know, as if I haven't heard the stories before.

"Can't," I tell her through a mouthful. "He has to be in the Seattle office two days a week. We'd have to have a place here, anyway. And besides, I don't want to leave. My life is here, my friends are here and I love my job." *True, true, not true.* I've never liked Portland; I thought of it as the poor man's Seattle: same scenery, similar weather, grubbier city. My grandparents lived and died there, never once leaving the state. Aside from their main house, they had a vacation home in the south, near California. The thought of Portland makes me feel claustrophobic.

My mother looks at me disapprovingly, a fleck of mayonnaise smeared across a pearly pink fingernail. She's old-school that way. In her mind, you went wherever your man went or he became susceptible to cheating. If only she knew.

"This was the agreement we made and it makes the most sense," I say firmly. And then I add, "For now," to appease her. And it is true. Seth is a builder. He recently opened up an office in Portland, and while his business partner, Alex, oversees the Seattle branch, Seth has to spend most of his week in the Portland office overseeing his projects there.

Monday and Tuesday are there, living in the city. *They* get to see the most of him and it makes me sick with jealousy. He often has lunch with one of them during the day, a luxury I don't have, since he spends most of Thursday traveling back to Seattle to see me. On Fridays, he spends the day in the Seattle office, and then sometimes meets me for dinner before heading back to Portland on Saturday. The rotating day the wives share is spent on travel for the time being, but with two of his wives living in Oregon, I've begun to think it will be permanent. It's hard being part of something so unusual and not having anyone to talk to about it. None of my friends know, though I've almost blurted the truth to my best friend, Anna, half a dozen times.

Sometimes I wish I could reach out to one of the wives, have a support group. But Seth is set on doing things differently than what he grew up around. We, the wives, have no contact with each other, and I've respected his wishes not to snoop. I don't even know their names.

"When will you try for a baby?" my mother asks.

Again. She asks this every time we're together and I'm quite sick of it. She doesn't know the truth and I haven't had the heart to tell her.

"If you had a baby, he'd be forced to be here more permanently," she says conspiratorially.

I stare at her, my mouth open. My sister and I were the sum of my mother's life. Our successes were her successes; our failures, her failures. I suppose it was fine and dandy to live for your children while you raised them, but what happened after? When they went off to live their own lives and you were left with nothing—no hobbies, no career, no identity.

"Mother, are you suggesting I trap Seth with a baby?" I ask, setting my fork down and staring at her in shock.

My mother is a bit of a live wire, known to make off-handed comments about other people's lives. But telling me to get pregnant to force my husband home is too far, even for her.

"Well, it's not like it's never been done before..." She's chuffing, her eyes darting around. She knows she's gone too far. I feel a wash of guilt. I never told my mother about the emergency hysterectomy. At the time I hadn't wanted to talk about it, and admitting it now would make me even more of a failure in her eyes.

"That's not who I am. That's not who we are as a couple. Besides, who would take over for Seth at the Portland office?" I snap. "You're talking about our finances and our future." Not just mine, either. Seth has a rather large family to support. I drop my face into my hands, and my mother stands up and comes around the table to comfort me.

"I'm sorry, little girl," she says, using her pet name for me. "I overstepped. You know what's right for your relationship."

I nod appreciatively and pick up a stray piece of chicken salad with my finger, licking it off my thumb. None of this is normal, and if Seth and I are going to make it work, I need to have a talk with him about my feelings. I've spent so much time pretending to be cool with everything that he has no clue about my struggles. That isn't fair to him or to me.

My mother leaves an hour later, promising to take me to lunch on Monday instead. "Rest up," she says, giving me a hug.

I close the door behind her and breathe a sigh of relief.

I'm desperately tired, but instead of heading to bed, I wander into Seth's little closet. Despite being gone for most of the week, he keeps a stash of clothes here. I run my hands over the suit jackets and dress pants, lifting a shirt to my nose to find his smell. I love him so much, and despite the awful uniqueness of our situation, I can't imagine being married to anyone else. And that's what love is about, isn't it? Working with what your partner came with. And mine came with two other women.

I'm about to turn off the little overhead light and leave when something catches my eye. Poking out of a dress pants' pocket is the corner of a piece of paper. I pull it out, at first worried the pants will be washed with the paper in the pocket and ruin the rest of the wash, but once I have it in my hands, I'm curious. It's folded into a neat square. I only hold it in my palm for a moment before opening it to have a look. A doctor's bill. I scan the words, wondering if something is wrong or if Seth went in for a checkup, but his name isn't anywhere on the paper. In fact, the bill is made out to a Hannah Ovark, her address listed in the top corner as 324 Galatia Lane, Portland, Oregon. Seth's doctor is in Seattle.

"Hannah," I say out loud. The receipt in my hand says she was in for a checkup and labs. Could Hannah be... Monday?

I turn off the closet light and carry the paper with me to the living room, unsure of what to do. Should I ask Seth about it, or pretend I never saw it? My MacBook is sitting next to me on the sofa. I shift it into my lap and open Facebook. I have a vague sense that I'm breaking some sort of rule.

I type her name into the search bar and tap my finger on my knee while I wait for the results. Three profiles come up: one is an older woman, perhaps in her forties, who lives in Atlanta; the other is a pink-haired girl who looks to be in her early teens. I click on the third profile. Seth told me that Monday was blond, but had never given any other details about her appearance. My vision of a chill-looking surfer girl is shattered as I stare at Hannah Ovark. She isn't a surfer, and she doesn't have the blond innocence I was hoping for. I shut my laptop rather abruptly and stalk off to the bathroom to find my sleeping pills. I desperately need sleep. I'm feeling loopy and it's starting to affect the way I see things.

A row of orange bottles stares out at me from the medicine cabinet. Little sentinels with purposes ranging from drowsy numbness to staying alert. I reach for the Ambien and lay a pill on my tongue. I drink water straight from the tap to wash it down and then I curl up on the bed and wait to sink into oblivion.

FOUR

I wake up disoriented and groggy. The sun sits high outside of the window, but hadn't it been early evening when I fell asleep? I reach for my alarm clock to check the time and see that I've been asleep for thirteen hours. I hop out of bed too quickly and the room spins around me.

"Shit, shit, shit." I grab on to the wall to steady myself and stay there until I feel sturdy on my feet. My phone sits facedown on the dresser, the battery almost depleted. I have seven missed calls from Seth, and three voice messages. I call him back without listening to the messages, a sense of dread growing with each ring.

"Are you all right?" is the first thing he says to me when he picks up. His voice is strained and I immediately feel guilty for making him worry.

"Yes, I'm fine," I tell him. "I took a sleeping pill and must have conked out for the night. I'm sorry, I feel like such a jerk."

"I was worried," he says, his voice sounding less tense than it did a moment ago. "I almost called the hospital to see when you left."

"I'm truly sorry," I say. "Is everything all right on that side?"

It's not. I can already tell by the sound of his voice. He couldn't possibly know that I'd found Hannah, could he? I wrap a strand of hair around and around my finger while I wait for him to speak.

"Just some trouble at work," he says. "Unreliable contractors. I can't talk about it right now. I just wanted to hear your voice."

I thrill that it's my voice he wanted to hear. Not the others'. Mine.

"I wish I could see you," I say.

"You could take a few days off of work. Drive down and spend a couple of days in Portland with me..."

I almost drop the phone in my excitement. "Really? You would...want that?" I'm staring at myself in the dresser mirror as I speak. My hair is longer than I've ever grown it; it needs professional attention. I touch a limp strand and wonder if my stylist can fit me in before I leave. A little getaway seems like a good reason for some grooming.

"Of course," he says. "Come tomorrow. You have all of that vacation time you haven't used."

My eyes rove over the bedroom furniture, the white-washed woods, and rustic baskets. Maybe a change of scenery is exactly what I need. I haven't felt myself lately.

"But where will I stay?"

"Hold on a sec…" His voice is muffled as I hear some-one on his end say something to him, then he comes back on the line.

"I have to go. I'll book a room at the Dossier. See you tomorrow?"

I want to ask him about Monday and Tuesday, if he plans on ditching them for me, but he's in a rush.

"I'm so excited," I say. "Tomorrow. Love you."

"Love you, too, baby." And then he hangs up.

I call work straightaway and arrange to have three of my shifts covered, and then I call my stylist, who says she's had a cancellation and can see me in an hour. Two hours later, I am home with a fresh color and cut, and heading to my closet to pack. I don't remember the paper I found or Han-nah Ovark until I go looking for my MacBook, which I plan on taking with me. I slump onto the sofa and stare at the screen, at the evidence of my stalking. My main screen is still open to Facebook, her smiling face staring up at me. It feels different to be doing this in the light of day, more deliberate and sneaky. I hesitate, my mouse hovering over her profile. Once I have information about her I can't go back; it will be there imprinted in my mind forever. I click on her profile, holding my breath, but when the screen loads, I see she has everything set to private. Frowning, I close the browser and shut down my computer.

Hannah is more of a supermodel than a laid-back surfer. Her lips are full and perfect and she has the type of cheek-bones you only see on Scandinavian models.

The next morning I wake up still thinking about Han-nah. I try to clear my mind of her face as I carry my over-night bag down to the carport. But at the last moment, I take the elevator back upstairs and retrieve the paper from my nightstand, tucking it into the deepest, most hidden pocket of my wallet. Just in case I need her address. *But why would you need it?* I ask myself as I buckle my seat belt and pull out of the carport.

Just in case... Just in case I want to see what she looks like in real life. Just in case I want to have a conversation with her. That type of just in case. It is my right, isn't it? To know who I am sharing my husband with? Perhaps I am tired of wondering.

The drive to Portland is around two hours if the traffic gods are feeling generous. I roll my window all the way down and turn up the music. When my hair is a tangled mess, I decide to give the music a break and phone my best friend, Anna, instead. Anna moved to Venice Beach a few months ago for a guy she met online.

"That's great that you're going to see him," she says. "Did you buy some new lingerie?"

"I didn't!" I say. "But good thinking. I can stop downtown and pick something up. Should I go with sexy trashy, or sexy beautiful?"

"Definitely trashy. Men like to think they're fucking a slut."

I laugh at how crass she is.

"Hey," she says when there's a lull in the conversation. "How have you been since—"

"Fine," I snap. I cut her off before she can say any more. I don't want to go there today. Today Seth and I are having a sexy getaway. "Listen, I have to go. Just pulling into the hotel now. Call you next week?"

"Sure," she responds, but she doesn't sound so sure. That's Anna, always worrying. We went to high school together and were roommates in college. When I first introduced her to Seth, she loved him, but then gradually something changed between them, her attitude turning distinctly sour. Like everyone else in my life, I chose to keep our true lives a secret from her, so Anna has no idea about the others. I figured he lost his glamour once she got to know him, and she changed her mind. Anna and I have very different tastes in men, and I hardly ever like her boyfriends, so how could I blame her for not liking my husband?

I park my car myself, avoiding the valet so I can slip out before Seth arrives and grab something sexy from one of the department stores. Hannah's photo looms in my mind. It's no wonder Seth didn't want me to know anything about her. Once I've checked into the hotel room, I study my face in the mirror, wondering what it is that Seth sees in me. I've always thought myself to be mildly attractive, sort of in the girl-next-door kind of way. But if you had a woman like Hannah, why would you go for a woman with boring brown hair and a smattering of freckles across her nose? I have a nice figure—my chest has been a focal point for men since I was sixteen—but I'm not tall, or slender, or graceful by any means. My hips are round and so is my rear. Seth, a self-proclaimed ass man, always reaches around to grope my backside when we hug. He always makes me feel sexy and beautiful—until I saw Hannah, that is. He's either a man of diverse taste or he's just gathering wives for the heck of it. Seeing Hannah's picture makes me curious about Tuesday, but there's no way Seth would tell me her name. He'd be angry enough knowing I snooped on his pregnant Portland wife.

Glancing at my watch, I see that it's lunchtime. I decide to drive over to the Nordstrom in the city and grab some lunch while I'm there. Portland is more low-key than Seattle, which is a crisscross of one-way streets and fast-limbed pedestrians. I have little trouble navigating the tight lanes of the city and parking in a garage a block away from the department store. I find a black lace bra and panty duo and pick out a sheer robe to wear over it, and carry the items to the register.

"Anything else I can get for you today?" the saleslady asks, walking around the register to hand me my purchase.

"Yes," I hear myself say. "Can you tell me how far Galatia Lane is? I'm not from around here."

"Oh," she says. "It's just on the outskirts of the city. About four miles. Cute little street, has those beautiful restored Victorian houses."

"Hmm," I say, pressing my lips together in a smile. "Thank you."

I drive there straightaway, then pull over, the tires grating along the curb. I dip my head to eye the houses, my hands still gripping the steering wheel. It isn't too late to leave. It is as simple as shifting the car into Drive and not looking back. I tap a finger as I decide, my eyes darting from house to house. I'm already here—what is the damage in having a look around? Even if Hannah Ovark isn't Monday, this neighborhood is beautiful. Leaving my Nordstrom bag in the front seat, I step out of the car and walk along the shaded pavement, eyeing the houses in wonder. They look like gingerbread houses: broad turrets, window boxes, white picket fencing, each one painted the color of a childhood fantasy. A soft pink, a Tiffany blue—there's even a house that is the color of mint chocolate chip ice cream, the shutters a rich brown. I remember the feel of the frozen chips of chocolate wedged between teeth, the way you'd suck at a tooth to loosen their hold. A neighborhood of nostalgia. How perfectly annoying that Monday would live here. I think of my condo downtown, stacked on top of a dozen others, people living vertically in little spaces in the sky. No magic, no mint chocolate chip paint, just long elevator rides and city views. I wonder what life would be like living in a place like this. I'm so lost in my thoughts that I walk right past number 324 and have to backtrack.

Hannah's house is cream-colored with a matte black door. There are green shutters on the windows and flower boxes that hold tiny evergreens. The garden is chock-full of plants—not flowers, but carefully tended greens. I have a new appreciation for her, a woman who tends evergreens over flowers, things that live. I spend five minutes staring, admiring it all, when a voice makes me jump.

"Shit," I say, holding a hand over my heart. When I turn around, she's staring up at the house, too, a blond with wispy pieces of hair framing her face. She has her head tilted to the side like she's really studying it.

"Lovely, isn't it?"

My thoughts arrange themselves around her face. It's a delayed response, recognizing someone in public who you've only known online. You have to match the features, the airbrushed skin to the real skin.

Hannah. My heart almost leaps out of my chest as I stare at her. I've broken a rule, breached a contract. I've always wondered about deer, why they don't run when they see a car barreling toward them. But here I am, frozen in place, heart whirring in my ears.

"It is," I agree, for lack of anything better to say. I add, "Is it yours?"

"Yes," she says brightly. "My husband owned it before

we got married. After the wedding we did a remodel. So. Much. Work," she says, rolling her eyes. "Luckily, it's what my husband does for a living, so he handled everything."

I love you all the same, wasn't that what he always said? The same! Yet here she is with a house right out of *Design and Home* while I wilt away in a high-rise. Clearly, she is the type you buy a house for and I am the type who gets a card. She is wearing a flowered kimono, a tank top and jeans. A sliver of her stomach is visible above the waistband of her jeans, smooth and taut. No wonder Seth doesn't want us near each other—I'd die of insecurity.

"Would you like to come in and see it?" she asks suddenly. "People often knock on the door and want a tour. I never knew that owning a house could make me so popular."

When she laughs, it's throaty, and I wonder if she's a smoker. *Not anymore*, I tell myself, eyeing her belly. It's too flat to contain life, too hollow. Thoughts of her pregnancy rouse images in my mind—of her long legs wrapped around Seth, him pushing relentlessly into her.

"Yes, I'd love to." The words are out of my mouth before I can stop myself. *Yes, I'd love to.* I could smack myself. But instead, I follow her up the path and to the front door, where she pulls out a key. A tiny plastic sandal dangles from the ring. Most of the word has been rubbed away but I can still make out the M-e-c-o of Mexico. There is an immediate tightening in my belly. Had she gone there with Seth? My God, all the things I don't know. Hannah is struggling with the key. I hear her swear under her breath.

"Damn thing always sticks," she says when it finally turns.

I shuffle behind her, glancing over my shoulder every few seconds to make sure no one is coming. *This isn't your neighborhood*, I think. *What difference does it make if someone sees you?* Hannah is even more beautiful than in her photos, and on top of that, she's nice, too. Nice enough to open her home for a private tour to a complete, gawking stranger. *Not such a stranger,* I think as I follow her inside. We share the same penis, after all.

I'm on the verge of maniacal laughter when my breath gets caught in my throat. I make a little *eh-ehm* sound to clear it while Hannah deposits her keys on an ornate hook and swings around to smile at me. The house creaks around us, gently asserting its age. The hardwood floors are gleaming and spotless, the type of rustic mahogany I'd wanted to put in the condo. Seth had vetoed my choice—he wanted something more modern, so we went with a slate gray instead. I stand at the foot of a curving staircase, unsure of whether or not I'm expected to remove my shoes. I have the eerie feeling that I've been here before, even though I know that's not possible. Hannah doesn't make a move to direct me either way, so I step out of them, leaving them near the stairs. Two bright pink flats in the midst of all this cream. A distressed table sits to my right; brightly colored bougainvillea spills from a vase on top of it. There are no family pictures hanging anywhere that I can see, and for that, I'm grateful. What would it be like to see your husband in family photos with another woman? Everything is tasteful and perfect. Hannah has an eye for decor.

"It's so lovely," I breathe, my eyes hungry to take everything in.

Hannah, who has removed her own shoes and slipped her feet into silk slippers, smiles at me, her Nordic cheekbones sharp and rosy. Seth's face is hard angles, too, a square jaw and a long, straight nose. I wonder what godlike creature these two have created together, and my stomach cramps at the thought of their baby. *Their baby. Their trip to Mexico. Their house.*

"I'm Hannah, by the way," she says as she leads me up the staircase. And then she's telling me about the man who built the house for his new wife a hundred years ago, and I think about how Seth's new, upgraded wife was living in it. It was just a year ago when I agreed to it all—our plans thwarted, but our love still there. I had wanted to please him, much like Tuesday, I imagine, when she agreed to me.

She leads me through several bedrooms and two restored bathrooms. I look for photos, but there are none. Then she takes me downstairs to see the sitting room and kitchen. I fall in love with the kitchen immediately. Three times the size of the tiny kitchen in my condo, there is enough space to cook several feasts all at once. Seeing the look on my face, Hannah grins.

"It wasn't always this grand. I gave up the second sitting room to expand the kitchen. We like to entertain."

"It's lovely," I say.

"It used to have yellow cabinets and a black-and-white checkered floor." Her nose is curled like she finds the whole idea distasteful. I can picture it, the ancient kitchen with buttery cabinets, probably hand-painted by the first owner.

"We hated it. I know you're supposed to appreciate that old charm, but I couldn't wait to change it."

We. Another shock. My Seth does not like to entertain. I try to picture him standing underneath the exposed beams of this ceiling, chopping onions at the marble island while Hannah pulls something from the double oven. It's all too much and suddenly I feel dizzy. I lift a hand to my head and reach for a chair to steady myself.

"Are you all right?" There is concern in Hannah's voice. She pulls a stool out from the island and I sit.

"Let me get you some water," she says.

She returns with a tall glass of water and I drink it, wondering when was the last time I had anything to drink. There was tea at lunch, and a glass of rosé. I'm probably dehydrated.

"Listen, Hannah, you invited a stranger into your house. I could be a serial killer or something. And now you're giving me water," I say, shaking my head. "You can't do things like that."

Her face looks impish when she grins, her eyes brightly mischievous. She's significantly younger than I am, but there's also something regal and old about her. I doubt she ever drank too many Mike's Hard Lemonades and retched into a toilet all night like I had in my teens. No, this woman is too put together, too responsible and too well-spoken. I could see what Seth saw, the elegance. The perfect mother to the perfect child.

"Well, now's the right time to make a snack," she says playfully. "I haven't eaten." She goes to the fridge and then the pantry, humming as she pulls things out. And when she comes back, there is an assortment of cheese, crackers and fruit on a wooden board, all arranged in a very artistic and grown-up way. I feel a kinship with her, her willingness to feed a stranger. I would have done the same. I eat a few pieces of cheese and immediately feel better.

As we eat, she tells me that she's a freelance photographer. I ask if the framed prints in the hallway are hers. She lights up when she tells me yes. And again, I wonder why there aren't any family photos around. You'd think a photographer would have a slew of pictures in their home.

"What do you do?" she asks me, and I tell her that I'm a nurse.

"Here at Regional?" she asks, interested.

"No, no. I'm here with my husband for the weekend. I live in Seattle." I don't expound on any of that. I'm scared to give myself away. We chat for a while longer about hospitals and the restoration of Hannah's beautiful home before I stand.

"I've taken enough of your time," I say, smiling at her warmly. "Look, this was so nice of you. Can I take you out to lunch next time I'm in town?"

"I'd love that," she says eagerly. "I'm not from Oregon. I moved here to be with my husband, so I haven't made many friends."

"Oh, where are you from?" I tilt my head to the side, trying to recall if Seth had told me where she was from.

"Utah."

My skin prickles. Seth is from Utah. Had he known Hannah when he lived there? No, that isn't possible. Tuesday is his first wife; he'd been with her in Utah. There is an age difference between Seth and Hannah, so it isn't likely they went to school together. Hannah pulls her phone from her back pocket and I tell her my number so she can program it in.

I head for the foyer and put on my shoes. I'm suddenly desperate to get out of here. What was I thinking, anyway? Seth could stop home during his lunch break and find me with Hannah. What would he say if he found two of his wives together? I make for the door and bend down to lift the lip of my shoe from where it's folded against my heel. It's then that I see the shards of glass on the floor near the window—two inches long and jagged. I pick it up and hold it in my palm. There is an empty hook on the wall where a picture once hung. I turn around to show the glass to Hannah.

"It was on the floor," I say. "Don't want you to slice your foot open..."

She takes it, thanking me, but I notice the blush that has crept up her neck. "Must have been the photo I had hanging there. There was an accident and it fell off the wall."

I nod. These things happen. But then, as she pulls her hand away, the glass held gingerly between her fingers, I notice a sizable cluster of bruises on her forearm. They're just turning purple. I avert my eyes quickly, so she won't catch me staring, and open the door.

"Goodbye, then," I say.

She waves before shutting the door.

I think about her bruises all the way back to my car. Had they looked like finger marks? *No*, I tell myself. *You're seeing things.*

FIVE

I have just enough time to get back to the hotel and take a shower before I'm supposed to meet Seth for dinner. I'm distracted this time, almost driving into the back of a delivery truck that is stalled at a red light. *Hannah, Hannah, Hannah.* Her face swims before my eyes. I wear the black dress he likes, tight in all the right places, and let my hair hang loose around my shoulders. Beneath the dress, I am wearing the lingerie I chose earlier in the afternoon. The lace is itchy and I've made comparisons in my mind about how Hannah would look wearing the same thing. It will be a good night, I tell myself. I am looking forward to being with him during our stolen time. It feels like cheating and that thrills me. Hannah might be everything I'm not, but he chose to spend tonight with me. I call him to check the time of the reservation, and when he answers, his voice warms me right where it counts.

"How much did you spend?" he asks.

He's joking, of course. He likes to act frugal when I spend money, but he always asks to see the things I bought and comments on them. He's an interested husband, and those are rare.

"A lot," I tell him.

He laughs. "I can't wait to see you. I've been distracted at work all day thinking about tonight."

"Will you come here, or should I meet you?" I ask.

"I'll meet you there. Did you bring that black dress I like?"

"Oh, yes," I say, smiling a little. Most days I still get butterflies when I hear his voice on the phone. Sometimes it makes me feel easy, like all he has to do is use that deep rumble and I'm putty in his hands. But today there is an absence of emotion as I listen to him. I can feel the slight disconnect in the recesses of my mind. We are bantering like we normally do, but my heart's not in it. Perhaps actually seeing Hannah, the other wife, changed things for me. Made it all real instead of a situation I emotionally detached myself from. *Their baby. Their trip to Mexico. Their house. I wish I had time for a drink*, I think miserably as I grab my coat off the seat.

Seth is waiting for me outside when I pull up to valet. The restaurant is quaint and romantic—a place where new couples come to connect and old couples come to reconnect. I thrill that this is what he chose for our night together, noting the crisp, white linen napkins and ankle-length aprons the servers wear. The hostess leads us to a table in the corner; I take the seat facing the window. Instead of sitting across from me, Seth slides in next to me.

I look around to see if anyone is watching us, if they care. When I discover that no one is pointing fingers and laughing, I relax.

"I never thought I'd be that girl," I say, sipping my water.

"We used to make fun of them, remember?" Seth laughs. "The gross couples…"

I smile. "Yeah, but now I feel like I can't get enough of you. Probably because I have to share."

"I'm yours," he says. "I love you so much."

His voice sounds flat to me. Has it always sounded like that? *You're being paranoid and nitpicking everything to death*, I tell myself. *He hasn't changed, you have.*

It's hard not to wonder how often he says that to the others. Hannah's face fills my mind and I feel a rush of insecurity. This is why Seth keeps us apart—so we won't focus on jealousy and each other, but rather on our relationship with him. I bite back my feelings. That's what I do: compartmentalize, organize, prioritize.

Seth orders a steak and I opt for the salmon. We chat about the hospital and the new house he's building over in Lake Oswego for a retired actress. It's all very banal and normal, a typical married couple discussing the small details of their lives. I almost feel better about everything, the wine softening the sharp corners of my anxiety, until I see a young blond woman walk up to the host stand cradling a newborn baby. The only thing visible is the crown of the baby's head where a patch of dark hair peeps past the blanket. Jealousy rolls over me hot and heavy. I feel as if I can't breathe, and yet I can't tear my eyes away. The woman's partner fusses over her, touching her tenderly, and then wrapping a protective arm around her as they stare down at their tiny creation, together. I freeze, watching them carefully, the familiar tide of pain creeping in. They share an intimacy because they made a child together. No, that's not true of everyone. Plenty of people have children together and that's all they have. But I can't help but think of Hannah and Seth, how they'll have something together that I won't.

Seth sees me watching them and grabs my hand. "I love you," he says, looking at me with concern.

Sometimes I think he can tell that I'm thinking about them—the others—and he rushes at me with words. Word salve for the second, barren wife. *You couldn't give me what I wanted most in the world, but hey! I still love you so very much.*

"I know." I smile sadly and look away from the happy family.

"You're enough for me," he says. "You know that, right?"

I want to lash out at him, ask if I'm enough, then why is he having a baby with someone else? Why is there anyone else? But I don't. I don't want to be that maudlin girl, a nagger. My mother was a nagger. I grew up seeing my father's pained expressions when she'd rant on and on and I felt sorry for him. And her biting comments seemed to intensify with age, as did the crease lines on my father's weathered forehead. His face was well-worked leather while hers was a veneer of Botox and filler.

"You look upset," I say.

"I'm sorry," he says. "Hard week at work."

I nod sympathetically. "Anything I can do to help?"

When Seth looks at me, his eyes are soft. He reaches for my hand, a sexy half smile on his lips.

"I chose this life and everything in it. I can manage. I worry about you, though. After—"

"You don't need to worry. I'm fine." I nod reassuringly. It's a blatant lie, and perhaps if he weren't so distracted—stretched so thin—he would see through it. I'm not fine, but I can be. In my weakness, I thought I could talk to him about my struggles, but he has enough of his own. Besides, if Hannah can do it, so can I. She's expecting a baby with a man who has multiple wives, and yet when I was with her, I didn't pick up on any insecurities. She appeared to be a happy woman. Then I think of the bruises on her arm, the purple marks, dark as plums, that resembled fingers, and my eyes narrow.

"What's wrong?" Seth asks. "You did that thing with your eyebrows..." His hand grips my thigh underneath the table, squeezing gently, and I feel a tingling between my legs. My body betraying my mind, typical of me; I have no discipline. Not when it comes to Seth.

"What thing?" I ask, but I know what thing. I just like to hear him say it.

"Where you scrunch them up and then your lips pucker like you want to be kissed."

"Maybe I do," I throw back. "Have you thought of that?"

"I have." Seth leans in to kiss me and I feel the softness of his lips press to mine. He smells of wine and himself and suddenly I want him to see the lingerie. I want to watch the lust rise in his eyes before he pushes me onto the bed. *It's a good thing to want your husband and to want him to want you*, I think.

We are full-on making out like two teenagers when I hear a woman's voice nearby—insolent, a little riled up.

Seth pulls back to look over his shoulder, but I am still hazy-eyed and picturing the bed at the hotel.

"Lovers' quarrel," he says, turning back to me. Over his shoulder, I see a couple arguing at the bar.

I run my finger around the rim of my wineglass while I watch his face. I can tell he's straining to hear what they're saying as he stares at his water glass in concentration. He seems to be enjoying the sound of their voices, which are strained with tension. I watch the set of his lips to see if he's taking a side, but no, he's just listening. Seth and I rarely fight, probably on account of how agreeable I force myself to be. Had I ever seen him lose his temper? I flip through my memories, trying to conjure an image of my husband being angry enough to hit...grab...push.

"Seth," I say. "How often do you fight with them?"

The wine has loosened my tongue, my facade of indifference dropping away as I study my husband's face.

He doesn't meet my eyes. "Everyone fights."

"Yes, I suppose," I say, already bored with his answer. "What sorts of things do you fight about?"

Seth looks uncomfortable as he reaches for his glass. It's empty, of course, and his head jerks around to look for our server so he can cushion my question with alcohol. My eyes stay glued to his face. I want to know.

"Regular things."

"Why are you being evasive?" I drum my fingers on the tabletop. I'm aggravated. I rarely ask questions, and when I do, I expect an answer. I expect answers for my compliance. My role isn't an easy one.

"Look, I've had a really hard week. Being with you is a break from all that. I'd rather just enjoy your company instead of drudging up every fight I've had with them."

I feel myself soften. Tucking my hands under the table, I smile at him apologetically. Seth looks relieved. I was being unfair. Why spend our time together talking about his other relationships when we could focus on strengthening our bond? I push Hannah and her bruises from my mind.

"I'm sorry," I say. "Would you like one more drink before we leave?"

Seth orders two more drinks, and after they arrive, he looks at me with what can only be described as solemn guilt.

"What? I know that look. Spit it out."

He laughs a little and leans over to kiss me on the lips. "You know me so well." He grins.

I lean back against the firm leather of the booth, waiting for the bad news.

"Actually, I really need to talk to you about something."

"Okay…"

I watch as he takes another sip of his bourbon, stalling for time, arranging the words in his mind. I imagine that if he had something bad to tell me all along, he's already rehearsed what he's going to say. It makes me prickly to think he invited me all the way here just to butter me up for bad news.

"It's about Monday," he says.

Something in my belly twists and I feel a wave of panic. He found out I've been to see Hannah. My lips are dry. I lick them, already composing the words—the excuses I'm going to give him.

"Monday?"

"Everything with the baby is fine. So far. But I was thinking that it's a bad idea for you and me to take our vacation this year with the baby due…"

His words drop between us and all I can do is stare at him, dumbfounded. It's not as bad as I thought, but also just as bad.

"Why?" I blurt. "What difference does it make? We can go before she has it."

"That's just it," Seth says. The waiter comes by and Seth passes him his credit card without looking at the bill. "I'll need the time off when the baby gets here. I can't take a vacation. On top of that, things are busy at work. I need to be there."

I fold my arms across my chest and stare out the window, suddenly not feeling as special and loved as I had hours ago. I feel cast off, abandoned. I am not the one having his baby—she is—and so my needs matter less. Oh my God, he invited me to Portland to soften the blow. This wasn't a stolen romantic getaway, it was a manipulation: the soft words, the flirting, the nice dinner—the realization stings.

"I've sacrificed a lot, Seth..." I want to cringe at the bitterness I hear in my voice. I don't want to act like a child, but being robbed of my time with him is unbearable.

"I know you have. It hurts me to ask you to do this," he says.

I balk at his tone. It's like he's speaking to a child, one he's about to discipline.

I look at him in alarm, weighing my urge to lash out and say something that will hurt him. "Ask me? It sounds more like you're telling me."

It begins to rain, and a couple dashes from the restaurant and across the street toward the parking garage. I watch their progress and wonder what it's like to be with a man who wants only you. I didn't date much before Seth. I was one of those serious students who avoided relationships to focus on my studies. If I had more experience under my belt, maybe I wouldn't have agreed to the life Seth offered me so easily.

"You know that's not true." He reaches out to touch my hand and I pull it away, placing it under the table on my lap. Tears sting my eyes.

"I'd like to leave," I say.

Seth actually has the audacity to frown at me. "You can't run away from this. We have to talk about things. That's how it works in a relationship. You knew when I married her what that would entail. You agreed."

I am so enraged I stand up, knocking over my empty water glass as I push out of the half-moon booth and rush toward the door. I hear him call my name, but nothing he says could make me stop. I need to be alone, to think about all of this. How dare he lecture me on marriage? His path is the easy one.

SIX

The next morning I'm woken by the sound of the door opening. In my haste to climb into bed, I'd forgotten to hang the Do Not Disturb sign. I hear a tentative "House-keeping…" and I call out a muffled "Later!" I wait until the door closes again before I roll over in bed and see that I have seven text messages and five missed calls from Seth. If I were to call this much when I didn't hear from him, I'd look needy and insecure. I turn my phone off without reading the texts and jump out of bed to pack the few things I brought with me. I want to be home. It was a mistake coming here. I am craving the familiarity of my condo, the cold Coke that waits in the fridge. I plan on climbing under the covers and staying there until I have to go back to work. I want to call my mother or Anna and tell them what happened, but then I'd have to tell them the whole truth, and I'm not ready for that. I'm on my way down to the lobby when I think of Hannah and have the sudden urge to see her again. She's the only one who knows what this is like, the torture of sharing your spouse. I send her a text as I march toward the parking garage, the straps of my duffel digging into my arm. I'd been so distracted last night I don't remember where I parked my car. I walk up and down the rows of cars, switching my bag back and forth on my arm when it becomes too heavy. When I finally find it and unlock the door, I see a bouquet of lavender roses propped on the front seat, a card propped against the steering wheel. I move them to the passenger side without opening the card and climb in, gunning the engine. I didn't want his flowers or his Hallmark apologies. I wanted him: his attention, his time, his favor. I am almost to the freeway, having momentarily forgotten about the text I sent to Hannah, when my phone chimes to tell me I have a text. I'd asked her if she was free to grab a late breakfast before I headed out of town. Her response causes my heart to beat wildly.

I'd love to! Meet you at Orson's in ten? Here's the address.

I type the address into my phone and make a U-turn. I barely glanced at myself in the mirror before I left this morning. As I wait for a light to change, I pull down the car's visor and, flipping open the mirror, I study my face. I look pale and washed out, and my eyes are puffy from last night's crying. I dig in my bag for a lipstick and quickly mop it across my lips.

Orson's is a hole-in-the-wall breakfast spot with a block-letter sign above the door. There is a golf-ball–size hole in the O with a series of spiderweb cracks around it. I walk inside, the smell of eggs and coffee thick in the air, and look around for an empty table.

The place is packed, filled with the type of people I can't imagine Hannah and her fine cheekbones being friends with. Mohawks, pink hair, tattoos—one woman has seven piercings in her face alone.

I find a table by a window where I can see the door and toss my purse into the empty seat across from me. Too often I'd been in coffee shops where desperate people try to pilfer your chairs. Hannah walks in ten minutes later, wearing a red dress and glossy black flats. Her hair is pinned back, but wisps of it fall around her face like she was caught in a strong wind.

She looks frazzled as she slides into her seat and pushes the strands behind her ears. "Sorry I'm late. I'd just gotten out of the shower when I got your text." She pulls off her sunglasses and sets them on the table while she presses her fingers to the bridge of her nose.

"Headache?" I ask.

She nods. "Caffeine headache. I've been trying to cut back, but I think I'll have one today."

"I'll go grab us coffees if you tell me what you want," I say, standing up. I have the sudden urge to protect her. She nods, looking around.

"Yeah, I suppose we can't risk losing our table."

She tells me her order and I walk up to the register and get in line. It's then that I start sweating. Like, what the hell am I doing? Is this to get back at Seth? *No*, I tell myself as I reach the front of the line. I'm searching for my own form of community. I need to understand myself, and the only way to do that is to get to know the other woman who has made similar choices. Besides, it isn't like I could find a polygamy group online, like one of those MOPS meetings mothers attend.

I place our order and carry the number on a stand back to the table. Hannah is chewing on her nails and staring at a coffee stain on the table.

I glance at her arm, to the place where I saw the bruise yesterday. It's gone from purple to a dim blue.

She sees me looking and covers it with her hand, perfectly manicured fingers wrapping around her arm.

"An accident," she says.

"Looks like finger marks." My comment is offhanded, but she looks startled, like I've just slapped her. I study her eyes. They're so perfectly blue they look painted, her lashes flicked up with expertly applied mascara. *It's all too perfect*, I think. When things are that perfect, something is wrong.

While we wait, she chats about another renovation she wants to do on the house, but her husband is dragging his feet. I gravitate between liking and hating her as I smile and nod. How ungrateful to live in such a beautiful place and to never be satisfied with it. Wasn't Seth exhausted by her demands? I imagine he'll tell me about it soon, ask what I think about the renovation she wants. Seth always confers with me about these things, almost like he's asking permission. I'd tell him to give her what she wants, of course. It would make me look good. Hannah suddenly changes the subject and asks questions about my condo and how I've decorated it. Her interest flatters and confuses me. I'm grateful when our food and drinks arrive. I stare down at my plate, at the omelet that is healthier than one I would have ordered had I been by myself, and have the desperate urge to tell her something personal. "I found out last night that my husband is cheating on me."

Hannah drops her fork. It clatters onto her plate and then does a flip landing on the floor. We both stare at it.

"What?" she says. Her response is so delayed it's almost funny.

I shrug. "I'm not sure how to process it. We had a fight last night and I stormed off."

Hannah shakes her head and bends to pick up her fork. Instead of asking for a new one, she pulls an antibacterial wipe from her handbag and polishes it clean.

"I'm sorry," she says. "My God, here I am blabbing about... I'm really sorry."

She sets down her fork and stares at me. "Seriously, that's terrible. I'd be an absolute mess. How are you even holding up?"

"I don't know," I say honestly. "I love him." She nods, like this is answer enough.

She studies me over her plate of egg whites. She's barely touched her food. I want to tell her to eat, that she has a baby to grow.

"I'm pregnant," she says.

I feign surprise. I don't have to try very hard because I'm genuinely shocked that she told me, a complete stranger.

My eyes travel to her belly, flat and firm.

"I'm not very far along," she admits. "I haven't told anyone."

"Your...husband?" I ask. Though I want to say, *"Our husband?"*

"Yes," she sighs, "he knows."

"And...is he...happy?" I already know the answer, of course—Seth was over the fucking moon—but I want to hear about it from Hannah's mouth. What does my husband's excitement look like to her?

"He's happy."

"You're saying something without saying it." I wipe my mouth and stare at her pointedly. My mother can't stand this side of me; she says I'm too forward, but Hannah doesn't seem bothered by my statement. She wipes her mouth with a paper napkin and sighs.

"Yes, I suppose I am." She looks at me with new appreciation. "I like how direct you are." I bite the inside of my cheeks to keep from smiling.

"So what's the deal? You have to talk to someone about it, right?" I'm trying to play it cool, but my toes are curled up in my shoes and my leg is bouncing sporadically underneath the table. I feel like a druggie. I need more, I need to hear it all, to understand.

She looks at me through spiky black lashes and presses her lips together.

"He hides my birth control pills."

I press the back of my hand to my mouth as I choke on the sip of coffee I've just taken. She has to be joking. Seth, hiding birth control pills? Seth is the type of guy who gets what he wants without tricks. Or maybe that's just with me.

"How do you know he hides them?" I ask, setting my coffee cup down. Hannah shifts in her seat, her eyes darting around like she's waiting for Seth to appear out of the walls.

"He's joked about it and of course my pills go missing."

"It's like when women poke holes in condoms to trap men with pregnancies," I say, shaking my head. "But why would he want to trap you with a pregnancy?"

Hannah's mouth pulls into a tight line and she looks

away. My breath catches in my throat as my eyes travel to the bruises on her arm.

"You wanted to leave…"

She looks at me but doesn't say anything. I can almost see the truth in her eyes, pressed behind her rapid blinking. My mind is spinning out of control. It's inconceivable to me, Seth hurting a woman, Seth hiding birth control pills. I want to ask if she loves him but my tongue is glued to the roof of my mouth.

"Hannah, you can tell me…"

A woman with dreadlocks and a baby strapped to her chest in one of those hippie sling things walks past our table. Hannah watches her with rapt interest, and I wonder if she's imagining herself with a baby. I'd done it a thousand times before, imagining the weight of a tiny human in my arms—wondering what it would feel like to know you made something so small and perfect. I stare at her beautiful face. Hannah is not who she seems: the perfect house, the perfect face, the perfect outfit…and then those bruises. I wanted to know her, understand her, but every second spent with her makes me more confused. A few hours ago I was furious at Seth, and now, as I sit across from my husband's other wife, my anger transfers to her. I feel absolutely bipolar in my emotions—one minute distrusting one, the next the other. Why would she have agreed to all of this if not to have a child with him? That's why…that's why he added a wife. Because I couldn't give him a child.

"Did he make that bruise on your arm?" I lean in, studying her face for signs of a lie before she's even answered me.

"It's complicated," she says. "He didn't mean it. We were fighting and I walked away. He grabbed my arm. I bruise easily…" she offers weakly.

"That's not okay."

Hannah looks put off, like she'd rather be anywhere else but here. She glances longingly toward the door; I lay a hand on her arm and stare her right in the eye.

"Has he hit you before?" My question is loaded. I'm not just asking Hannah Ovark if her husband hits her, I'm asking if *my* husband hits her.

"No! I mean, he doesn't hit me. Look, you have it all wrong."

I'm about to ask her exactly *how* I have it all wrong when someone bumps into our table. I lean out of the way, but it's too late, a cup tilts toward me, emptying its contents over my clothes. The girl who'd been holding the cup widens her eyes, her mouth dropping open.

"Shit," she says, jumping back. "I'm so sorry. It's iced, thank God it's iced."

I grab my purse, moving it out of the way as a puddle of brown crawls across the table. Hannah is shoving napkins at me, pulling them one by one from the holder. I look at her helplessly as I dab at my pants. "I have to go," I say.

"I know." She nods like she understands. "Thanks for the breakfast," she says. "It was nice to talk to someone. I don't get to do that very often."

I smile weakly at her and think of the woman with the dreadlocks and the baby. She's lying. There's something off about Hannah Ovark and I'm going to find out what it is.

SEVEN

When Seth calls a few days later I am home, snuggled up under a blanket on the couch. I've been screening his calls for days, sending him to voice mail on the first ring. I'm mellow after two glasses of wine and so I answer. I've been going over what Hannah said, replaying her words over and over until I want to cry from frustration. He says hello first; his voice sounds tired but hopeful.

"Hi," I breathe into the phone. I hold the device to my ear with one hand, and with the other I trace the patterns of a throw pillow on my lap.

"I'm sorry," he says right away. "I'm so sorry." He sounds it.

"I know..." My anger dissolving, I reach over for the remote and mute the mindless fodder I was watching. Reality TV is the ultimate distraction from a broken heart.

"I spoke to Hannah," he says. "That's Monday's name."

I hold my breath, pushing myself into a sitting position and tossing the pillow onto the floor. Did he really just tell me her name? It feels like a triumph, Seth trusting me with something he's never shared. I am fairly certain neither of the other wives knows my name. And then it hits me: Hannah holds all the power. She is the pregnant wife. I suddenly feel claustrophobic, my prior softness replaced with nerves. If Hannah decided that it was important for Seth to stay with her instead of going on vacation with me, that's exactly what he would do. I may be Seth's legal wife, but this baby shifted me to the position of middle child, and everyone knows that the middle child is the forgotten one. I clear my throat, determined to act normal, despite what I am feeling.

"What did she say?" My heart is pounding and my nails find their way to my mouth where my teeth begin their ripping assault.

There's a pause on his end. "I told her that it was important for me to take the trip," he says. "You're right. I can't take time away from you. It isn't fair."

I should be nice, play the role of the good wife, but the words bubble from my lips before I can pull them back.

"I don't want your charity. I want you to *want* to take a trip with me."

"I do. I'm doing my best here, baby."

"Don't call me that, Seth."

There's a long pause on his end, followed by a sigh. "All right. What do you want me to say?"

Annoyance blooms in my chest.

What do I want him to say? That he chooses me? That

he only wants me? That's never going to happen. It's not what I signed up for.

"I don't want to fight," he says. "I just called to tell you that I'm figuring it out. And I love you."

I wonder if he made me the bad guy, told her I was kicking up a fuss. Why would I even care what Hannah thinks of me? But I do care what Hannah thinks, even if she doesn't know who I am. *Well, she does know, doesn't she?* I think. *She just doesn't know she knows, you fuck.*

"I told her that it was important I go," he tells me.

That sounds like Seth actually. Never wanting to *be* the bad guy. He needs to please and be pleased. He makes love to me in the same way, alternating between a tender reverence and wild grip of fingers and thrusts until I sound off like a porn star.

Suddenly, his voice changes and I press the phone closer to my ear. "I didn't know if you still wanted me there... on Thursday..."

I swipe away the guilt I'm feeling for being so harsh and consider my feelings. *Do I want him here? Am I ready to see him?* I could just outright tell him what I did and ask for an explanation. But he could deny the whole thing, and then I'd never get to talk to Hannah again. He'd tell her who I was and she'd feel betrayed by what I'd done. There's a huge chance that I am blowing all of this out of proportion, and then I'd look like a pathetic idiot to the only person in the world I am close to.

"You can come," I say softly. Because if he doesn't, he'll go to one of them. I may be angry with him, but I am still a competitive woman.

"Okay," is all he says in return.

We hang up with barely more than an *I love you* from Seth. Who I know genuinely does love me. But I don't say it back. I want to make him suffer. He needs to know that there are no lies in a marriage—no matter how many women you're married to—which makes the truth even more complicated. But still…

I don't know what to do. I grow sour with each day, like curdled milk left in the heat. When Thursday arrives, in an act of defiance I decide not to make dinner. I'm not going to cook for him, put on a show like everything is all right. It isn't. I don't do my hair or put one of my usually sexy dresses on, either. At the last minute I spray some perfume on my wrists and at the neckline of my shirt. *That was for me*, I tell myself. *Not him*. When Seth walks through the door, I am sitting on the couch in sweatpants, my hair rolled into a bun, eating ramen noodles and watching Bravo. He pauses in the doorway to the living room, surveying my state with a look of amusement. I have a noodle hanging out of my mouth, my lips cupped around it.

"Hi," he says. He's wearing a cardigan pushed up to his elbows and a light blue V-neck T-shirt. His hands are stuffed into his jean pockets like he doesn't know what to do with them. Sheepish. How charming.

Normally, I'd be on my feet by now, rushing toward him so that I could be wrapped in his arms, so relieved that I could finally touch him. This time I stay seated, and the only acknowledgment I give him in greeting is a slight raise of my eyebrows as I suck the lone noodle into my mouth. It slaps my cheek on the way in and I feel a spray of the salty chicken water hit my eyeball.

I watch as he ambles into the living room and sits across from me on one of the floral chairs we chose together: deep emerald green with creamy gardenias floating across the fabric. "Almost like they're caught on the wind," he'd said when he first saw it in the store. I'd bought it just because of his description.

"There's ramen in the pantry," I say cheerfully. "Chicken and beef." I wait for a startled reaction, but he doesn't have one. This is the first Thursday in our marriage that I have not cooked an elaborate meal.

He nods, hands clasped between his knees now. I marvel at the change. All of a sudden, it's like he doesn't belong here and I do. He's lost his power and I sort of like it. I lift the bowl of broth to my lips and drink it down, smacking my lips when I'm done. Delicious. I forgot how good a brick of noodles could be. *Oh my God, I'm so lonely.*

"So," I say. I'm hoping to prompt Seth into saying whatever he's holding behind his teeth. By the strained look on his face, he appears to be choking on all of his unsaid bits. I can't believe I even entertained the thought that this man could rough up a woman. I study his face, his weak chin and too-pretty nose. It's strange how perception is altered by bitterness. I've never thought his chin weak before, never considered his nose too pretty. The man whose face I've always loved and cradled between my palms suddenly looks weak and pathetic, transformed by my flip-flopping opinion of him.

I flip through the channels, not really seeing what's on the screen. I don't want to look at him for fear he will be able to see in my eyes the ugly things I'm feeling.

"I thought I'd be good at this," he says. I spare him a glance before I keep flicking.

"Good at what?"

"Loving more than one woman."

The laugh that bursts from between my lips is sharp and ugly.

Seth looks at me, chagrined, and I feel a stab of guilt.

"Who can be good at something like that?" I ask, shaking my head. "God, Seth. Marriage to one person is hard enough. You're right about one thing," I say, setting the remote down and turning my full attention on him. "I'm disappointed. I feel betrayed. I'm…jealous. Someone else is having your baby and it's not me."

The most I've said about our situation. I immediately want to reel the words back in, swallow them down. I sound so jaded. It's not a side of myself I've ever let Seth see. Men prefer the purrings of a confident, secure woman— that's what the books say. That's what Seth said about me in the first months of our dating: "I like that you're not threatened by anything. You're you no matter who else is in the room…" It isn't that way now, is it? Two other women are in the room, and I notice them every minute of every day. I look around my small living room, my eyes touching the knickknacks and art that Seth and I chose together: a painting of an English seaside, a driftwood bowl that we found in Port Townsend in our first year of marriage, a pile of coffee table books that I swore I needed but have never paged through. All the things that comprise our lives, and yet none are filled with memories, or represent a joining of lives, like a baby would. He shares that bond with someone else. I suddenly feel depressed. Our existence together is a shallow one. If not for children, what is there? Sex? Companionship? Is anything more important than bringing life into the world? I reach up absently to lay a hand on my womb. Forever empty.

EIGHT

It has been a miraculous three sunny days in Washington and the night sky is rejoicing with a spray of stars. I opened the blinds right before bed so we could feel like we were lying underneath them, but now they almost seem too bright as I lie awake next to my snoring husband. I glance at the clock and see it's just past midnight when suddenly the screen on Seth's phone lights up. His phone is on his nightstand and I lift myself slightly so I can see who is texting my husband. Regina. I blink at the name. Was that… Tuesday? A client wouldn't text this late at night, and I know the names of everyone in his office. It had to be. I lie back down and stare at the ceiling saying the name over and over in my head: Regina… Regina… Regina…

Seth's first wife is Tuesday. I don't know if it was me or

if it was Seth who gave her that nickname, but before Hannah, it was just Seth and the two of us. Three days went to Tuesday, three days to me, and one day was reserved for his travel. Things felt safer back then; I had more control over my own heart and his. I was the *new* wife, shiny and well-loved—my pussy a novelty rather than a familiar friend. Of course, there was the promise of babies and family, and I would be the one to provide them—not her. That boosted my position, gave me a power.

Tuesday and Seth met sophomore year in college at a Christmas mixer thrown by one of his prelaw professors. Before Seth was business, he was law. When Seth walked in, Tuesday, a second-year law student, was standing by the window sipping her Diet Coke alone and illuminated by Christmas lights. He spotted her right away, though he didn't get to speak to her until the very end of the night. According to Seth's account, she was wearing a red skirt and four-inch black heels. A departure from the dowdy attire of the rest of the law students. He doesn't remember anything about her top, though I doubt it was anything scandalous. Tuesday's parents were faculty members of the college, observing Mormons. She dressed modestly except for her shoes. Seth said she wore fuck-me shoes right from the get-go, and that over the years, her taste in footwear has intensified. I try to picture her: mousy brown hair, a blouse buttoned to her collarbone and hooker shoes. I asked once what brand she prefers, but Seth didn't know. She has a whole closet filled with them. "But check if their soles are red," I wanted to say.

Toward the end of the night, as people were starting to leave to head back to the dorms, Seth made his way over.

"Those are the sexiest shoes I've ever seen."

That was his pickup line. Then he said, "I'd ask them on a date, but I think they'll just reject me."

To which Tuesday had replied, "You should ask me on a date instead, then."

They were married two months after they graduated. Seth claimed that they never fought once during the two and a half years they dated. He said it with pride, though I felt my eyebrows lift at the ridiculousness. Fighting was the sandpaper that smoothed out the first years of a relationship. Sure, there was still plenty of lifelong grit after that, but the fighting stripped everything down, let the other person know what was important to you. They made the move to Seattle when a friend's father offered Seth a job, but Tuesday hadn't acclimated well to the constant shade and rainy mist of Seattle. First, she became miserable, then outright hostile as she accused him of dragging her away from her family and friends to mold away in wet, dreary Seattle. Then, a year into their marriage, he caught her with birth control pills, and she confessed that she didn't want to have children. Seth was distraught. He spent the next year trying to convince her otherwise, but Tuesday was a career woman and my dear Seth was a family man.

She was accepted to a law school in Oregon, her dream. Their compromise was a relationship commute for the two years it would take her to finish. Then they would re-evaluate and Seth would look for a new job somewhere closer to her. But the business Seth ran was doing well, and his investment in its success grew. When the owner had a stroke, he agreed to sell the company to Seth, whom he had trusted to run it for two years. Seth's move to Oregon was thwarted. He would never leave Tuesday, he loved her too deeply, and so they worked around their respective states, driving, driving, driving. Sometimes Tuesday would drive to Seattle, but mostly it was Seth who made the sacrifices. I resented Tuesday for that, the first, selfish wife. Seth opened an office in Portland partially to be closer to Tuesday, and partially because it was a good business opportunity. When we first met, I asked him why he didn't divorce her and move on. He'd looked at me almost pityingly, and asked if I'd been left before. I had, of course—what woman hasn't experienced being left? A parent, a lover, a friend. Perhaps he was trying to distract me from the question, and it had worked. Tears sprang up, resentful memories came, and I believed Seth my savior. He wouldn't leave me, no matter what. That's where jealousy came in, when someone or something threatened my happiness. I'd understood Seth in that moment, admired him, even. He didn't leave, but the downside of that was he didn't leave *anyone*. He merely adapted. Rather than divorce, he took a new wife—one who could give him children. I was the second wife. Tuesday, in a compromise to remain without children, agreed to legally divorce Seth while I married him. I was to be the mother of his children. Until…Hannah.

"Seth…?" I say it again, louder this time. "Seth…"

The moon is bright outside the bedroom window, and its glow illuminates my husband's face as he slowly opens his eyes. I've interrupted his sleep, but he doesn't look angry. Earlier, Seth stood behind me and wrapped his arms around my waist, kissing my neck slowly, as we looked out at the city below. I must have forgiven him sometime between his bowl of ramen and our lovemaking, because the only thing I feel for him at the moment is intense love.

"Yes?" His voice is heavy with sleep and I reach out to touch his cheek.

"Are you angry with me for what happened to our baby?"

He rolls onto his back and I can no longer see every detail of his face, just the slant of his nose and one blue-green eye.

"It's midnight," he says, like I don't already know.

"I know that," I say softly. For good measure, I add, "I can't sleep."

He sighs, rubbing a hand over his face.

"I was angry," he admits. "Not at you…at life…the universe…God."

"Is that why you found Monday?" It takes all of my courage to form those words into a sentence. I feel as if I've cut open my own chest and splayed out my heart.

"Monday hasn't replaced you," he says after some time. "I want you to believe that my commitment to you is real." He reaches out a hand and caresses my face, the warmth of his palm reassuring. "Things didn't quite pan out the way we wanted, but we're still here and what we have is real."

He hasn't really answered my question. I lick my lips, thinking of a way to rephrase. My footing in our marriage is unsteady, my new purpose unclear.

"We could have adopted," I say. Seth turns his face away.

"You know that's not what I want." His voice is clipped. End of story. I'd brought up the topic of adoption before, and he'd immediately dismissed it.

"What if the same thing happened to Monday…that happened to me?"

His head snaps right so he's looking at me again, but this time there's no kindness in his eyes. I'm startled by it.

"Why would you say that? That's a terrible thing to imagine." He pushes himself to a sitting position, so I do, leaning back on my elbows until we're both staring at the bay windows and the stars beyond.

"I—I didn't mean it like that," I say quickly, but Seth is flustered.

"She's my wife. What do you think I'd do?"

I bite my lip, gripping the sheets in my fists; such a stupid thing to say, especially after things had been going so well all evening.

"It's just…you left me. You found her after…"

He stares straight ahead, not really seeing anything. I see the muscles in his jaw jump.

"You knew I wanted children. And I'm here. I'm right here with you."

"But are you?" I argue. "You need two other women—"

"Enough." He cuts me off. He gets out of bed and reaches for his pants. "I thought we were done with this."

I watch as he steps into them, not bothering to button them when he pulls on his shirt.

"Where are you going, Seth? Look, I'm sorry. I just—"

He walks toward the door and I swing my legs over the side of the bed determined not to let him leave. Not like this.

I throw myself at him, grabbing onto his arm and trying to pull him back. It happens in an instant, his hand shoving me away. Caught off guard, I fall backward. My ear clips the nightstand before I land on my rear on the wood floor. I cry out but Seth has already left the bedroom. I raise my hand to my ear and feel the warm trickle of blood on my fingertips, just as I hear the front door slam closed. I flinch at the sound, not because it's overly loud, but because of the anger behind it. I shouldn't have done that, woken him up in the middle of the night and put thoughts of dying babies in his head. What happened wasn't just hard on me; Seth had lost his child, as well. I stand up, wobbling on my feet. Squeezing my eyes closed, I cup my bleeding ear and wait for the dizziness to pass, then I walk slowly to the bathroom, flicking on the light to assess the damage. There is a centimeter-long cut on the outside of my ear, running parallel to the cartilage. It stings. I clean it with an alcohol wipe and dab some Neosporin on the wound. It's already stopped bleeding, but not hurting. When I return to the bedroom I stare at the bed for a long time, empty, the sheets rumpled. Seth's pillow still holds the indentation where his head rested.

"He's under so much stress," I say out loud as I climb into bed. I think my problems and insecurities are extreme, but I only have one man to keep happy. Seth has three women: three sets of problems, three sets of complaints. I'm sure we all pressure him in different ways: Monday and her baby, Tuesday and her career…me and my feelings of inferiority. I pull my knees up to my chest, unable to close my eyes. I wonder if he'll go back to Hannah. Or maybe it will be Regina this time.

I tell myself that I won't search for them online, that I'll respect Seth's privacy, but I know it's not true. I've already crossed a line, befriended his other wife. Tomorrow, I will type their names into a search box so I can see who they claim to be. So I can study their eyes, search for regret, hurt…or anything that looks similar to what's in my own eyes.

NINE

Regina Coele is tiny, maybe five feet on a good day. I walk away from my laptop where it rests on the kitchen counter, and pull open the freezer. It's only ten o'clock, but I need something stronger than the Coke I poured to drink with breakfast. I pull a bottle of vodka from where it's wedged between a bag of frozen peas and frostbitten hamburger patties. I study the photo of her on Markel & Abel's website: a family law firm with two offices, one in downtown Portland and one in Eugene. In the website photo, she wears dark-rimmed glasses perched on a slightly upturned nose. If not for the smear of red lipstick and her sophisticated hairstyle, she'd easily be mistaken for a girl in her late teens. I top off my juice with the vodka and add a few cubes of ice to the tumbler. Most women would feel fortunate to have such a youthful appearance. But I imagine that in Regina's line of work, she needs clients to respect her, not question if she's old enough to drink. The orange juice does little to disguise the heavy pour of vodka. I suck my teeth, deciding what to do next. I told myself that I just needed to see her, just one quick look. I'd made the silent promise even as I typed her name into the search box, but now that I'm looking at her I just want to know more. I throw back the rest of the vodka and the juice and pour another before carrying my laptop to the living room.

I uncap my pen and lean my notebook on the armrest of the couch, ready to work. In neat letters, I write *Regina Coele* at the top of the page and then the name of the law firm where she practices. I follow that with her email and the firm's phone number and address. Recapping my pen and setting it aside, I leave the law firm's website and go to the most obvious place to look for a person. Facebook has never heard of Regina Coele—not the one I'm looking for at least. There are a dozen profiles of wrong Reginas, none of them matching the details my sleuth skills have already uncovered. But no, I think ruefully; she wouldn't use her name on social media, not if there was a chance her clients could search for her.

I type in *Gigi Coele, R. Coele* and *Gina Coele* with no results. I lean back on the sofa, linking my hands and lifting my arms above my head in a stretch. Maybe she's not on Facebook; there are plenty of people who steer away from the intrusive probing fingers of social media. But then I see the freckles in my mind, the round nose—and I remember a little girl who lived on my street when I was growing up. Georgiana Baker—or Barker—or something like that. She was a tomboy to my girlie girl and she liked to be called Georgie.

Something about my childhood memory of Georgie reminds me of Regina. Perhaps it's the freckled nose.

I type *Reggie Coele* into the search bar on Facebook and I strike gold. A different version of Regina Coele pops up, this one with wavy hair, heavy eyeliner and glossy lips. Her privacy settings restrict me from seeing anything past her profile picture, but the casual way she embraces a friend, wearing spaghetti straps, tells me that this is the real side of her—a stark opposition to her stiff-backed lawyerly look. Once I find her, it's a rabbit hole of information. I can't stop, my finger moving the cursor of my MacBook from website to website. I'm manic in my research, hating her one minute and liking her the next. My eyes are wide with the information I've been thirsty for the past two years, my stomach a tangle of anxiety and excitement. This is my husband's *other* wife. One of them, anyway. I've looked up her Instagram (private), her Twitter account, which is not private, but the last time she tweeted was a year ago. On an off chance that she's doing something she shouldn't, I search her name on a website that would link Regina (or Reggie) to any of the popular dating sites. My search pings two results: Choose—a site that allows you to swipe left or right to pick and eliminate matches in your area, and GoSmart—a more elaborate dating website that matches you according to the results on the Myers-Briggs personality test.

Why would Regina be on dating websites? She'd been with Seth since college, when he barely had any hair on his chin, so there was no lapse in their relationship when she would have been single. I rearrange myself on the couch, tucking my socked feet underneath me and staring at the screen with grim determination. I have to find out, don't I? Seth couldn't possibly know about this, and it's the sort of information that changes people's lives. I think of the deep hurt it would cause him to know that his beloved Regina is being unfaithful, and almost shut my laptop.

Perhaps this is better left alone. I could finally put my white-hot jealousy to rest, knowing that Seth's other wife is an unfaithful witch. I carry my tumbler to the kitchen, then circle around the living room with the fingers of one hand pressed to my forehead as I think. And then I realize: I can't *not* know. I must uncover the secrets of my husband's first wife or I'll go mad.

To access Regina's full profile, I have to sign up for an account. I decide to be Will Moffit, a website owner who recently moved to Portland from California. When I'm asked for photos to upload, I use pictures of my cousin Andrew, who is currently in prison for identity theft. Ironic. I feel guilty about it, but not enough to stop me. It doesn't really matter, anyway. Once I have the information I need, I'm going to delete the account. No harm caused. I just need to take a quick peek. I fill out the information, my fingers gliding easily over the keys of my MacBook, filling line after line with perfect nonsense. Will's favorite movie is *Gladiator*. He runs marathons and has a horde of nieces and nephews whom he loves very much, but he has no children of his own. I type faster and faster. I am lost in the information I am creating. And suddenly this man, Will Moffit, feels very real. That's good. It's perfect actually. Regina will think him real, too. I want the information that will condemn my husband's first wife. Paint me in a favorable, faithful light. *Look what I have found, my love! She doesn't love you like I do!*

And then the information is there in front of me. Compiled on a website with a hopeful green banner that reads

Your soulmate is just a few clicks away! I click on Regina's profile with one hand while the other bounces on my knee. I am lucky there is no one in the room to witness my exposure of nerves. Seth always says my body language is a dead giveaway to whatever I'm feeling.

She's listed as a thirty-three-year-old divorcee from Utah. Her interests include hiking, sushi, reading autobiographies and watching documentaries. *What a bore*, I think, cracking my knuckles. I've never known Seth to watch a documentary in the years we've been together. I picture them on the couch together, holding hands underneath a blanket, her leg tossed casually over his. It doesn't seem right. But maybe I know a different Seth than Regina. That is something I haven't considered before now. Could a man be a different person with each of his wives? Could he like different things? Is he gentle when he has sex with them or does he like it rough? And perhaps that is why Regina is on a dating website in the first place. Because they have nothing in common and she is looking for someone to share her life with, someone with the same interests.

I click through her photos, recognizing some of the places in her pictures: the Arlene Schnitzer Concert Hall—Seth took me there to see the Pixies two years ago. Regina is standing in front of a poster of Tom Petty, hands perched on her hips, wearing a broad smile. In another photo she sits in a kayak, a Mariners cap shading most of her face as she holds an oar above her head in triumph. I reach the last photo and it's then that I see her. I have to blink a few times to clear my vision. How long have I been looking at the computer screen? Is my brain playing tricks on me?

Standing up, I set my MacBook on the coffee table and walk over to the bar to make myself a real drink. No orange juice to cushion the taste of the liquor this time. I pour myself two fingers of bourbon and carry it back to the sofa. I'm not sure of what I saw and maybe I didn't see anything, but the only way to know for sure is to walk back to my laptop and look at what spooked me in the first place. I bend over and hit the space bar. The screen lights up, and Regina's photo is still there. I stare at it for a moment, my eyes narrowing before I turn away. I can't be sure, there isn't enough to be sure. The picture is of Regina standing in front of a restaurant, her arm casually thrown around a friend's shoulders. She's cropped the photo to show only herself, but there next to her is the slight profile of a much taller, much blonder woman. A woman who looks shockingly like Hannah Ovark. I click the icon that says *Send Message* and begin typing.

TEN

When I drive to work the following afternoon, I'm so distracted by thoughts of the wives that I miss my turn into the hospital and it takes me twenty minutes to loop back around in traffic. Swearing, I jerk my car in a spot in the employee garage and take the steps two at a time instead of waiting for the elevator. I'd spent my afternoon composing a message to Regina from Will. I kept it short: Hey! I'm new to the area. You're an attorney. Badass. You showed up in my matches so I thought I'd reach out. This is me reaching out...awkwardly. No one said I was good at this dating thing. I ended the message with a smiley face and hit Send. It was just enough self-deprecating charm to catch a woman's attention. Will screamed: *I'm honest and not threatened by your success*—or at least I thought so. On the off chance that Regina messages him back I'll have an "in" to getting to know her.

"You're late." Lauren, one of the nurses, frowns at me as I walk through the doors. Why do people always feel the need to tell you you're late like you don't already know it yourself? My jaw clenches. I hate Lauren. I hate her always-on-time perfectness, the easy way she handles difficult patients like it's her absolute pleasure to do so. She loves to take command; a perfectly pretty, blond general.

I relax my face in an attempt to look apologetic and mutter something about traffic as I try to squeeze past her. She pushes her chair away from the computer, blocking my way and staring me down.

"You look like shit," she says. "What's up?"

The last thing I want to do is explain myself to know-it-all Lauren Haller. I stare right through her as I consider what to say.

"Didn't sleep well. This schedule sometimes fucks with me, you know?" I look longingly toward the break room, wishing she'd let me pass.

Lauren studies me for a moment like she's deciding whether or not she believes me, then finally nods. "You'll get used to it. I was like that my first year, didn't know my ass from my elbow, I was so tired."

I restrain the eye roll and smile. It isn't my first year. And technically she's only been here a year longer than I have, but she brandishes the seniority around like a cheerleader in uniform. *Rah rah, I'm better than you!*

"Yeah? Thanks, Lo, I'm sure it'll get better." I head for the break room, head down, to stash my stuff in my locker.

"Have a glass of wine," she calls after me. "Before you go to bed. That's what I do."

I lift a hand to signify I've heard her and duck out of

sight. The last thing I want to do is absolutely anything Lauren does. I'd rather be sober for the rest of my life than imitate her bedtime behaviors.

The break room is mercifully empty when I slip inside. I breathe easy and eye the lockers like I do every day. Same ol', same ol'. People have decorated the front sides of their lockers with photos of husbands, children and grandchildren in various shades of happiness. There are anniversary cards, vacation magnets and the occasional dried flower—all taped up with pride. I kick aside a green balloon, which dangles limply in front of my own locker, the remnants of someone's birthday. Happy 40th! it declares in primary colors. There is a smudge of white frosting on the top of it, a slip of a sticky finger. The front side of my locker is empty, save for the remains of a Sub Pop sticker its last occupant crookedly slapped on the metal. When maintenance tried to remove it, it left behind gray fuzz that stubbornly lingers despite how many times I've tried to scratch it off. I really should put something up, a picture of Seth and me, maybe.

The thought depresses me. I suppose that's why I haven't done it. I don't feel like he is all mine, and the knowledge that somewhere out there, that two other women may have a picture of Seth on their desks or taped to a locker, makes me sick to my stomach. I reach up absently to touch the sore spot on my ear and think of Hannah's bruises. An accident, she'd said. Same as what happened last night. An accident.

My eyes stray to Lauren's locker, which is four spots over from mine. Most days I try not to look, keeping my eyes trained on my blank space, reminding myself it doesn't matter—but today I stare at each one of her photos, a strange feeling bubbling in my belly. Mostly there are glossy four-by-six selfies with an occasional card stuck between them, a sappy *You are the love of my life* in pink cursive across the front. The cards seem like a dare. Anyone can go over and flip it open to read what's inside, and part of me thinks Lauren wants that. I take a step closer to study the photos: Lauren and John posing in front of the Eiffel Tower, Lauren and John kissing in front of the pyramids, Lauren and John hugging next to a trolley in San Francisco. How many times had I heard her tell people that they were an "adventure couple"?

I've suspected that the only reason Lauren and John travel so much is because they can't have children, and my suspicion was confirmed when I was pregnant and she suddenly stopped talking to me. I asked one of the other nurses about it and she'd told me in a hushed voice that it was hard for Lauren to be around pregnant women what with all of her miscarriages. I'd brushed it off, giving her room and making sure never to mention my pregnancy around her. A few months later when I lost our baby, Lauren had taken an immediate interest in me again, acting like we were long-lost sisters. She'd even gone as far as sending a huge bouquet of flowers to the condo when I took the week off of work to grieve. The whole thing made me uncomfortable, having something so ugly and devastating in common with someone. Maybe if we had books in common, or an interest in makeup, or a television show—empty wombs weren't a bonding topic. I'd ignored her invitations for Seth and me to come over for dinner until they finally stopped coming. Her texts eventually stopped, too, and now we barely make eye contact unless she's busting my balls about something.

The truth is, Lauren's happy vacations and attentive husband stories make me jealous. She doesn't have to share her husband with anyone else and I crave that, as much as I try to tell myself that I don't. Things would be so much easier if the other two weren't in the picture. Holidays whenever we wanted to take them, dinners out in public where everyone could see what a beautiful couple we were, a husband who opened the front door every night rather than two days a week. Even the fight we had last night would be avoided since it had, in essence, been instigated by the situation.

I've just collected my stethoscope and pocketed my trauma scissors when a text comes through from Seth. I cheer up as soon as I see his name. Slamming my locker, I brace myself for what has to be an apology text. I'd accept his apology, of course; I'd apologize myself for causing our argument. No use holding grudges. But when I open my phone, it's not the message I was expecting to see. My mouth goes dry as I squint at the screen.

I picked some up. I'll make an excuse and get out of it. Love you.

I stare at the words, trying to make sense of them and then it hits me: this text wasn't meant for me. Seth made a mistake, typed his message to the wrong name. It's a painful thing when you realize you've received a text your husband meant for another woman. It's even more painful when you gave him permission to do so. *Which one is it?* I think bitterly. Regina or Hannah? I squeeze my eyes closed, pocketing the phone, and take a few deep breaths before pushing through the door. I can do this. I signed up for this. Everything's fine.

In between patients, I alternate between reading Seth's mistakenly sent text, wondering what exactly it was he was trying to get out of, and scrolling through Regina's photos. I decide to text Hannah—see if she'll let on about anything.

Hi! Hope you're well. Checking how everything is. I send it and pocket my phone until five minutes later when I'm changing someone's IV and there's a buzzing on my leg.

"Shoot, I forgot to put that on silent." I wink at my patient, a middle-aged man who came in with chest pains.

"Go ahead and check it, honey," he says. "I know how you young people are about your phones."

The text is from Hannah. Thanks for checking on me. Feeling great! When are you in town next?

Her text is almost too cheerful. Last time I saw her, she'd said that Seth hid her birth control pills to get her pregnant.

Everything okay with you and hubby? I text back. And then, as an afterthought, I add, Maybe later this month. Let's get together!

All sorted out. ☺ And that would be great.

I stick my phone back in my pocket, a frown on my face. Hannah is a happy woman at the moment. "Look at you, Seth," I say under my breath.

Four hours later, Seth has still not acknowledged that he sent the wrong text to the wrong person. I can't imagine how exactly he will address it when it does come up. How does one deal with a situation like that? *I'm sorry, honey, I meant that text for my other wife.*

As for Regina, it's impossible to stay away now that I know all of the information is out there—just floating around on the internet. It's creepy actually, that a person can just scroll through your life without you knowing. I've studied the photos and visited her friends' pages, searching for comments she might have left on their posts. I want to know more—everything—even the way she interacts with people.

"You've been bent over that phone all night…" Debbie, a middle-aged nurse, swings around the nurses' station, carrying an armful of charts. Her French braid is the same bright yellow as the suns on her scrubs. I turn back to my phone without acknowledging her, hoping she takes the hint. The last thing I feel like dealing with is questions, especially since Lauren already gave me the third degree.

Debbie drops the folders onto the counter, then scoots next to me, standing on her tiptoes to catch a glimpse of my phone. Her broad expanse of hip and breast brushes against my arm, and I shoot her a look that I hope says, *Back off!* Some of the other nurses and I have a running joke about it—if anyone gets too nosy you call them Debbie and tell them to back off.

"What are you looking at?" she chirps as I lift my elbows to prevent her from seeing the screen.

Some people have no concept of personal space. I hold the phone to my chest, the screen hidden, and frown at her.

"An ex-girlfriend," she says matter-of-factly, folding her arms across her ample bosom. "I check on Bill's all the time."

Debbie and Bill have been married for as long as I've been alive. What ex-girlfriends could still be around to pose a threat to their deep-rooted marriage? I want to ask, but asking Debbie anything means an hour-long conversation. But my curiosity is piqued, so I ask, anyway. "What do you mean?"

"Oh, honey. When you've been around as long as me…"

I soften at her tone. Clearly, I'm not the only woman who

suffers from insecurities, who lets them get to me until I act irrationally. I structure a question in my mind, one that won't give anything about my situation away.

"How do you deal with it—the doubts about whether he loves you?"

Debbie blinks at me, surprised. "It's not his love I'm worried about," she says. "It's theirs."

Someone walks past us carrying a Styrofoam cup of coffee. Debbie waits until she's around the corner and out of earshot before continuing.

"Women can be very conniving, if you know what I mean." She gives me a look that says I *should* know what she means. But I've never had many friends, just Anna, really, and my mother and sister. But yeah, if you pay attention to TV and movies, they paint women in an untrustworthy light.

"I guess so," I say.

"Well, I wouldn't put anything past them. Or myself for that matter. I know what I'm capable of."

Our heads bent together, I try to picture cheerful, plump Debbie as the conniving type she's referencing and can't.

Debbie looks around to make sure no one can overhear us, and then she leans so close to me I can smell the cherry blossom shower gel she uses.

"I stole him from my best friend."

"Bill?" I ask, confused.

Bill has a potbelly that sits on top of two spindly legs and only a horseshoe pattern of hair left on his head. It's hard to believe he ever needed stealing.

"And you still, um…look at her profile?"

"Of course." Debbie pulls a stick of gum from her pocket

and offers me half. I shake my head and she folds the stick onto her tongue in a perfect half.

"Why?"

"Because women don't ever stop wanting what they want. They see another man who's considerate and handsome, and it reminds them of what they're missing in their own lives."

There is a bitter taste in my mouth. I wish I'd taken the half stick of gum she'd offered. If Debbie is worried about Bill's exes twenty years past, how much should I be worrying about the women my husband fucks on the regular?

Just then, her pager buzzes, and she shoots me a wry look as she unclips it from her hip and glances at the screen.

"Have to run, doll. Talk later."

I watch her go, the wide gait of her steps as her white Reeboks squeak down the hall. Before she reaches the junction near the elevators, she turns around and faces me. Her arms pump at her sides while she walks backward.

"It's even better when you spy on them in person, by the way." She winks and then she's gone.

Nosy, annoying, no-personal-space Debbie just might be my new best friend. I hear a *ping* on my phone. When I look down, a notification has appeared at the top of the screen. It's from the dating app I downloaded. Regina has sent you a message.

ELEVEN

The front door swings open and Seth walks in, carrying two large bags of takeout. Ah, it's Thursday. I'd forgotten. Lately, all I think about is my husband's wives. Somewhere along the way, Seth has been replaced. I give him half a smile. We both know it's forced. A bouquet of white roses rests in the crook of his arm. Roses for no reason, or roses because he sent me a text meant for one of the others? Normally, I'd rush over to relieve him of what he's carrying, but this time I stay where I am. He never even attempted to explain his mistaken text. And I waited all week for something…anything. My mood is dour—and I don't plan on faking a good mood for his sake.

I picked some up. I'll make an excuse and get out of it. Love you.
The lines on his face are relaxed, his eyes alert. I fold a

towel and place it carefully on the put-away pile as I watch him kick the door closed and come sauntering down the hallway toward me. Everything about his demeanor bothers me. He's not playing the part of the contrite husband.

"For you," he says, handing over the flowers.

I stand awkwardly with them in my hand for a few seconds, and then set them aside to deal with later. I'm a mess again—hair loose and air-dried to waves. I'm wearing my favorite yoga pants, the ones with the hole in the right leg. I brush hair out of my eyes as he holds up the take-out bags and shakes them at me.

"Dinner," he declares.

The smile he's wearing is almost contagious, except I don't feel like smiling. I wonder if he's pleased with himself for picking up dinner, or if he has good news. It's a risk grabbing takeout without knowing if I cooked, but I suppose he suspects I am on strike.

"Why are you so happy?" I fold my last towel and pick up the pile to carry to the towel closet. Seth smacks my butt as I move past him. I think about shooting him a death glare, but I keep my head stiffly pointed forward. Why does his effort bother me now? I would have reveled in this attention a few weeks ago.

"Can't a man be happy to come home to his girl?" *Can't a man be happy to come home to just one girl?*

I press my lips together to keep from actually saying those words and busy myself arranging the towels in the linen closet.

When I'm finished with the laundry, we sit down at the kitchen bar to eat. I've said no more than a few words since he walked through the door, though he hasn't seemed to notice. Or perhaps he's ignoring my silence as a way to pretend everything is fine. I watch as he unloads grease-stained containers onto the counter, glancing at me every few minutes to gauge my reaction.

The smell of garlic and ginger wafts from the boxes and my stomach grumbles. He stands up to get plates but I wave him back.

"No need," I say, leaning forward and pulling a container of garlic chicken toward me. Flipping open the lid I pinch a piece of chicken between my chopsticks, watching him over the rim of the box as I chew. He eyes my UGGs, which are propped up on the counter next to the food, bewildered amusement on his face.

"First ramen, now Chinese takeout," I say. "Next comes pizza…" It's meant as a joke, but my voice is devoid of emotion. It sounded more like a threat, I think.

Seth laughs, dragging his bar stool closer to mine, reaching for the lo mein. "And shoes inside," he says of my UGGs. "I like it."

"To be fair, UGGs are practically slippers." I'm flirting and I hate myself for it.

"I didn't know you were capable of allowing yourself to breathe," Seth says.

My toes curl in protest. I have the urge to yank my boots off the counter and grab proper plates from the cabinet, but I stubbornly stay where I am, staring squarely at my husband. Maybe I want to focus on knowing the man instead of impressing the man. Probably something I should have done in the first place. Instead, I'd been swoony, full of dreams and the belief that we had something.

I set the container of chicken on the counter and wipe my mouth with one of the flimsy napkins Seth hands me. For the first time, I notice that he's wearing a T-shirt underneath a hoodie I've never seen before. When was the last time I saw my husband this casual, in a T-shirt? For the last year, Seth's wardrobe has consisted of dress shirts and ties, distressed loafers and sports coats—work Seth, married Seth. He looks like an entirely different man in scuffed Chucks and a worn T-shirt. I feel something stir in my belly... Desire? *Someone I'd like to hang out with*, I think.

"You're different tonight," I say.

"So are you."

"What?" I'm so lost in my thoughts, his voice alarms me.

"You're different, too," he notes.

I shrug; it feels terribly juvenile to do so, but what is there to say? *I've found your wives and now that they have names and faces everything feels different? I don't know who you are anymore? I don't know who I am?*

It's difficult to put into words all the things I've been feeling, so I say the only thing I've actually worked out. "People change..."

I'm almost afraid of the casual way he's looking at me, and then I remind myself that I'm trying to care less about what he thinks and to focus on what I think.

"You're right." He picks up his beer and holds it out to me. "To change," he says.

I hesitate only for a moment before raising my bottle of water and tipping it toward his beer. His eyes hold steadily on to mine as we toast and sip our drinks.

"Let's go for a walk," he says, standing up and stretching his arms above his head. His T-shirt lifts to reveal a tanned, toned stomach.

I quickly look away, not wanting to be distracted. I am a sexual creature—he controls me with sex, and I control him with sex. It's a merry-go-round of pleasure and servitude that I've always enjoyed. But being dick-whipped or pussy-whipped can sate you just enough to blind you. My mother once told me that a relationship could withstand almost any trial if the sex was good. It had sounded shallow and ridiculous at the time, but now I see that's exactly what has happened with Seth and me. A lot happens in a relationship, probably a lot that you really need to pay attention to, but you're too busy fucking to notice.

At the door, I shrug on my jacket and pull a beanie over my hair. I turn to the door and find Seth staring at me, a strange expression on his face.

"What?" I ask. "Why are you looking at me like that?"

"Nothing," he says, a little sheepishly after being caught. "Just appreciating the view."

He leans in and kisses me lightly on the tip of my nose before opening the door. I follow him into the elevator, my nose tingling. We ride to the lobby in silence, and when we step out, he grabs my hand. What's gotten into him? Flirting, public displays of affection… It's like he's a different man. As we step out onto the sidewalk, a feeling lurks in the back of my mind, something I've forgotten. I push the thought away. *Here and now*, I tell myself. *Be here and stop thinking about everything else.*

Normally, Seth and I don't venture out of the condo on the days he visits, part of the reason being we prefer to stay at home and just be together. The other part, of course, is being spotted by someone who knows him as Regina's husband. In the beginning it bothered me; I'd try to get him to go out to a restaurant or the movies, but he insisted on staying home. It hadn't seemed fair at the time—I was his legal wife, after all. Eventually I gave up, resigning our relationship to be one that stayed behind closed doors. And

now here we are, stepping out into the wet streets of Seattle, my hand firmly gripped in his. *Brava for me!*

Seth glances at me and smiles, like this is as much of a
treat for him as it is for me. My boots plow through puddles
as we make our way to a cider stand on Pike. Seth unrolls
dollars from his money clip, one after another. He leaves a
generous tip and hands me a paper cup of liquid gold. The
money clip was a gift from me a few Christmases ago. I've
not seen him use it until now; he always carries a worn
leather wallet in his back pocket.

We huddle underneath an awning with our drinks and
listen to a street musician play a Lionel Ritchie song on his
fiddle. As we sip, we glance almost shyly at each other, and
it feels like it did on our first date—charged and unfamiliar. There is a change between us tonight, a new chemistry we've not tapped into before. I imagine we could have
had this all along if there were two instead of four people
in the marriage. Our bond would be strengthened instead
of pulled thin.

Seth pulls me close and I lean into him, resting my head
on his shoulder, humming along with the song. I'm pressed
so tightly against him that when his cell phone rings I can
feel the vibrations against my leg. Seth, who normally has
his phone turned off when he's with me, pats his pocket
with his free hand. I angle my body away from his so he can
reach it, taking a careful sip of my cider. It scalds the roof
of my mouth; I press the tip of my tongue to the burned
spot as I wait to see if he'll answer.

When he pulls his phone from his pocket, he makes no
move to hide the screen from me. Regina's name flashes across
his wallpaper—a group photo of his nieces and nephews in

their Halloween costumes. I bite my lip and look away, feeling like I've done something wrong.

"Do you mind?" he asks, holding up the phone. The name Regina stares at me. I blink at him, confused. Is he asking me for permission to take a call from his other wife?

I shake my head dumbly, shifting my eyes back to the fiddler, who is now playing a Miley Cyrus song with gusto.

"Hello," I hear him say. "Yeah... Did you put it in peanut butter? She'll take it that way... Okay, let me know how it goes."

He's talking to Regina in front of me. It's like a metal ping striking at the center of me with sharpness. *Ouch, ouch, ouch.*

He slides his phone back into his pocket, nonplussed.

"Our dog," he says, watching the fiddler with renewed interest. "She's old and sick. She'll only take her pill with peanut butter."

Seth has a dog.

"Oh," I say. I feel stupid, emotionally clumsy. Had I ever noticed dog hair on his clothes? "What type of dog?"

He grins his lopsided grin. "A Sheltie. She's an old lady now—has trouble with her back legs. She had surgery a few days ago and won't take her medicine."

I listen, fascinated. His other life, a detail most would consider mundane, but I cling to it, want more. A dog. We briefly considered getting a dog, but living in a condo seemed unfair to an animal—that and my work hours.

"What's her name?" I ask cautiously.

I'm afraid that if I ask too many questions he'll shut down or get angry with me for prying. But he doesn't.

He tosses his empty cup into an overflowing trash can and says, "Smidge. Regina named her. I wanted something generic like Lassie." He laughs at the memory and then waves at a toddler who bellows, *"Hi!"* as his mother pushes him past in his stroller. I look away quickly. I can't look toddlers in the eye.

"You've never said her name," I say.

Seth tucks his hands in his pockets and stares at me. "Haven't I?"

"No," I say. "And last week you sent me a text meant for one of them…"

His head jerks back and I can see the uncertainty in his eyes. "What did it say?"

I study his face, not believing the pretense. "You know what it said, Seth."

"I'm sorry, baby. I don't remember. If I did, it was my mistake and completely hurtful to you. Forgive me?"

I pull my lips tight. There isn't really another option, is there? I could drag this out and sulk for a few more days, but what good would that do anyone? I nod, forcing my lips into a smile.

"Come on," he says, holding out his hand. "Let's get back. It's freezing out here."

I let him twine his fingers with mine and suddenly we're running across the street, me holding my beanie to my head and skipping up the curb. I hear myself laughing as we dodge slow-moving bodies on the sidewalk. He looks back at me and I smile shyly, the wings of infatuation beating in my belly.

We kiss as we ride the elevator to our floor, even though there's someone else in there with us—a middle-aged woman with a trembling Yorkie. She draws as far away from us as she can, pressing herself to a corner of the elevator as if we're contagious.

"Where have you been?" I whisper against Seth's lips.

"Here, I've been here." He's as breathless as I am, his hands groping through the puffiness of my coat. He yanks the zipper down, the noise startling in the confines of the elevator.

On the mirrored wall behind us, I see the woman's face pale. She clutches her purse tighter to her chest and stares at the numbers above the door, willing herself away from us. The Yorkie whines. I laugh into Seth's mouth as he pushes my coat off my shoulders and reaches to cup my breast. The doors slide open and she charges out. They slide closed and we climb higher. His hand is between my legs, his thumb rubbing circles. When the doors open on our floor, we move together, not wanting to let go.

Later, we lie in bed, our limbs tangled and our skin damp from exertion. Seth traces a line with his fingertips up and down my arm. I curl into him, enjoying the moment, everything but us forgotten. Just for tonight. Tonight, I will forget. Tomorrow is a different story. And then I remember the thing that's been bothering me, swimming in my mind right out of reach: Regina's message.

Hi, Will,
I don't mind the compliments at all! I worked hard to get through law school—lay 'em on me. ☺
I have a heavy workload right now, but I can make time for fun. You mentioned that you like to hike. Maybe we can do that sometime. I'm up for drinks, too, if you prefer that. Your nieces and nephews are adorable. You seem great with kids.
Talk soon,
Regina

With Seth snoring softly beside me, I read her message to Will three times before I write my response. There is more I want to know, to confirm, and Will is the only way I can do that.

Hey, Regina,
Since you've given me permission to load on the compliments I guess I should tell you that you're stunning. I'd love to go on a hike with you! And yes, my nieces and nephews are adorable. Do you want kids? I guess that's a really personal question but somewhat important to know when you're dating.
Will

It's been just a few minutes since I hit Send on Will's message when my phone lights up on the nightstand. I glance over my shoulder at Seth to see that his back is to me as he snores. Lifting my phone carefully from where it lies, I'm surprised to see a notification that Regina has sent me/Will a message. It's late and I wonder why she's awake, and then I remember Seth telling me that she'd stay up long after he went to bed, working—always working.

Will, what are you doing up so late? Looks like you're a night owl like me. I can never sleep. There's a really great hiking trail near my house. It takes about four hours round trip. Let's do this!
And yes, I do want children. Let's have a phone conversation soon.
Talk later,
Regina

TWELVE

It's Sunday and I'm at my parents' for lunch. My mother is nowhere to be found. I've just read Regina's last email to Will for the tenth time and I slam my phone down on the kitchen counter. Worried I've cracked the screen, I flip it over to check for damage. To my relief, there is none. I'm still angry enough to slam it again so I walk to the window and stare at the mist rolling across Elliott Bay while I get my feelings in order. Regina is cheating on Seth; the flirtatious tone she uses in the messages to the man she thinks is Will is escalating. And on top of that, I don't know why she's lying to him about wanting kids. Just this morning, she'd sent Will a suggestive photo of herself in a bikini (probably because she liked the flattery about her looks). It had really irked me to think the photo was from a vacation she'd taken with *our* husband. I don't know if I'm more upset by the fact that she's going to hurt Seth, or that I have to share him with a woman who can't even stay faithful, and who orders pizza, for God's sake. I have to tell him. He needs to know.

My father walks into the kitchen a moment later, a case of Diet Coke under his arm.

"I found a box of Diet in the garage fridge," he says. "That okay?"

"Fine," I say. Though it's not fine. I don't drink Diet. He pops a can and pours the contents into a glass with ice. I take it from him and sip. Perfume: it tastes like perfume. Or maybe that's just the bitter taste that's been lingering in my mouth since breakfast when I read Regina's fourth message to Will. She finally told Will she was divorced, not expounding on when, or why. It is partly the truth—Seth divorced Regina to legally marry me, but their relationship hasn't ended.

"Where's Mom?"

My father pulls a beer from the fridge. He doesn't offer me one because it's not ladylike for women to drink this early in the day, or so he's told me. "At the store. Where else?"

"Ladies' church group, Nordstrom, the gym, with Sylvie, the spa…"

"Good point." He winks at me before rummaging around in a drawer for a bottle opener.

"It's in there," I say, pointing to the drawer closest to the back door. My parents have lived in this house for twenty years and my father still doesn't know where things are kept. I blame my mother for this, for never allowing him to open his own bottle of beer.

As if on cue, my mother bustles into the kitchen, plastic grocery bags crackling in her hands, eyeing us like we're wolves trying to eat her. "What are you two on about?" she asks.

I watch as she sets the bags down and reaches up to pat her hair, something my grandmother used to do when she was nervous. I get a whiff of her perfume: Estée Lauder something or the other.

"We're gossiping about you, Mom, were your ears burning?" She touches her ear, frowning.

"Where's Seth?" she asks. "We haven't seen him in weeks."

My husband is being someone else's husband tonight.

"He's in Portland till Thursday."

She knows this, I told her yesterday when she called, asking about his whereabouts. She likes to rub in the fact that he puts work before me. I take a sip of my drink, the bubbles fizzing close to my nose. In her mind, it is because I don't wife hard enough. She once told me that the fact I had a job was probably driving Seth to be away more.

"How do you figure that?" I'd asked her.

"He feels like he needs to compete with you, work more. A woman's place is in her home. And your father never let a business meeting keep him from being home for dinner on time," she'd said.

My father doesn't even know where the bottle opener is, I want to say to her. I think about the last dinner I made for Seth— hadn't he opened the bottle of wine that was sitting on the table? Yes, and he knew in which drawer I kept the cork-screw.

"You should really think about joining a gym to keep yourself busy." Ah, we've moved on to ridiculing my body.

She rinses her hands under the faucet, glancing back to eye my thighs. I push up on my toes, lifting my thighs off the seat of the chair so they don't look so wide.

"Seth is doing what a man should do," my father chides my mother. "Working hard to build his future, to be a good provider." My father—sticking up for me and promoting patriarchy all in one sentence. *Bravo!*

I smile at him gratefully, anyway. I have more mommy issues than daddy ones. It doesn't matter that I have the trust fund and a stable job that pays the mortgage on our condo, Seth is the one working to provide for his family— three of them actually.

"Of course," my mother says quickly. "It would just be nice if we could see him every once in a while. Michael was over here last weekend with your sister. He got a promotion and bought her a new BMW. They're going to Greece for their three-year anniversary." My mother announces all of this like it's her who got the car and is going to Greece. This is my normal; I live in the shade of my sister's great big life. If I'd had a baby first, she'd be living in mine, but alas, that was never in the cards for me.

"I have to get back to work. I'll leave you two hens to your girl stuff." He kisses my mother on the cheek before removing himself to his study.

"Girl stuff," I say out loud. "Should we be fertilizing eggs or cooking them?"

She hears the disgust in my voice and immediately shushes me. "You know what he means."

"Mom," I sigh. "I actually do…that's what upsets me."

She looks at me sharply, the cat-eye glasses she's wearing catching the light from the window.

"I don't know what's gotten into you," she says.

She's right. I would never normally say things like this. Hannah has gotten into me…and Regina. Deep, deep, deep into me. I stare down at my half-empty glass of Diet Coke, tears stinging my eyes, then I reach up gingerly to touch my almost-healed ear. You could give your all to a man, every last thing, and you'd still end up with a bruised ear. Why had I sought out Seth's other wives? I've ruined everything. *But for whom?* I ask myself. *You or Seth?* Now nothing seems fair, not even my parents' marriage. I am falling apart, picking at my relationship like it's a scab. I think of Regina's messages to Will. I've poured through them over the last few days, reading them over and over till I have her writing style memorized. She is to the point but flirtatious, paying attention to the little things he says. Addicted to the details. Is that because Seth is too preoccupied with three relationships to notice the details? Regina, who placed herself on a dating website, who is eagerly writing messages to a man named Will just because he is saying all the right things. Am I next? Will I become so disillusioned by my marriage that I'll seek relationships elsewhere? If only my baby hadn't died. There would be no Hannah, Regina would be the distant, pizza-ordering wife and I would have all of Seth. I failed him in the most important way and he had to go to someone else to give him what I couldn't.

My mother sets down a plate of salad in front of me, the cherry tomatoes from her garden an angry red among all the green. There is still a chance for me. I could expose Regina for what she is. Seth would see that I have his best interest at heart, that I am his true champion. He didn't realize how much of a toll this lifestyle was taking on him: the angry outbursts were just one of the ways his stress was manifesting. It wouldn't matter that I couldn't give him children. I would leave Hannah to that. And besides, she would be preoccupied with their baby. Aren't new mothers notorious for neglecting their men once they have a tiny person to take care of? I would step in where she failed.

My mind is made up. I know what I have to do. If I can't beat Hannah, I will beat Regina. Take the nest from three to two.

Hi, Regina,
I love Tom Waits. Saw him in concert a few years ago. It was probably my favorite concert of all time. I'm sorry to hear about your marriage. My sister got a divorce last year and she's still a mess about it. I'm glad you're okay and ready to get back out there again! His loss is my gain. If you don't mind me asking, what was the reason you decided to end things? Do you have any regrets about your marriage? As for me, I haven't had a serious relationship in a while. I've thrown myself into my work these last few years. But I'm ready to settle down (I think). Will be visiting my sister in Montana this weekend—what are you doing?
Talk soon,
Will

THIRTEEN

Pathetic. I can't even get having a fight with my husband right.

I replay our conversation over in my head, the one we had after I left my parents' house. I'd called Seth as soon as I pulled out of their driveway. I wanted to tell him how great our time had been together, how much I enjoyed being with him the other night, but he sent me to voice mail. He called back twenty minutes later when I was walking into the elevator of our building.

"Hey," he'd said. "I was on the phone..." His voice had cut out and as I held the phone closer to my ear I heard the word "...parents..."

Seth's parents: I'd never met them. Their lifestyle meant keeping to themselves most of the time, and they rarely traveled outside of Utah. As the elevator door opened and I spilled out, I had an idea. I'd suggested it to Seth.

"We should take our vacation to Utah! How long has it been since you've spent time with your family?" I'd expected him to love the idea, jump on the opportunity to use our time together to go home, but Seth's reaction shocked me, his voice immediately going cold.

"No," he'd said, followed by a deep sigh, like I was a child. Seth has been putting off a face-to-face meeting with his parents for the two years we've been together. "My family is fucked up," he'd always said. "Busy people." He says "busy" like I'm not busy, like I couldn't possibly understand the demands of their life.

"You have half siblings!" I'd argued. "Surely they can spare some time. I'd like to meet them…"

Seth had shot down the idea somewhat aggressively, and we'd argued about it until I gave in. That's what I do to avoid losing Seth's favor—I give in. I will not be the nagging shrew. I will not be the difficult wife. I will be the favorite, the one who makes his life easier. Who volunteers to suck his cock to ease his bad day and moans like it's her receiving the pleasure.

The truth is, I'm not even sure I want to meet his parents. They're polygamists, for God's sake. Not the kind we are, either. They all live together and wear odd clothes and raise children collectively like they're some sort of rabbit-fucking hive. Imagine looking the *other woman* in the eye every day, washing her dishes and changing her children's diapers, and knowing she was clawing your husband's back in pleasure last night. It seems so twisted, but who am I to talk? The reason I haven't told any of my friends or family the truth is because of how twisted it would sound to them.

Either way, they are his parents, and on principle, it feels right that I should meet them. I've earned that. A thought occurs to me that I'm not entirely comfortable with: What if they've already met Hannah? Would Seth even tell me if they had? After his reaction that left me bleeding, I'm too afraid to ask.

I pour myself a glass of wine, my second for the hour, and wander into the living room to watch some TV. The only thing I can find to watch are episodes of trash reality shows that I've already seen. Somehow, the messy lives of reality stars make me feel better about my own. There is something dull and vapid about the plastic-looking women on those shows, despite their fame and fortune—no matter if they deserve it or not. There is something hopeful about that for the rest of us. *We're all fucked up, every single one of us*, I think.

But twenty minutes later, I can't seem to focus. I turn off the TV and stare at a wall, my anger still festering. I go to the hall closet to retrieve the cards his parents have sent over the years, eight in total, and study the signatures at the bottom. The cards are generic, flowers or teddy bears on the front of them—all the same, never with anything personal aside from their hastily scratched names: Perry and Phyllis. That seems strange, doesn't it? They might not know me, but they could at least express their desire to. *Can't wait to meet you! Hugs!* Or maybe even, *Seth says such wonderful things about you.* I think about all the cards I've sent them, my eagerness spelled out in the notes I've written, telling them about our condo in Seattle and—before the miscarriage—the names we'd chosen for the baby. I feel silly about it now, sharing all of those details with them and them not caring enough to respond. I wish I could ask

Hannah or Regina about them—what they thought, if they ever had any meaningful interaction.

I've not so much as emailed with his mother, though I've asked on several occasions for her email address. I figure that if we can make some sort of connection online, we've made progress. Seth always tells me he'll send it over and never quite gets around to it.

The day before our wedding, his dad, Perry, had been rushed in for emergency gallbladder surgery and his mom hadn't wanted to leave her husband's side. I hadn't seen the problem, since there were four other wives to tend to him, weren't there?

"She's his legal wife. She has to be there to oversee things in case something comes up," Seth told me.

After they missed the wedding, they promised to come up for Christmas, but then his mother came down with pneumonia. For Easter it was strep throat, and the following Christmas it was something else. When I lost the baby, they sent flowers, which I'd thrown straight in the trash. I didn't want any reminders of what had happened. They always send a card on my birthday, fifty dollars tucked inside.

I finish my glass of wine and pull up Regina's Facebook profile. Maybe she has pictures with them somewhere. It's a long shot but worth a try. Seth doesn't have any pictures of them. He says they hate cameras and cell phones, and for legal reasons never take any photos together. Just as I thought, Regina's profile yields no information. Neither does Hannah's. I don't know if I should feel relieved or more upset.

I turn away from my MacBook, frustrated. If I want answers there is only one thing I can do, and that includes me continuing to go behind Seth's back. A message in my email says Regina has messaged Will back. I sign in to the site, feeling anxious. I've been wondering when she will request a meet-up, and trying to decide what I'll say, but so far she seems okay to take things slow. The message is a long one. I upgrade from wine, pouring myself a vodka instead and settling on the couch, sucking on my bottom lip while I read.

Hi, Will,
Just got home after a day full of meetings. I'm blown. Will probably just order takeout and watch Netflix. It's nice that you're visiting family this weekend, have fun!

My marriage...hmm, that's a tough one. We worked hard at it for a few years, probably even after we both knew it was over. In the end, we were just very different people who wanted different things. He's married to someone else now...happy, I hear.

Sometimes it bothers me that he was able to move on so quickly while I needed time to heal, but I suppose we all deal with things differently. Why did your last relationship end? Were you together long?
Regina

I stare at the screen for a long time contemplating her words. *Different people who wanted different things.* Why is she lying? What does she have to gain by developing this relationship with a man over the internet? I know the answer even before I complete the thought: she's lonely. Seth's attention wanes thin and at times seems nonexistent, so the attention of a stranger would sate a deep need to be seen...and heard. Regardless of why, the fact is she actually *is* cheating. And Seth has no clue. I close the lid to my MacBook and stare out the window. I contemplate taking a walk; things can get claustrophobic in a high-rise. You can spend days going to the in-building gym, visiting the vending machine for drinks instead of walking the block to the market and staring out at the world beneath you instead of venturing out into it. I've found that more and more I am opting to stay home when I'm not at work, feeling less inclined to brave the drizzle when it isn't for a good reason. Before, in my old life, you couldn't keep me inside. If I've changed so much in the last few years, maybe Regina has, too. Perhaps she realizes she doesn't want to be with Seth anymore, and this is her way of feeling out the dating scene. In which case her messages to Will are a good thing. For me at least. If I tell Seth what I know about her, I'll have a lot of explaining to do. I decide not to say anything to Seth. I'll wait to see what else she writes to Will before I decide. I'm flicking through channels on the TV ten minutes later when I stop on one of those shows about internet relationships. The show brings people together who've interacted solely through the internet, often to find that one or the other has been lied to in depth. I flinch, thinking of "Will," the photos of my cousin I've uploaded to the site. What people present on the internet is seldom true to real life. If I want to know who Regina Coele really is, I need to see her in real life like I saw Hannah.

I call the law firm of Markel & Abel and tell the receptionist that I would like to schedule an appointment with Regina Coele. I'm put on hold, and as I wait, there's a twist in the pit of my stomach. I ask myself what I'm doing. This isn't like me; for years I've accepted everything quietly... submissively. But it's too late now; I opened one too many doors, and the lust for knowledge overpowers rationality. She transfers me to Regina's secretary, who tells me that her earliest available appointment is three weeks from today. I feel a surge of disappointment. Three weeks seems like an eternity.

"Are you sure there's nothing sooner than that?" I ask.

"I'm afraid not. Ms. Coele is booked through. I can put you on a wait-list, but to be honest, we hardly ever have cancellations." Her voice is nasally and matter-of-fact—a real Hermione Granger if I've ever heard one.

"All right, then," I sigh. "I suppose I have no choice."

"I'll just get you set up in the system with some basic information, then," she tells me. I hear the clacking of computer keys and then she begins to ask me questions.

I tell her that my name is Lauren Brian from Oregon. When she asks about the nature of my visit, I tell her that it's concerning divorce, and suddenly she's different, her voice much kinder. So much so that I wonder if she's experienced a divorce herself. The thought of divorcing Seth makes me sick to my stomach. I don't want to divorce him—I want him for myself. But first I need to know the nature of his relationship with Regina. She asks me a series of questions—are children involved, did we sign a prenup, how long have we been married? "Don't worry," she says before she hangs up. "Ms. Coele is one of the most competent attorneys in Oregon."

Competent Regina. I wonder if someone would describe me as the most competent nurse in Seattle? Lo most certainly wouldn't.

When I hang up the phone, I walk directly to the bar and make myself a vodka and soda. I'm lonely, I realize as the ice cubes crack beneath the vodka. Lonely and sad. I shouldn't be; I am young and vibrant, and these are my best years. *This is necessary*, I tell myself, pushing aside the guilt of sneaking around. *You have to figure this out.*

FOURTEEN

I think about Hannah all morning. It's becoming an obsession to wonder where she is and what she's doing. I'm not sleeping well; even when I swallow the sleeping pills my doctor prescribed me, I wake in the middle of the night, my body covered in a sheen of sweat. I have forgotten what my own happiness means. What the definition is to me as a person. This influx of emotion was brought on by Regina's last message to Will, when she asked him what makes him truly happy. I'd answered as Will: my family, my job. But when I switched gears and contemplated what made *me* happy, I was unable to come up with a good answer. I know what makes Seth happy, and I know that I feel happiness when he does, but doesn't that point to the fact that I've completely lost my own identity to identify *with* him? I've become that woman—the one who is made happy by the happiness of others. It's disappointing to me, that I've forgotten myself entirely. When Seth found me in that coffee shop, I was in the pursuit of it to some degree. I was metaphorically wet behind the ears, lacking experience. Sometimes I wonder if he'd known that and if that was why he chose me. How easy to convince a young girl in love that she can emotionally do the impossible. And plural marriage by all means is impossible on the heart and mind. But I am determined. Seth and I have gotten off track; the way he shoved me the other day proved that. We can make it back to each other—I just need Regina out of the picture.

I decide to take a walk to clear my head. It's probably too cold, but I've been cooped up in this condo with my thoughts for too long. If I had a friend nearby, things would be different. Someone to confide in, glean wisdom from. But this secret in my marriage prevents me from developing meaningful relationships. There are too many questions, too many lies you inevitably have to tell. It is almost comical to think of someone giving advice on something as bizarre as plural marriage: *Be supportive of the other women! Remember to suck his dick as often as you can so you can be the favorite…*

Shrugging on my warmest coat, I slip my feet into my rain boots and head toward Westlake Center. The tree trunks in the square are painted cobalt blue for the Seahawks, and as I weave my way between them, I catch sight of a stand selling mulled wine and roasted chestnuts. I've already had too much to drink today, but one cup of mulled wine won't hurt. As I wait in line, I tell myself that they probably cooked all of the wine out of it.

I order a large and carry my steaming paper cup toward the shops on the other side of the street. I'm about to cross when I hear my name being called. I turn around and search the faces around me, surprised. I don't know many people in the city. Most everyone has their heads bent against the rain, and as I stall on the sidewalk, they push past me in a herd, crossing the small intersection.

And then I see her, her impossibly perfect blond hair tucked beneath a beanie and then the hood of a bright red raincoat. She looks innocent and eager, like a hipster version of Little Red Riding Hood. "Hey, I thought that was you." Lauren approaches, her face pink from either exertion or cold. She rests a hand on my shoulder as she bends over to catch her breath. "I ran to catch up," she says. "You were in your own world, didn't hear me when I called."

"Sorry," I say, glancing over my shoulder. The light has changed back to red and I missed my chance to cross. Great. That means I'll be stuck at this intersection with Lauren for another few minutes.

"Um…so what are you doing here?" I ask.

I half expect her husband, John, to appear through the crowd, cheesy grin plastered to his face. John is forever smiling, begging the world to like him. *I'm a good guy! Look at me smile!* He wears beanies, too, always with three perfect curls strategically hanging over his forehead. I look around wearily. The last thing I need right now is their couple-ness.

"Oh, I thought I'd come walk around the center for a bit," she says. "Grab something to eat."

"Where's—"

"Working," she says quickly. Someone bumps into me and my mulled wine sloshes out of the cup and onto my jacket. I stumble, unable to right my footing. Lauren grabs me before I can fall. I smile at her gratefully as I right myself.

"Whoa," she says. "How many of those have you had?" She means to be funny, and of course she has no idea that I've spent the greater part of my day drinking, but something in her voice makes me angry.

"You don't have to be so goddamn judgmental," I snap. I dump the rest of the wine onto the sidewalk and march the empty cup over to the trash. There is no room for it, the garbage can overflowing. I set the empty cup on top of it and return to wait for the light. Lauren looks like I've slapped her, the smile falling off her face. I feel guilty right away. She was being really nice, and here I am, spewing my frustration all over the place.

"I'm sorry," I say, lifting a hand to my head. "I had a really shit day. Look, would you like to get a drink?"

She nods without a word, and suddenly outside of my own troubles I see something else on her face. She's not happy, either; there's something wrong. I sigh. The last thing I need is to be someone else's shrink today.

"All right, then," I say, glancing around. "There's a tap house up that way, or we can go to a real bar, one with the hard stuff."

She contemplates this for a few seconds before nodding her head decidedly. "Hard stuff."

"Good," I say. "I know where all the best places are. Follow me."

I lead her past the tourist spots and well-lit restaurants to Post Alley, where I swing a left. We have to pass the gum wall, and Lo crinkles her nose at the sickly sweet smell of half-chewed bubble gum.

"Gross," I hear her say. "I can't believe this is a tourist spot. What is even wrong with people?"

"You're being uptight again," I call over my shoulder. A teenage girl to our right pretends to lick the mounds of gum as her friend takes a picture, and Lauren shudders.

The foot traffic thins out and soon we're the only ones walking down the alley. Lauren presses close to me like she's afraid we're going to be mugged.

"How long have you lived here?" I ask. Her mouth is buried beneath a scarf; the only thing visible is her red-tipped nose.

"Four years."

I nod. Four years is relatively new to the city. You're still trying to figure out which streets to avoid and frequenting chain restaurants.

"You were born here?" she asks.

"Oregon, but my parents moved here when I was little."

I lead her down another alley and stop in front of a grass wall. "You okay with this place?" I ask. Lo eyes the place warily, then nods.

The interior of the bar is lit by neon pink lights that run along the walls and the ceiling. It's the type of place one might call seedy. The first time we came here, Seth said the place had eighties porn vibes. It was one of the few times we were out in public together, and as Lauren and I walk through the doors it hits me that he probably brought me here because there was little chance of being seen by any-one he knows.

We find a little table in the corner and begin the task of unwrapping ourselves from scarves and jackets. I try not to look at her because I don't know why I'm doing this, except there is something sad in her eyes, something that matches how I feel. I tell myself that if she brings up our lack of children I'm going to leave. I order shots to start. We need something to cut the edge, and fast.

"What do you normally drink?"

I expect her to say rosé or champagne, but she says, "Whiskey," matter-of-factly and then downs her shot like she's at a college frat party. *Nice.*

We order fries, and by the time our food arrives, we've had three shots each and are sufficiently sloshed. Lauren can't figure out how to work the lid on the ketchup and, in a fit of giggles, drops the bottle on the floor. She retrieves it and wedges the lid open with her teeth.

"And you thought I was uptight," she says, eyeing me over the bottle.

"You're drunk," I tell her, dipping a fry into the ketchup and folding it into my mouth. "Your picture-perfect life doesn't allow you to be anything but uptight."

Lo snorts. "So perfect." She closes her eyes, an exaggerated expression on her face. "It's not what you think."

"What do you mean?" I ask. I know she's had more than her fair share to drink, but I don't stop her when she begins to talk. If she's going to regret telling me things, she can do it tomorrow when I'm not around.

"Do you really want to know?"

"I wouldn't have asked if I didn't," I say. She toys with her napkin, ripping it in half, then balling it up in her fist. When she's destroyed it, she drops the wadded-up paper in her water glass. I watch it float before lifting my eyes to her face.

"He cheats on me," she says. "All the time. The trips we go on are always after I've caught him. To buy me back, I suppose."

I don't know what to say, so I stare at her dumbly until she speaks again.

"It's all a farce. I'm a farce. I thought if we had a baby, things would get better, he'd be more hesitant to break up our family, but then it was hard to get pregnant and even harder to keep a baby in my body. Now I can't have children at all and this is just my reality."

I reach across the fries and empty shot glasses and touch her hand—lightly at first, and then I hold it. "I'm sorry," I say, though the words sound shallow and uncomforting even to my own ears. "Have you thought about leaving him?"

She shakes her head. Her nose is throbbing red, and I see that she's started to cry. "No, I can't. I love him."

That makes me pull my hand back and stare at the plate of half-eaten fries. I'm all too familiar with that feeling, aren't I? Not knowing if I should leave, trying to make things better—never quite being able to. I'm drunk and inspired by Lauren's honesty, so I say, "My husband has two other wives." And then feel the heat rise to my face. She's the first person I've told, and she's someone I've always claimed to hate. It's funny how things work.

Lauren laughs, thinking I'm kidding, but the serious expression on my face causes her mouth to drop open. Her own hurt forgotten in the wake of my shocking news, she stumbles over her words. "You're joking. Oh my God, you're not joking…"

I feel part relief and part fear. I know I shouldn't have told her, that it was dangerous both to Seth and the other women, but alcohol and sadness have loosened my tongue, and, well, it's too late to take it back now.

"I'm a polygamist," I say, just to clarify. "Though I've never met either of them, they don't even live near here."

"Let me get this straight," Lauren breathes. "You knowingly let your husband cheat on you...with two other wives?"

I nod. She bursts into laughter. At first, I'm upset. This wasn't really something to laugh about, but then, as if through a haze, I see what she sees and I can't help but start laughing, too.

"What a fucked-up pair we are." And with that she stands to go to the bar to get more drinks. We really don't need to drink anymore, but also we do. When she carries them back to our table I smile wanly at her. Lauren looks at me over the rim of her water glass—the paper removed—with a smile equally as weak.

"What a mess we've made of our lives, eh? Well, what's he like—your Seth? Is he worth it?"

"I'm not sure," I say honestly. "I used to think so, otherwise I wouldn't have married him. But lately, I've been feeling different. I've even gone as far as finding them online just so I can spy."

Her eyes grow big, two saucers of vulnerability. "It's like a movie," she says. "In fact, if I were sober I don't think I'd believe you about any of this."

"Are you going to leave John?" I ask her.

"Are you going to leave Seth?" she shoots back.

"I really just want those other women to go away."

"Here, here," she says, lifting her glass in a toast. But she doesn't look convinced; she looks concerned.

We part ways right where we met, only now it's too dark to see the blue tree trunks. She gives me a brief but meaningful hug, after promising to never tell my secret, and I say I'll do the same. It feels good to have someone know, even someone I've always disliked. That's what I keep thinking on my walk back to the condo. Like someone has taken some of the burden off my shoulders and I can move around a little easier. I wonder if she feels the same. If we can somehow help each other.

FIFTEEN

I'm lying on the couch listening to sad music: The 1975, The Neighborhood, Jule Vera. My eyes are closed; my hangover has seized my head and my stomach. I shift onto my side, keeping my eyes closed. Amazing how once you open a door for something, there's no going back. All you can do is brace yourself as you get sucked in, deeper and deeper. Regina and Hannah, Regina and Hannah—they're all I can think about. I stack myself against what I know about them, I measure our flaws, sieve through them. I texted Hannah this morning, just to check on her, but she hasn't answered. She is my ally without knowing it. My fate feels tied to hers. I wonder if she ever wishes she could get rid of Regina.

Regina is more successful than I will ever be, more confident. Hannah is younger, prettier. I am somewhere in the middle of both of them, a medium to balance out the extremes. Seth has texted me more than usual this week—he's trying.

I heave myself from the couch around noon and head for the bathroom. When I get out of the shower, I look at myself naked in the bathroom mirror and try to imagine what Seth sees when he looks at me. I'm short, without the petiteness of Regina, my hips wide and my thighs full and muscular. My breasts spill over whatever shirt I'm wearing; out of a bra they hang loose and full. All three of us are completely different body types, and yet the same man desires us. It doesn't add up. Men have a type, don't they? Especially one as particular as Seth. Seth, who likes Mary-Kate Olsen but not Ashley—definitely not Ashley, he says.

His type would have to be Regina, since she's who Seth married first. But weren't we still finding ourselves in our twenties? Perhaps he discovered his type is me. That's wishful thinking, when you're one of three. He once told me that he was drawn to everything about Regina at that party, enough so that he approached her on the off chance that she'd shoot him down. He'd been attracted to me, too—the way he'd flirted with me, his eyes always filled with what I considered lust. I don't know how he met Hannah, and I need to know. The photo of Regina flashes in my mind, the taller, younger blond standing next to her—is it Hannah? Did they know each other? I can wait until I go to Portland for my appointment with Regina, or I can find out now.

Yes, that's a good idea—a little sleuth work to distract me. I text Hannah again, and before she replies, I'm already throwing things in a small overnight bag. If she's busy, I could always go snoop around on my own. To my relief, she texts back, delighted that I'm coming. She suggests dinner and a movie. I must be mad, truly, going to dinner and a movie with my husband's other wife. Some might call me a stalker, some might say I was off my rocker—but what did it matter? *Love certainly makes people crazy*, I think, zipping up my bag. I imagine she'll opt for a romantic comedy—something light and sexy. Women her age still have such a rosy outlook on life. But instead, she asks me if I like horror films. I'm a little taken aback. I don't, of course, but I say I do. I want to see what she has in mind, the type of things that amuse her. Her charming historical house and perfectly put-together meat and cheese board didn't exactly scream *slasher film fanatic*. She tells me there's a psychological thriller she wants to see; it has Jennifer Lawrence in it. I ask if her favorite movie is *The Sixth Sense*, and she texts back that she hasn't seen it. I've just pulled out of the parking garage. I'm not really paying attention and someone honks at me. It's *The Sixth Sense*; who hasn't seen *The Sixth Sense*, especially a horror movie fan? She's *that* young.

I leave Seattle just a little after noon with a fresh coffee in the cup-holder, cheerful music playing through the speakers. Oh, how things change from hour to hour. I'm upbeat, the radio station is playing eighties music and I sing along. If I drive fast, I'll have just enough time to check into the hotel and freshen up before meeting Hannah for dinner. I feel a fizz of excitement in my belly, not just at the prospect of garnering information about our husband, but at doing something other than sitting at home waiting for Seth. Waiting, waiting—my life is all about waiting.

Traffic to the neighboring city is thankfully light and I make good time. Seth would have called me a speed-demon; he would pump an imaginary brake in the passenger seat when I made him nervous. When I get to the hotel, I toss my things on the bed and take a quick shower. I only brought two outfits: one for the drive back tomorrow and one for tonight. Now, as I stare down at the brown cardigan, cream silk top and jeans, I wish I'd chosen something with more color, something eye-catching. I'll look plain and drab next to Hannah's gazelle-like figure, my large breasts making me look plumper than I really am. I rub the fabric between my fingers and stress. Eventually, I've stressed too long and I don't have time to dry my hair. The air curdles it into messy waves. I do my best to tame them a little, but in the end I have to go.

Portland's weather is in a better mood than Seattle's. There is no mist in the air, just the smell of exhaust fumes and pot. Hannah opens the door on my first knock, a bright smile on her face. Too bright. I give her a quick hug and that's when I see it—a dark, brooding bruise skims the underside of her cheekbone, a sickly green color, like pea soup. She's made an attempt to cover it with makeup, but on her fair skin, the color blooms with alarming vibrancy.

"I just need to grab my coat," she tells me. "Come in for a second."

I step into the foyer, not sure if I should mention the bruise or pretend she's done an excellent job with her makeup like she's probably hoping. I look around the foyer, checking for the missing photo that was once hanging next to the door—or so she said. In its place is a framed print of a pressed poppy. It depresses me. Pressed flowers are an attempt to hold on to something that was once alive. They're desperate and lonely.

"Do you like it?" she asks, coming down the stairs. "I found it at a flea market. I've always wanted to be able to do it myself but never had the time."

"I do," I lie. "Didn't you say you had a family photo there before?"

Hannah seems to flush under my gaze. "Yes," she says, and then quickly turns away.

I think of my empty locker at work and realize she's playing the same game I play. Hide the husband; avoid the questions. But bruises? I've never had to hide bruises. I think of my ear and absently lift a finger to trace the spot. Beneath my relaxed exterior, my heart beats hard against my ribs. Before the night he pushed me, I never would have been able to imagine Seth doing something to hurt a woman. And even after the night he shoved me I made excuses, blamed myself. But there's no denying Hannah's bruise. I press my questions down my throat until it feels like I'm choking on them.

"Hey, let's drive separately so you don't have to come all the way back here after the movie," she suggests. I nod, wondering if there's another reason. Tonight is her night with Seth; he'd arrive late after leaving Regina's. Perhaps she didn't want him knowing she'd made a friend. A friend would ask about her bruises, a friend would direct her eyes at the husband.

I follow behind her SUV, gripping the steering wheel so tightly my knuckles turn white. We pass through downtown, the square of food trucks, the shops, the people bundled up, all whizzing past. I barely see it. I'm too busy thinking.

We've just pulled up to the restaurant when I get a text from Seth.

Hi. Where are you?

I stare at his text, puzzled.

It's six o'clock. Which means Seth should still be with

Regina. It's an unspoken rule that when you're with one wife, you don't text the others.

Dinner with a friend, I text back.

Nice. Which friend? The hair on my arms prickles. Seth's not in the habit of quizzing me. In fact, he's never asked about my friends, except to caution me not to tell them about us.

Where are you? If he's being nosy, I have the right to be, too.

Home.

That's an interesting answer, I think. Especially when he has three homes.

Hannah is walking toward my car, having already parked. I shove my phone deep into my purse and step out of the car to meet her.

Seth will have to wait. It'll be a nice change, since I'm always on the waiting end. It's funny how I care about him less when I'm with Hannah.

"Ready?" Hannah grins. The restaurant she chose reminds me a little of the Italian place Seth took me to the first time he told me about his wife. As soon as we walk in the doors, she's approached by who I suppose is the manager. He rushes over to say hi, fussing over her as he leads us to a table. Hannah thanks him and he runs to the kitchen to get us a specialty appetizer.

"How do they know you?" I ask after a server waves at her.

"Oh, we come here a lot." By *we* I assume she means her and Seth.

I notice that she keeps the bruised side of her face turned away so that when she looks up at them, they only see her good eye. It's only once we've ordered our meals that I finally ask her what's been bothering me all night.

"Hannah, how did you get that bruise?"

She lifts her hand as if to touch it and then drops it into her lap.

"If you tell me that you walked into a door or hit your face on a cabinet, I'm not going to believe you, okay? So why don't you just tell me what really happened."

"So you want me to make something up?" she asks, raising an eyebrow.

I bite my lip thinking about what to say. "No. I want you to trust me, though," I say carefully. "God knows I've made some really stupid decisions, so I'm not ever going to judge you."

She wipes her mouth with her napkin and takes a long sip of her water. "Really, it's like you want me to confess to something scandalous," she says.

"Last time I saw you, you told me that your husband hid your birth control pills so you'd get pregnant. That sounds pretty controlling and manipulative to me. I'm just checking."

She looks down at her hands, which are now folded neatly on the tabletop. She looks completely relaxed and in control, minus the U-shaped bruise beneath her eye. I stare at her, mentally willing her to tell me everything. If Seth is hitting her, I need to know. My God—it would be hard to believe, but...

"My husband..." She chews on the inside of her cheek. I want to nudge her forward, encourage her to talk to me, but I'm afraid that if I say anything at all the spell will be broken and she'll shut down, so I wait.

"He does have a temper. Sometimes..." Her voice falters like she's not exactly sure how to word things. "I think his past affected him more than he's willing to admit. But I can assure you, he doesn't hit me." I'm hung up on part of her explanation, the part about his past. Does she know something that I don't?

"His past?" I interrupt. "What do you mean?"

I manage to keep my face neutral, but I can feel my eyebrows pushing toward each other, my forehead wanting to crease with worry.

Hannah clears her throat, and it's a very ladylike sound. I can barely take it; I want her to spit it out. There are already feelings of intense jealousy curdling in my stomach that she would know something that I do not.

"Well," she says finally. "He comes from a large family..."

No shit, I want to say.

"Someone in his family...well, someone hurt him."

I shake my head. "Hurt him how?"

"Oh, I don't know," Hannah says, and I can tell she's already regretting saying anything. "Roughed him up for fun, bullied him. I'm making it sound lighter than it actually is..."

I stare at her, confused. So Seth was teased by his siblings? What's new? My sister once tossed my favorite doll into the fireplace and looked on contentedly while I sobbed.

She waits until the server filling her water glass has walked away and then she leans close to me. "He had an older brother who was a psychopath," she whispers. "Would do terrible things to him, like hold him down in his bathwater until he thought he was going to die, and would sneak into his room at night and...well...touch him."

I balk. "He was *molested*?" I search my memory for anything—anything Seth has said about his brother. But the truth was that he hardly spoke about him; I didn't even know his name. I feel a rush of anguish; I was less important. He didn't share his hurt with me. I take a long drink of water, hoping she doesn't notice my expression.

Hannah draws back at my outburst and then quickly looks around to see if anyone's heard us. There's no one in the direct vicinity, and her face relaxes.

I'm impatient with her. Screw caring what people think at a time like this. My heart is racing a mile a minute and I feel positively sick to my stomach. If that were true, how could he not have told me? As I stare at Hannah, at her perfectly sharp cheekbones, and full lips—pursed disapprovingly at me—I feel both betrayed and hurt. She can see it on my face because she reaches across the table to grab my wrist. Squeezing it softly, she watches me with her big blue eyes.

"Are you okay?" she asks. "Did I say something to upset you?"

"No, not at all. It's just a terrible thing…" I try to pull myself away from her as gently as possible, keeping a tight smile on my lips. I hate her in this moment. She seems to buy my lie, because she lets me go, retiring her hands to her lap.

"How many years did it continue?" I ask.

"On and off through most of his childhood. Until his brother left for college."

"So you're saying he sometimes…does things…out of anger, because of what his brother did?"

"No. Yes. I don't know. We argue like all married couples and sometimes things get very heated. I've slapped him," she admits. "I felt terrible after, of course. And he grabbed my arm after, to stop me from doing it again—those were the bruises you saw last time." She looks away, ashamed.

In that moment, I have the urge to tell her everything. Who I am, what I know about her and Regina. The way he shoved me and never apologized, which made me think he didn't realize he'd done it. Wouldn't everything be so clear if we could lay it all out between us? I'd certainly understand more about Seth. Or I could just ask Seth about it, but then he'd know I'd been talking to Hannah.

"What about the bruise beneath your eye?" I swallow the emotion lodged like a hunk of bread in my throat and look her squarely in the eyes.

"No, it's not like that. I was doing a house project and walked into an open cabinet. Really. He just gets moody, withdrawn... He needs his alone time, you know? Sometimes I think it's because he was always surrounded by people." She presses her lips together. I try a new tactic. I came here to get information, after all, although perhaps not of this dark nature.

"Okay, tell me the good things about him, the things you love." I smile encouragingly as Hannah chews on her lip. "You are having his baby, after all. There are some things you must like..."

"Of course, yeah, of course." She seems relieved that I've changed the subject to something more palatable.

I notice the immediate change in her. When Hannah talks about Seth this way, her eyes take on a glow and her lips soften to the smile of a young girl entirely smitten. I recognize the symptoms, as I've so often seen them in myself.

"He's charming, and he's kind. He spoils me, always

asking if I need anything and if I'm okay. He bought me a baby name book and he likes to hear my ideas…the small things…" I remember Seth telling me about the baby name book saying that Hannah—or Monday, as he called her— wanted a boy.

"He's fun," she continues. "Likes to joke around and laugh. I really love that about him."

Have I ever considered that Seth's sense of humor is his strong suit? I tend to be the witty one in the relationship, always quipping something or the other while he laughs.

"Right," I say when she pauses. "Those are all wonderful things." She nods, encouraged, and I think her eyes fill with tears, but then our server arrives to refill our water.

"Can we change the subject?" she says after he leaves.

"Sure." I smile. "Where is he tonight?" I don't know why I ask, except that when people ask me where my husband is, I always falter before making up some lame excuse.

"He's… He should be home," she says. "I told him I'd be out for the night."

"Does he mind that you have friends?"

"He doesn't know," she says. "He's protective of me, of who I spend time with."

I don't miss the way her eyes dart left, searching for the right answer…the easiest answer.

I nod, but I can't help wondering if she's working things out with him or herself, resigning herself to be the type of woman he wants. She's so much younger than me, close to my age when I met Seth in that coffee shop. If anyone had tried to warn me back then I would have laughed, brushed off their concern. Seth was a good man, family-focused; if he was occasionally moody, that was fine.

Our food arrives before I can think any more on it. For

the rest of our dinner we discuss banal things, and when it's time for dessert, I stand up to use the restroom. I can feel her eyes on me as I leave the table. I wish I could know what she's thinking.

SIXTEEN

When I get back from the restroom, Hannah is gone. I stare at the empty table, a sinking feeling in my stomach. Our server is ceremoniously clearing away the last of our glasses when he looks up and sees me. He grins sheepishly, shrugging his shoulders and stepping back.

"Thought you left," he says. "She ran out in a hurry."

As I step closer, I see that she's paid the bill in cash and left a note on the back of my beverage napkin. I pick it up, frowning. Why would she leave so suddenly? Had our conversation spooked her that much? Maybe Seth called and summoned her home. The words are scribbled; her pen tore through the napkin at several spots. *Had to run, felt sick. Rain check on movie.*

That's it? I turn it over in my hand, hoping for a more

detailed explanation, but there's only the pink lipstick residue I left earlier when I wiped my mouth.

"Did she look sick?" I ask the server. He's waiting for me to leave so he can get his money and get the table ready for the next round of guests.

"Not really." He shrugs.

I take out my phone to text.

What's up? Why did you leave without saying goodbye?

Didn't feel well. Had to run.

I consider asking her more, but then think better of it. I've already scared her enough with all of my questions. Things are probably better left alone. It could be the baby, I remind myself. She's still in her first trimester. I was sick as a dog for the first five months of my pregnancy; the bathroom floor had become a hangout. I push the memories from my mind, their resurgence a cold knife against my thin control. If I thought on that too much, I'd—

I consider going to the movie by myself, but the more I think about it, the more I realize how tired I am—I realize that all I want is to drive back to the hotel instead.

As I'm waiting in the hotel valet for an attendant, tapping my fingers impatiently on the steering wheel, something begins to nag at the back of my mind. Seth's texts to me earlier had been strange—the tone of them. Was it possible that he'd seen me there with Hannah? I decide to take a quick spin past Hannah's house. Just to see if her car is there. No harm in that. I wave off the attendant as he approaches my car and speed past, ignoring his look of disapproval. Twenty minutes. It would take me twenty minutes tops to spy on Hannah and my husband. Excitement whips through me as I rush through a yellow light, eager to reach their quaint home.

I can tell she's not home even before I reach the house. The windows are dark and lifeless and her car is missing from its usual spot against the curb. I can't see Seth's anywhere, either. I consider creeping up to the house and taking a peek inside, but it's still early enough that a neighbor could spot me.

Shit. *Shit.*

Could she have left the restaurant and gone straight to the hospital? There's no finding out tonight. I head back to the hotel, feeling defeated. Something's going on and I feel like I'm the only person in this marriage who doesn't know what.

By the next morning, I've barely slept. My mind wouldn't stop ticking and I had too many ugly thoughts. If I can't find a way to sleep soon, I'll have to see a doctor. It was torture lying awake half the night, being tired but not knowing how to shut off your brain. I fall into a fitful sleep around five and wake at seven to find a voice mail from Hannah on my phone. I roll onto my back, wondering why the phone didn't ring, and remember that I'd put it on silent before we went into the restaurant. My two hours of sleep had been wrought with dreams—dark things about being chased and being caught. I don't remember the details of the dreams, but the feelings they left behind linger in my mind. I listen to the message with half of my face hidden under the comforter, my eyes squinting against the light that sneaks in through a break in the curtains. Hannah's voice shakes and I press the phone closer to my ear so I can make out what she's saying.

"I'm really freaked out." Her voice quavers, and it sounds like she's blowing her nose. "We had a fight. I don't feel safe. I just… I—" Her voice cuts off like she lost reception in the middle of the call.

I hold the phone away from my face and see that the voice mail is still playing. Pressing it back to my ear, I strain to hear, in case she's said anything else.

"Leave…alone…he's—" It cuts out for the final time. Damn my shitty reception.

I lie there frozen for a few minutes, her words ricocheting around in my head. Seth. She had a fight with Seth and now she is scared. What did he do to scare her? I throw my arm over my eyes. I was scared, too, wasn't I? Ever since… his outburst, he'd seemed more unpredictable. If I said the wrong thing, would he do it again? If I call Hannah back I'll be irrevocably involved in this…this thing. I wouldn't be able to make any more excuses for him. I'd have to admit that what he'd done to me was deliberate. I'd been the one to seek Hannah out, to keep the truth about who I am from her. Perhaps it's time to tell her that Seth is my husband, too. I roll back over onto my stomach and bury my face in the pillow. I call Anna.

"What's up," she says when she answers the phone. I'm not deterred by the briskness of her greeting; it's Anna's way.

"Hi," I say. "I need moral guidance."

"Are you facedown in a pillow?"

Anna knows my ways, too. I shift my head so she can hear me better.

"Not anymore," I say.

"Oh, boy, are you sure I'm the one you should be asking for moral guidance?"

"No, but I don't have anyone else, so moral-up and give the type of advice Melonie would give you." Melonie is Anna's mother, a psychologist who spent most of our teenage years observing us like we were science projects and then dissecting everything we did. As teens we thought it was terrifying and thrilling at the same time. At that age, most adults aren't interested in the details of your thoughts, unless it's to tell you those thought are wrong. But Melonie had been different. She'd validated us by saying we were on our own adventure, exploring the world. She made self-destruction seem normal and so we'd destructed without guilt. Nowadays, I wonder how healthy that had been: an adult egging us on. And here I am as an adult, seeking the same type of assurance, asking my best friend to validate me like her mother had.

"Okay," Anna breathes. "Hit me with it, I'm in Melonie mode."

"I have a new friend—I know her through someone else," I add, because I know Anna will ask. "I've seen some bruises on her before but didn't think much of it, but then today, she leaves a message on my phone, saying she got into a fight with her husband and she's scared. Two things you should know—she's pregnant, and I know her husband fairly well and he doesn't seem like the type of guy who'd toss his wife around, you know?"

Anna sighs. I can picture her seated at her kitchen table, a cup of her nasty instant coffee cooling in front of her— she likes it lukewarm rather that hot. When she's frustrated, the ankle of her crossed leg swishes from side to side, the ankle bracelet she wears glinting against her olive skin.

"First off," she begins, "I don't give a flying fuck how innocent a man appears, if a woman has the tits to come forward and say she's scared, something is going the fuck on to make her scared. You don't need to get too involved, but you can get involved enough to give her the push to leave. We're all just waiting for someone to stand behind us, aren't we? Even if it's just one person, it gives you strength."

I bite my lip. Anna is right. I sit up in bed, pulling my knees to my chest and wrapping my arms around them. This is so fucked. I'm compartmentalizing without even realizing it.

"But what if she's blowing things out of proportion? I mean, I know this guy. He's a good man…"

"Don't be dense. Parishioners think they know their priests, aunts think they know their husbands, and meanwhile they're molesting little boys behind closed doors. Can we really know anyone?"

I think of myself and all of the things my best friend doesn't know about me, and drop my head. Anna is spot-on, isn't she? Maybe we're all pretending everything is fine when it itsn't. *He pushed me*, I think. I can try to rewrite that story, blame myself, excuse my husband, but he pushed me.

Anna and I chat for a few more minutes, and when there's a break in the conversation, I thank her and say I have to go. She hesitates when she says goodbye, almost like she suspects I'm not telling her everything and she's giving me the chance to 'fess up. She's given me a lot to think about. I hang up quickly and head to the bathroom to take a shower.

I'm going to call Hannah back and tell her everything. Together we could… What? Leave Seth? Find Regina and ask if Seth had ever been aggressive with her? It doesn't matter. We can approach the options together. Like a team.

I plan what I'm going to say to her as I soap my hair and let the hot water ease some of the tension out of my shoulders.

Once I'm wrapped in my towel and sitting on the edge of the bed, I call her back. I'm nervous. I chew on my lip. It rings half a dozen times before I hear her voice. *Hey, it's Hannah. Leave a message!*

"Hi, Hannah. It's me. I'm worried about you so call me back as soon as you get this. I'll be driving back to Seattle, so anytime in the next two hours and I can answer right away. Okay, bye."

I move to get dressed and gather up my things, glancing at the phone every few minutes to see if I've missed her call, but my phone remains dark and silent. I call again and this time I'm sent straight to voice mail.

"Hannah, damn it! Call me back!" I make a noise of frustration as I pull the phone from my ear, and then realize I haven't hung up the call yet. Great. I stuff my phone in my pocket and, snatching up my bag, I head for the lobby.

I drive past their house one more time, but neither of their cars are there. Not knowing what to do, I decide to head for home. I can turn around and come back if she needs me. But four hours later, I'm pulling into the garage under my building not having heard from her. Traffic was backed up for miles. Hungry and needing to use the restroom, I waited it out instead of losing my place in the never-ending line of brake lights. I drag my things up the elevator and into my condo, kicking the door shut behind me. I drop my purse near the door and race for the half bathroom.

I emerge hungry and thirsty, about to raid the fridge, when I see movement through the door to the bedroom.

My heart seizes in a panic and I freeze. Where is my phone? In the foyer where I'd dropped my handbag?

I look around for signs of my mother, who usually leaves her things on the kitchen counter when she comes over, a pile of designer leather. But everything is just as I left it, right down to the scattering of bagel crumbs near the toaster. I hear movement, feet shuffling against carpet, and then suddenly Seth is standing in the kitchen doorway. I grab at my heart, which is pounding painfully in my chest, bending over slightly at the waist and laughing at myself.

"I thought someone broke in," I say. "You scared me."

It takes a minute for a few things to sink in: the first that today is not Thursday; the second, Seth is not smiling; and third—there is a bandage on the knuckles of his right hand. I lick my lips, my brain working frantically. *He knows!* I think. That's why he must be here, to sort me out. I'm not the type to lie. Omissions, yes, but if he asks me point-blank about Hannah I'll tell the truth.

My eyes travel to his face, and for a moment, neither of us say a thing. It's a staring match, one I'd rather not be in.

"What are you doing here?" I finally say.

His eyes look tired and dull, not the normally mischievous sparkle that is my Seth. *My Seth!* I almost laugh. I don't know who that is anymore. Suddenly, I feel frightened.

He answers my question with another question. "Where have you been?"

Ah, a standoff. *Who wants to answer first?* I think.

I turn to the fridge, remembering my thirst, and grab a bottle of water from the shelf. I offer Seth one before closing the door, holding it out to him. He nods, that stony look still on his face. I toss him the bottle and lean back against the counter while I screw off the lid and drink.

"I saw a friend. I told you."

"I know what you're doing," he says.

I notice his clothes for the first time, a pair of jeans and crewneck sweater that I'd laundered last week. Things that belong here at the condo.

"Have you been here since last night?" That thought hadn't crossed my mind until I saw the clothes. Had he come here after his fight with Hannah only to find me gone?

"Yes," he says.

"I'm sorry. I didn't know or I would have come home. Why didn't you call?"

Seth glares at me and my stomach turns. He has strong squared shoulders, like a Lego man. Women get swoony over his shoulders, but right now they just scare me. How much would it hurt if he hit me? How hard had he hit Hannah? I picture her lithe body and milk skin—one hit, and she'd be bloody and mottled. *The baby!* I think in a panic. His eyes are searching my face but not in an imploring way; there's a hardness to them that makes me shiver. This is his way: he prods without actually asking. It's beneath him to ask questions. We are here for his pleasure.

I raise my chin at how bitter this makes me feel. Something has changed in me. Did it take days…? Weeks…? I cannot pinpoint when or how, but if the shift is noticeable to me, it's definitely noticeable to my husband, who's staring at me like I have Egyptian hieroglyphics tattooed on my face. That is male folly; they expect you to always be the same, reliable cow, but women spend their lives changing. Our change can swing for you or against you depending on how fairly we've been treated. I swing against, though I can feel the gravity of my love for him trying to pull me back down. *He's a good guy. There has to be an explanation for all of this…*

"What have you done?" he says. His eyes, I notice, aren't a sharp white. They are dingy pink, the shade you get after a long night of drinking.

I try to hide the trembling in my voice. "I don't know what you're talking about," I say.

"Yes, you do."

I'm breathing through my mouth now. I don't want him to see how scared I am. I don't want him to have the upper hand.

The sink drips—it's the only noise in the room. I hear myself swallow as the seconds tick by, my eyes still on his face.

"What happened to your hand?" I ask.

We both look at his hand. Seth registers the bandage like he's seeing it for the first time. He splays his fingers, twisting his wrist from side to side, as he blinks at it. A piece of hair falls onto his forehead and it's the first time I notice that his hair is wet from a shower. *What are you trying to wash off?*

If his knuckles look like that, what does Hannah look like?

"I hit something." That's all he says, like it's a good enough explanation.

"Doing what?" My question seems to throw him off balance. He opens and closes his mouth.

"Seth," I say. "What have you done?"

SEVENTEEN

He lunges for me. It happens in slow motion, my brain desperately trying to catch up to reality. My. Husband. Is. Attacking. Me. I'm not prepared for it, and when his hands close around my upper arms, I scream. It's a short, brittle sound—pathetic, really.

It's cut off when Seth begins to shake me, his fingers digging viciously into my arms. My head snaps back and forth, back and forth, until he stops and then he's just an inch from my face, breathing hard against my skin. I can smell liquor on his breath, and the mouthwash he tried to cover it up with. I try to break free, but he has me pinned, the lip of the marble counter digging into my back. His fingers pinch painfully into the skin of my arms and I whimper. He's never touched me this way; it's like I'm looking into the face of a stranger.

"You bitch," he breathes. "Nothing is ever enough for you. I've risked everything…"

A fleck of spittle lands on my lip. I wrench my shoulders out of his grasp, pushing at his chest with my forearms, but instead of letting me go, his hands move to my wrists. I'm a prisoner. I can't believe he's saying that. I'm the one who's risked everything. I'm the one who's made the sacrifices.

I pant into his face, not daring to move. I couldn't deny any of this now, her bruises, my shove. *I'm awake!* I think. There would be no going back. It feels like he's going to snap the bones in my wrists, meager bones against strong hands. I've always liked that Seth is so much bigger than I am, but now as I cower under his strength, I curse myself. I'm in shock, trembling like a cornered animal.

He says it again, this time his words pronounced louder, more carefully, like I was too stupid to understand them the first time.

"Who. Were. You. With?"

"Hannah," I say smoothly. "I was with Hannah."

Both of our eyes make a choreographed move to his bandaged hand.

For a moment, his grip on me falters, his fingers go slack. I think he's willing himself to have misheard me. I realize I've confirmed his fear and I need to get away from him.

I yank one arm free and shove at his chest to get him to move. If I could just get to my phone I could call somebody to help. But who? Who would believe me? What would I tell the police? My husband is yelling at me because he thinks I've cheated on him? Seth barely budges and now his eyes are narrowed, boring into me with intensity. I've never seen that look on his face before. It's like I'm seeing a different man.

"Why?" His eyes flutter. "How? We had an arrangement. Why would you do that?"

"Yeah?" I seethe. "Or you had an arrangement. I'm sick of it. I wanted to know who she is. See her face. You get everything you want, three wives, and we're just left to pine after you."

"We had an agreement," he says. "You wanted this."

"I wanted it because it was the only way to have you. You're hitting her. I saw the bruises."

He shakes his head. "You're crazy." He looks aghast that I would accuse him of such an ugly thing.

He releases me, and all of the pressure that was pushing against me a minute ago is gone. I slump against the counter, massaging my wrists as Seth paces across the small kitchen.

His face is blanched white, causing the dark circles under his eyes to look even more pronounced. He looks sick. But I suppose you'd feel a little sick after hitting your pregnant wife, drinking all night and then being confronted by your barren wife. I feel my anger build as I watch him—the man I'd always thought so beautiful, a chiseled god. He looks a little melted, if I'm being honest—a discarded idol low on luster. I want to check my phone, see if Hannah called. What if he hurt her really badly? I move slightly toward the doorway; if I make a dash for it I can reach my handbag in the foyer. My phone is in the pocket, next to a half-eaten roll of Life Savers and my pill compact.

"Listen to me. You're sick. It's happening again..."

I stare at him in astonishment. "Sick...? You're the sick one," I spit. "How can you even say something like that to me after you asked me to live this lifestyle? You get to have as many women as you want, and we are your emotional prisoners." Once the words are out of my mouth I realize how much I mean them. I've never allowed myself to think it; I was overcome by love—pressing, pressing, pressing my feelings down to accommodate him. Isn't that what we do as women?

"Have you been taking your pills?"

"My pills?" I echo. "What would I need to take pills for?" I think of the compact, the one I'd bought at a touristy shop at Pike Place Market with the pink rose on the lid. What was inside of it? Aspirin…a couple of old Xanax from Anna? The *drip, drip, drip* of the sink is grating on me. There are no pills I need to be taking. That ended a long time ago.

Seth's lips part as he blinks rapidly—gunshot blinks. He looks around as if searching the kitchen for help, all the white and silver we painstakingly chose together is blinding in this moment. I want to close my eyes and be somewhere warmer. I almost suggest moving this little accusation party to the living room when his eyes narrow sharply on me.

"I was at your house," I say boldly. "Why didn't you tell me you bought her a house and remodeled it? Did you think I would be too jealous to deal with it?"

"Are you fucking kidding me?"

He holds up his hands, palms splayed toward me, his eyes wide. I flinch even though he's clearly not threatening me. His chest is heaving, which causes me to look down at my own chest. I seem to be holding my breath, because it doesn't move at all.

"This is over," he says, closing his eyes. "I thought you

could handle this. We had an agreement... I can't believe this." He says that last part to himself.

Anger and pain tangle in my chest. A sob escapes my lips. I'm so confused. I reach up and touch my face, feel my features; this isn't a dream, this is real.

Seth's face softens. "Listen to me. I've been trying so hard. What we had was real, but things change. After you lost the baby, you changed."

"No!" I shout. "I'm going to tell everyone who you are and what you've done. You can't keep your lifestyle a secret anymore. Even Regina is cheating on you."

There is a sharp silence following my words. His eyes grow wide and I can see the red streaks on the whites as he says, "Stop it."

I throw back my head and let my throat churn out a hoarse chord of laughter. "Are you kidding me right now?" My fear has morphed into anger. It's better to be angry than to be afraid, I decide. "You're going to be exposed for what you are."

"I'm calling your doctor," he says. He roots for his phone, pulling it from his back pocket, never taking his eyes off me as he places his thumb on the screen to unlock it. A deep furrow appears between his brows as his fingers dart across the screen.

"I found the doctor's bill in your pants pocket—Hannah's. I went to see her." I say all of this calmly, watching his face for a betrayal. He's pretending that this is all in my head, why?

"What doctor's bill?" He shakes his head, and then I see it. A spark of recognition. He sets his phone on the counter next to the coffeemaker, forgotten. "Oh my God," he says. "Oh my God." He shakes his head. "When I was at the doctor, a woman checked out in front of me. She got distracted by her phone and walked out of the office without it. I ran it out to her, except once I was out there I couldn't find her. She must have driven off. I stuffed it in my pocket. I should have turned it into the receptionist, but I didn't even think to do that. That's what you found."

I don't believe him, not even for a second. This is crazy. He's lying.

"You need help. You're having delusions again."

Again? I'm so angry that it's me who launches at him this time, my hands extended like I can claw his eyes out with my bitten-down fingernails.

"Liar," I scream.

I ram into his chest—that was a mistake. Once I'm in his range, he uses his strength against me, holding me at arm's length. I can't reach him, but my arms flail, anyway, as I try to make contact with something. His open water bottle falls from the counter and makes a dull thud against the wood floor. Water pools around our feet, and as I struggle to get away from him I feel myself slipping. Seth tries to catch me, but as my feet lose grip and slide out from under me, so do his. We fall in a tangle; I slam into the ground, my shoulder blades hitting the floor with Seth's weight on top of me, and then I see nothing but the dark.

EIGHTEEN

"Hello, Thursday. Can you hear me?"

A voice tugs at my consciousness, unfamiliar. It pulls me forward like a hand in the fog. A blinding headache pounds behind my eyes and I know that the moment I open them it will be ten times worse. I roll my tongue over the roof of my mouth and I wake to a bright room—not naturally bright, but lit by the fizzing hum of fluorescents overhead.

A woman leans over me and I register navy blue scrubs and the stethoscope, which hangs like jewelry from her neck.

"There you are," she says brightly—too brightly. "You're going to have a headache—we've given you something for that. You should feel better in a bit."

I let my head fall to the right where an IV stands senti-nel beside the bed. I am terribly thirsty.

"You were extremely dehydrated," she says. "We're fix-ing you up. Would you like some water?"

I nod, and a pain shoots through my head, causing me to flinch.

"Try not to move around too much." She disappears and comes back with a thick plastic cup, color unidentifiable, straw perched from its lip. The water tastes like plastic, but it's cold, and I close my eyes as I suck it down.

"Which hospital am I in? Where's my husband?"

I listen to the squelch of her shoes as she crosses the room, a familiar and soothing sound. Years ago, a patient told me that the sound a nurse's shoes make on a hospital floor made her have a panic attack. *It's when you know they're coming to inject you with more shit, or to tell you bad news*, she'd said.

"You're in Queen County. I haven't seen a husband, but it's past visiting hours and I'm sure he'll be back tomorrow."

Queen County! I try to sit up in bed, but yelp when a pain shoots through my head.

"Easy," she says, rushing over. "You have a concussion. It's minor but—"

"Why am I in Queen County? Where's the doctor? I need to speak to him."

She opens my chart, glancing at me disapprovingly over the top of it. Her eyebrows are two sandy brown caterpillars—she's in need of a good pluck. I don't know why I'm being so mean except that she has answers and I don't.

"Says here you came in by ambulance. That's all I can tell you for now until you speak to your doctor." She snaps it shut with an air of finality and I know it won't do me any good to keep hounding her. I know her type; she has the whole nurse hard-ass thing going on. We have three or four of them at my hospital. They're always assigned the more difficult patients as a mercy to the rest of us.

Momentarily defeated, I allow my back to rest against the flat hospital pillow and squeeze my eyes shut. What happened exactly? Why didn't they take me to Seattle General? My friends and colleagues are there. I'd receive the best care among my own. Queen County has a reputation for bringing in a rougher sort of crowd. I know, because this isn't the first time I've been here. Queen County is your criminal uncle you only see on holidays: grubby, sagging and tagged up. It's the house whose lawn has soda cans and beer bottles dotting its yard like weeds, the shopping cart abandoned on the street corner. It's a place where dreams never have the soil to grow, everything lost in the cracks.

I have a flash of memory: a wheelchair, blood—plenty of blood—and the tense face of my husband as he leaned over me, assuring me everything was going to be all right. I'd half believed him at the time because that's what love does. It gives you a sense of well-being—like bad things will evaporate under the strength of two people who adore each other. But it hadn't been all right, and I'm much emptier in my marriage than when I arrived that first time.

I grimace at the memory. I bunch the sheets up at my neck, suddenly cold, turning on my side as I lie as still as possible. My head feels tender, like even the slightest movement could make unbearable pain explode. I want to see Seth. I want my mother. I want someone to tell me that everything is going to be all right, even if it's not true. Why would he leave me here alone with no note, no explanation?

My eyes snap open, and very carefully I look around the room for my handbag or phone. No, the nurse said I'd been brought in by ambulance; my phone would be at home. I have the faintest memory of my handbag sitting near the front door—in the foyer. I'm suddenly very tired. *The drugs*, I think to myself. They've given me something for the pain and it's going to knock me out. I let my eyes close and drift backward like a leaf floating in water.

When I wake up, there is a different nurse in the room. Her back is to me, a narrow braid hanging down the center of it, almost reaching her waist. She's young—I'd guess not a year out of nursing school. Sensing my eyes on her, she turns and sees that I'm awake.

"Hello there." She moves fluidly, like a cat—her shoulders rolling forward as she walks. She checks the monitor while I watch her, still too out of it to speak.

"I'm Sarah," she says. "You've been sleeping for a while. How do you feel?"

"Better," I croak. "Groggy. Do I have a concussion?" My throat hurts and I glance at the plastic water jug to my right. Seeing my look of longing, she pours me a fresh cup and I glance at her gratefully. I already like her better than Nurse Hard-ass from yesterday.

"Let me get the doctor to come talk to you now that you're awake."

"Seth…?" I ask as she heads for the door.

"He was here while you were asleep. But I'm sure he'll be back soon…"

My lips pull away from the straw and a line of water runs down my chin. I wipe it away with the back of my hand. "What day is it?"

"Friday." And then with an almost embarrassed laugh, she says, "TGIF."

I refrain from rolling my eyes—actually, I don't think I *can* roll my eyes. I feel like I'm underwater, my body moving like a piece of seaweed dragged along the ocean floor.

"Sarah...?" I call out. She's halfway out the door, an almost-escape, when she peeps her head around the corner.

"What medication do they have me on?" Is my voice slurring or am I imagining it?

She blinks and I can see she doesn't want to answer without the doctor speaking to me first.

"Haldol."

I struggle to sit up, the lines in my arm tugging uncomfortably as I push aside the sheets. *Haldol, Haldol, Haldol!* My brain is screaming. Where is Seth? What happened? I try to remember the events that led me here and I can't. It's like trying to pound through a brick wall.

Sarah comes rushing back in the room, her face pinched with worry. I'm the patient they trained her for—*keep her calm, call for help.* I see her glance over her shoulder, trying to catch a view of someone in the hallway. I don't want her to do that; they'll fill me with more medication until I can't remember my own name. I calm, relaxing my hands, smoothing out my face. Sarah seems to buy my show because she slows down, approaching the bed like someone would approach a live scorpion.

"Why am I on Haldol?" I've been on it once before. An antipsychotic that doctors only use in extreme cases of violent behavior.

Sarah's face is blanched, her lips pursing and squishing for an answer. Silly girl, she'll get the hang of it in a year or so. She's required to tell me what drugs they've given me; she's not required, however, to tell me why. I want to take advantage of her lack of experience before someone with more knowledge comes in, but then the doctor is there, his pinched face stern and unyielding. Sarah scurries from the room and he narrows in on me, tall and bent—the kind of figure that could be frightening, if you watch too many horror films.

"Haldol?" I ask again. "Why?"

"Hello to you, too, Thursday," he says. "I'm hoping you're comfortable."

If comfortable means drugged up, then yes, I'm sure I am. I stare at him, refusing to play this game. I'm terrified, my stomach in knots, my brain fighting through the drugs to gain control. I want Seth to be here; I long for the reassurance of his unwavering confidence, and yet I'm disgusted with him, too. Why? Why can't I remember?

"I'm Dr. Steinbridge. I was a consulting doctor on your case last time you were with us."

"The last time Seth had me locked me up in the nuthouse?" My voice is hoarse. I lift a hand to touch my throat, then change my mind, dropping it to the sheet instead.

"Do you remember the circumstances that brought you here, Thursday?"

I hate the way he keeps saying my name. I grind my teeth, the humiliation sinking deep into my body. I don't remember and admitting that will make me sound crazy.

"No," I say simply. "I'm afraid the memories have disappeared along with my husband."

Dr. Steinbridge makes no indication that he's heard my snark. His long, gangly legs make their way over to the bed, and it looks as if the bones in them could snap at any moment and send him sprawling to the floor.

I don't suppose if I ask directly where Seth is, he'd answer me, either. That's the thing about these doctors—they answer questions selectively, often turning your own questions around on you. It's funny that I've spoken to enough shrinks to know how they do things.

"I'm going to ask you some questions, just to rule out a concussion," he says. "Can you tell me your name?"

"Thursday Ellington," I answer easily. *Second wife of Seth Arnold Ellington.*

"And how old are you, Thursday?" he asks.

"Twenty-eight."

"Who is the current president?"

I scrunch up my nose. "Trump."

He chuckles a little at that one, and I relax.

"Okay, good, good. You're doing great."

He's talking to me like I'm a child or slow of understanding. I'm irritated, but I try not to let on. I know how hospitals deal with uncooperative patients.

"Any nausea?" he continues.

I shake my head. "No, none."

He seems pleased by my answer because he marks something off on his chart.

"Why can't I remember coming here?" I ask. "Or what happened before?"

"It could be the hit your head took, or even stress," he says. "When your brain is ready, it will impart those memories to you, but for now all you can do is rest up and wait."

"But can you tell me what happened?" I plead. "Maybe it will trigger something..."

He twines his fingers, letting them drop to his waist as he stares up at the ceiling. He looks like a grandfather getting ready to recount a long-ago memory to a room full of grandkids instead of a doctor talking to a woman in a hospital bed.

"On Tuesday evening, you were in the kitchen. Do you remember?"

"Yes," I say. "With Seth."

He consults his chart. "Yes, that's right. Seth."

I keep my face even as I wait for him to say more. I won't take the bait and prompt him, though I desperately want to know.

"You attacked him. Do you remember that?"

I do. It comes back to me, a wave crashing over my head. I remember the anger, flying across the kitchen toward him. The feeling of wanting to claw at his skin until he bled. The reason for my anger comes back, too, and I grip the sheets as I remember—first Hannah, and then his denial.

"Why did you attack him? Do you remember?"

"Yes. He hit his other wife. I confronted him about it and we fought."

He cocks his head to the side. "His other wife?"

"My husband is a polygamist. He has three." I expect him to react, to be shocked, but instead he writes something down on the notepad in front of him and then looks up at me expectantly.

"Did you see him hit his wife?"

"One of his wives," I say, frustrated. "And no, but I saw the bruises on her arm and face."

"Did she tell you that he hit her?"

I hesitate. "No—"

"And you all live together, you and these other wives?"

"No. We don't even know each other's names. Or we're not supposed to."

The doctor lowers his pen, looking at me over the rim of his glasses.

"So you're a polygamist in that your husband—"

"Seth," I say.

"Yes, Seth, has these relationships with two other women whose names you don't know."

"I know their names now," I say. "I...found them."

"And you confronted him about these other relationships?"

"Yes!" I drop my head. My God, this is getting so twisted.

"I knew about them. I confronted him about the bruises...on Monday's arm." The inside of me feels hollow as alarm bounces through my chest and settles like a weight in my stomach. I try to keep my composure; breaking down now would only result in me looking crazier than I already do.

Dr. Steinbridge picks up his pen and writes something on my chart. His pen scratches against the paper in quick little successions. The sound triggers an echo of memories, memories that make my entire body clench in emotional agony. I imagine it says something like *delusional*. Maybe underlined two or three times. Isn't that something? I'm the one being called delusional when it was Seth who thought he could pull off three marriages at once.

I decide to stick to my guns. Pulling myself up, I stare Dr. Stein-whatever right in his beady little eyes and say, "I can prove it. If you bring me a phone and allow me to make a call, I can prove the whole thing to you."

Nurse Sarah reappears in the room, a food tray in her hands. She glances at the expression on the doctor's face and then at me, her cat eyes bright with interest.

"Dr. Steinbridge," she says, her voice light and friendly. "Thursday has a visitor."

NINETEEN

Seth strolls in, looking every bit like he's going for a casual Sunday brunch instead of visiting his wife in the psych ward. He's wearing a button-down with a cardigan and distressed gray jeans. I don't recognize the outfit; it must be something he keeps at one of *their* houses.

I see that he's had a haircut recently and strain to remember if he had it a day ago when he surprised me at our condo. Wouldn't that be something? His wife in the psych ward and he goes to get a haircut. Who am I kidding? He has two others—when one of the spares falls off the wagon, life keeps moving.

He smiles, looking refreshed and well-slept, and walks over to kiss me on the forehead. I almost turn away but think better of it; if I want to get out of here, I'm going to have to play nice. Seth is my shot at freedom.

The spot where his lips touch my skin stings. It's his fault that I'm here, his fault that no one believes me. Isn't he supposed to be on my side, trying to keep me out of places like this? And then I remember his lie, his denial, as I stared him down in the kitchen. He'd tried to make me believe that I'd made Hannah up. I look up at his face in alarm, wondering if I should wait to confront him when we're alone, or if I should just do it now. I glance at Dr. Steinbridge, who is watching us. Everyone's always watching in this place, hawk eyes waiting for you to mess up and betray your mental state.

"Maybe you can clear something up for us," the doctor suggests, looking to Seth. *Yes!* I think, settling deeper into the bed. Finally. Put him on the spot and make him answer. My husband nods, his brow furrowed like he's dying to help.

"Thursday has mentioned that you have—" Dr. Steinbridge glances at me like he's embarrassed to say it "—additional wives…" His sentence drops off, and Sarah freezes where she's writing something on my white board. She glances over her shoulder at me, and then, embarrassed to be caught, turns back to her work.

"I'm afraid that's not true," Seth says.

"No?" Dr. Steinbridge glances at me. His tone is light. It's like they're discussing the weather.

"I divorced my first wife three years ago," Seth says, looking embarrassed.

"But they're still together," I say.

"We're divorced," Seth says firmly. The doctor nods. "I left her for Thursday—"

I shake my head in disbelief. I can't believe it. "That's bullshit, Seth. You can't spin this story any way you like. Tell the truth—you're a polygamist!"

"I am only married to one woman, Thursday," Seth says. His face is earnest, so convincing. I falter, because his performance is so excellent I am temporarily tongue-tied.

"Okay, then," I say. "But how many women do you have a sexual relationship with?"

"Thursday claims you have two other wives that you refer to as Monday and Tuesday," the doctor says.

His face colors underneath the doctor's gaze. I watch it eagerly. There's no way he'll be able to talk himself out of this. "It's a game we play."

"A game?" Dr. Steinbridge repeats. My mouth drops open. I'm shaking.

"Yes." He looks at me for support, but I turn my face away. I don't understand why he's lying like this. He isn't legally married to the other two, so it's not like he can get arrested for bigamy. Everything between us has been consensual. Making it seem like I've made all this up is ensuring that they won't let me out of this place—not without a lot of counseling and medication, anyway.

"This thing Thursday and I would do to joke about all of my time spent away. I'd always come home on Thursday and since her name is Thursday, we said there was a Monday and a Tuesday, as well." He glances at me nervously. "I didn't know she took it this far, but considering..."

"What? Considering what?" I snap. Anger surges through me. I can't believe he went *there*. I'm suddenly hot all over, even though I know they keep the rooms cool. I have the urge to shove off the sheets and lean out the window so the cold air can touch me.

"Thursday, you have a history of delusion," the doctor interrupts. "Sometimes, when a trauma…" His voice continues, but I block it out. I don't want to hear it. I know what happened, but that isn't what's happening now.

Seth's eyes are pleading with me; he wants me to go along with whatever he's doing. My headache has suddenly gotten worse, and I need to be alone, think all of this through.

"Get out," I say to both of them, and when it's not enough and nobody moves, I scream it. "Everyone get out!"

A new nurse comes charging around the corner and looks at Dr. Steinbridge for instruction.

I look pointedly at him, ignoring Seth. "I don't need to be sedated. I'm not a danger to myself or anyone else. I need to be alone."

The doctor considers me for a moment, making up his mind about my mental state. Then he nods. "All right, then. I'll be back later to check on you and we can talk further." He looks at Seth, who appears ready to pass out. "You can come back for afternoon visitation and see if she's ready to talk then," he says. "I'd like to talk to you in my office."

I can see the tension building in his shoulders; he's lost control of the situation. Seth doesn't like to lose control; he's not used to anyone else getting their way. Why haven't I realized this before? Why am I just seeing it now?

Seth glances at me once more before nodding.

"All right. I'll be back later." He announces this to the room, not to me. He doesn't look at me before he strides out the door.

When they're all gone, I take a deep, shuddering breath before turning on my side and staring out the small slat of window. The sky outside is a murky gray, its tears a fine mist of rain. I can just see the tips of some trees from my angle and I focus on those. I think of the window in our— *my*—condo. The one that overlooks the park, how hard I'd fought for that unit when Seth wanted the one with the view of the Sound. I'd needed that view into the lives of strangers; it was an escape from my own life.

I doze off and wake up to Sarah carrying in my lunch— or is it dinner? I don't even know what time it is. As soon as I smell the food, my body remembers it's hungry. It doesn't even matter that the meat loaf is gray, or that the mashed potatoes are instant. I shovel food into my mouth at an alarming rate. When I'm finished, I settle back against the pillows with a stomachache. My eyes are closed and I'm dozing off again when I hear Seth's voice. I consider not opening my eyes, pretending to be asleep, in hopes that he leaves.

"I know you're awake, Thursday," he says. "We need to talk."

"Then talk," I say, without opening my eyes. I hear the rustling of a paper bag and the smell of food reaches my nose. When I open my eyes, Seth has laid out containers between us—five of them. Despite the heaviness of the hospital food sitting in my stomach, my mouth begins to water.

"Your favorite takeout," he says, one side of his mouth lifting in a smile. It's his most charming smile, the one he used on me that day in the coffee shop. He glances up at me, his head still ducked, and for a moment he looks like a little boy—vulnerable and eager to please.

"I've already had delicious hospital meat loaf," I say, eyeing the container of mushroom risotto.

Seth shrugs and his smile turns sheepish. I almost feel

sorry for him, but then I remember where I am and why I'm here.

"Seth…" I stare at him hard and he stares back. Neither of us quite knows what to do with the other, but we're preparing for some sort of emotional warfare—I can see it in his eyes.

"Why won't you tell the truth?" I say finally. That's really the bottom line, isn't it? If he told the truth, I could get out of here.

But if he told the truth, things could…things could never go back to normal. That's when I understand it, the steely look in his eyes. It all comes to me. Not only do I know who Hannah is, I know that he's been physical with her—hit her—and things between us can never be the same. Initially, my hopes were that he'd want to be with me, only me. But that will never happen, and I don't even want it to happen anymore. I don't know who my husband really is. I don't know anything at all. What he says next is not what I expect.

"The truth is that you're very sick, Thursday. You need help. I tried to pretend it wasn't happening, I played your games…" He stands up and the containers of food wobble precariously on the bed.

I'm so angry I could toss them at him. He walks to the window, stares out before he turns back to me. His face has changed from one instant to the next; there's a grim determination written across it now, like he has something awful to say to me.

"You changed," he says slowly, cautiously. "After the baby…"

"Don't," I say quickly. "Don't bring the baby into this."

"You won't talk about it, and we have to. You can't

just move past something like that," he says. There's more conviction on Seth's face than I've ever seen. His fists are balled at his sides and my mind flashes to last night in the kitchen. He looks just as angry, but also sad.

He's right. I've always refused to talk about what happened. It was too painful. I haven't wanted to relive those feelings, drag over them again and again in some shrink's office. My hurt is a living thing—sick and swollen, still festering under the surface of my calm. It's personal; I don't want to show anyone else. I nurture it on my own, keep it alive. Because as long as my hurt is still there, the memory of my son is, as well. They have to coexist.

"Thursday!" he says. "Thursday, are you listening to me?"

The smell—even the sight—of the food makes me sick. I begin pushing the containers off the bed, one by one.

The sound of them hitting the floor with wet thuds diverts Seth's attention. He races for the bed, which is just five steps away, and grabs my wrists before I can get to the pea soup. I lift my knee under the white sheet and try to topple it off. That's the one I've been looking forward to most—seeing it spread across the hospital tile like sludge.

"Our baby died, Thursday. It wasn't your fault. It wasn't anyone's fault!"

I writhe, throwing myself back against the pillows and then rearing up again. My wrists ache where Seth holds them and I bare my teeth at him. That isn't true and we both know it. It isn't true.

"You have to stop this," he pleads. "All the lies you tell yourself. They won't let you out of here until you tell the truth…"

An alarm goes off, high and ear-piercing. I wonder if

it's because of what I've done. Sarah races into the room, her braid flying comically behind her. She's followed by a man and another woman—all flashes of blue scrubs and determined faces.

The alarm is here, in this room, I realize. Seth must have set it off. But no…it's not an alarm…it's me. I'm screaming. I can feel the burn as the noise churns through my throat and out of my open mouth.

One of the nurses slips, and she goes down hard into the smear of food across the floor. The male nurse helps her up, and then they're on me, pushing Seth aside to hold me down. He backs away, against the wall, watching.

I expect his eyes to be wide with fear, or his face distorted with worry—but he looks quite peaceful. I feel something cold slide into my veins and my eyes flutter back. I force them open; I want to see Seth. He blurs for a minute, but he's still there, watching. The drugs tug at my eyelids, pulling me down. What was that look on his face? What did it mean?

TWENTY

When I come to, I am cold. I don't remember where I am, and it takes a few minutes for the events of the last few days to settle over me. Scratchy memories—they don't feel good. The smell of antiseptic fills my nostrils and I struggle to push sheets aside and sit up in bed.

A hospital… Seth… Food on the floor.

I rub my forehead, which is throbbing painfully, and peer over the side of the bed; there's no trace of the collage of color I left behind before they cocktailed me out. Why did I do that? It's a stupid question because I know. *Because Seth thinks food fights are wasteful and stupid.* I hadn't thrown anything at him, but throwing it on the floor had felt like enough—a childish display of acting out.

Practical, dry, somewhat stern Seth—that's not how I would have described him a few weeks ago. What changed?

Hannah! That name hits me harder than the rest. Because it's been how many days since I last heard from her? Three…four? I remember the look on Seth's face before the drugs pulled me under… I couldn't make out his expression; it was a mix of things I hadn't seen on his face before. Isn't that something? Being married to a man for years and seeing an expression for the first time.

I have to contact Hannah—see if she's all right. But without my phone, I don't have access to her number, and what if Seth has already been through my phone and deleted the texts we'd exchanged? Does he know my password? It's not hard to figure out—our dead baby's due date.

A new nurse walks in, this time an older man with a buzz cut, white eyebrows and a face like a bulldog. I slink down in bed. His shoulders are too wide and I can tell he won't take my shit. I was hoping for someone younger and inexperienced, like Sarah, who I could talk into helping me.

"Hello," he says. "I'm Phil."

When did his shift start? When will he be gone?

"I spoke to your doctor. Seems like everything looks good with your head…" He knocks on his own skull with his knuckles as he pages through my chart and I grimace at the gesture. He's a caveman in a nurse's uniform. "They'll be transferring you over to the psych ward."

"Why? If I'm fine, why am I not being discharged?"

"Hasn't the doctor spoken to you about this?" Phil scratches over his left nipple and flips another page.

I shake my head.

"He should be over in a bit and he'll discuss it with you then."

"Great," I say dryly. I'm sour. I don't like Phil. He is obviously ex-military and thinks everything should be done a certain way: discipline and order. I want a young, easily manipulated nurse like Sarah, who will feel sorry for me.

Before Phil leaves, I ask if I can make a call.

"To whom?"

"My husband," I say sweetly. "He's working in Portland and I'd like to check on him."

"There's no husband listed in your chart," he says.

"Are you calling me a liar?"

Phil ignores me. "Why don't we leave the checking in up to him? After all, you're the one in the hospital."

I glare at him as he leaves the room. I used to like guys like Phil—they were helpful in sticky patient situations, always willing to play bad cop when a nurse needed a break—but being on this side of a Phil is a terrible thing. I'll wait for the next nurse and hope she's more my type.

Dr. Steinbridge tells me that all is well in my head, nothing swollen or bruised.

"Looking good, looking good," he says, tapping a bent finger against my chart. His knuckles are dusted with white hairs. "We're transferring you to the psych ward, where you'll have your evaluation and we'll get your new medication sorted out."

"Wait a minute," I say. "I don't need to go to the psych ward. I'm fine. I fell and hit my head."

His lips fold in like he's disappointed with me.

"You're having extreme delusions, Thursday. Violent outbursts. Don't worry," he tries to reassure me. "We'll work on getting you better. We all want the same thing."

I doubt that. Seth wants me in here. I want to scream,

swear at him…force him to see the truth, but I know that if I do I'll only confirm what he's thinking…what Seth's telling him. I'm not crazy. *You're not*, I tell myself. *Even when you feel like you are, remember you're not.*

An hour later, a nurse pushes a wheelchair into the room and flips on the brakes.

"I'm here for your transfer," she says.

"My husband…?" I hate the whine in my voice, hate that I have to ask where my husband is instead of knowing.

She shrugs. "I'm just here for your transfer. That's all I know."

I feel woozy as I walk over to the chair. The backs of my legs hit the soft leather and I sink down in relief. It's not the head injury making me feel this way, it's the drugs. I can barely think clearly. I don't remember the wheelchair ride up to the eighth floor, or getting into the bed in the tiny room. I'm assigned a nurse, but I have no recollection of her coming in to see me. Nothing feels real. I question my existence, I question Hannah's… Did I imagine everything, like they said? I want to talk to Seth, I want my head to clear, but they keep pouring pills down my throat.

I spend the next seven days in a sort of haze. Nothing feels real, the drugs making me feel detached from my body: a limp helium balloon bobbing about a room going nowhere. I go to group, eat my meals in the dining hall and see Dr. Steinbridge for sessions. I've lost so much weight that I don't recognize myself when I look in the mirror. My jaw has definition and there are hollows above my collarbone, deep compressions that were once filled with fat. How can a week do this to a person? I wonder, but I'm not sure I care. Everything is muted, even my feelings about myself.

I stop asking about Seth after a few days; even the thought of him makes me feel desperate and crazy. The nurses look at me with pity in their eyes. I have the vague feeling that I don't like it when they do that. They probably don't think there is a Seth. And maybe there isn't. Also, fuck him for putting me in this position where I am questioning myself.

On the ninth day, my mother comes to see me. Visiting hours are in the common area, where all of us crazies wait eagerly for our people to arrive. We sit on mustard-colored couches or at the gray tables on foldout chairs, our hair greasy and our faces pale and splotchy from too little or too much sleep. An attempt at normalizing the room is made with potted plants and framed artwork. I've studied each piece of art and the plaques next to them telling of the local artists who painted, or sketched, or photographed. Seattle likes to keep it local, homegrown artists to soothe the homegrown sick.

I find an unoccupied couch near the vending machines. They won't allow us caffeine or too much sugar. The machines are stocked with vitamin water and bruised-looking apples. I sit with my hands in my lap, staring at the floor. When my mother walks in, she doesn't recognize me at first. Her eyes move right over my face, then bounce back like they're on a bungee cord.

I see her mouth my name before she clutches her purse tightly to her side and scurries over. I stand as she approaches. I'm not sure if she wants to hug me or if she's too disappointed. The first time I landed myself in a psych ward, she refused to come, saying it was too painful to see me that way. Too painful for *her*. Now she lowers herself onto the sofa without taking her eyes from my face.

"Your father—" she starts.

"Yeah, I know, Mom. It's fine."

We look at each other like it's the first time we're truly seeing each other's faces. My father would never come to a place like this. To see one of his daughters locked in a psych ward would mean that he had done something wrong as a parent, and my father likes to maintain the illusion of perfection. As for my mother, I am her crazy, unhinged offspring—she gave birth to me and has no idea of who I am or of the life I live. She doesn't want to know. We're both thinking the same thing. I pull my sweater down over my hands as I gaze at her Botoxed forehead. She doesn't want to admit how old she is any more than she wants to admit that her daughter is a first-class fuckup.

"I'm not here because I'm crazy," I tell her.

She immediately opens her mouth to deny she's ever had that thought. Of course, that's her job as a mother.

"I'm not sick, either. I'm not having an emotional breakdown because I lost my baby a year ago." I cut off all the roads her mind is taking, all the ways she's trying to make excuses for why I'm here.

She closes her mouth and stares. I feel like a child as my bottom lip quivers. She won't believe anything I say. Seth has already gotten to her.

"Mom, Seth already had another wife when I met him. Her name is Regina Coele. She didn't want children. I was the one who was supposed to give him a baby. But then I had the…" My voice trails off.

My mother drops her head like this is all too much. I watch the tips of her lashes, the bridge of her nose, as she stares down at her shoes. From this angle she looks ten, twenty years younger. Just a girl who has bent her head in exasperation…frustration…hopelessness? I've never been good at telling what she's really feeling. I know all of the brands she likes, I know her thoughts on shallow, useless topics, but I don't know how to uncover what she's truly feeling. I'm not quite sure if she knows, either.

"Regina is Seth's *ex*-wife. He was married before you, yes. You're right—she didn't want children and so they parted ways." My mother leans forward, her eyes imploring. It's true. How can I argue with that? Regina is technically his ex-wife. He divorced her to marry me, after all. But they're still together, still a couple, just without the title.

"Mother," I say. "Please listen to me. Seth is trying to cover his tracks. They're still together."

She drops her face into her palms. When did I become the type of woman who isn't believed by her own mother? *When you started lying to yourself*, I think.

When she looks up, her eyes are wet. She reminds me of a cocker spaniel with those wet eyes. "You have an unhealthy fixation on his exes. But, Thursday, he's not with them. He's with you. Seth is worried sick about you." She reaches for my hand, but I pull it away. I won't be coddled that way—spoken to like I'm a child. Her hand drops uselessly back into her lap.

"Why do you think he's always in Portland? He has two other wives." I stand up, begin pacing.

"He works there," she hisses. "He loves you, we all do. We want you to get well."

"I am well," I say stiffly. I stop to glare at her. "Why hasn't he come? Where is he?" That's when she gets shifty, averting her eyes, crossing and uncrossing her ankles. She doesn't know what to say because she doesn't know where Seth is, or why he hasn't come.

"In Portland…" she says. It sounds more like a question. "He still has to work, Thursday. Life goes on."

"No, it doesn't. Not when I'm in the hospital. He has other wives to tend to his needs," I say. "Why come see the loony toon in Tonker Town?"

She looks at me quizzically for a moment before she stands up. We face each other and I can read the disappointment on her face.

"I need to get going," she says. Fifteen minutes. She lasted fifteen minutes in the psych ward. I watch as she retreats toward the doors, her shoulders sagging with the weight of my failures as her daughter. At least this time she came.

TWENTY-ONE

I am alone. I realize that it's always been this way, my whole life, and anything my mind constructed to convince me otherwise was a lie. A comfortable lie I needed. My parents were occupied with my sister, Torrence, who was always getting into trouble at school or with her friends. I was the good child; I parented myself well while they were busy. I knew the rules, the moral confines they'd built around me: no drinking, no premarital sex, no drugs, no sneaking out, top-notch grades only. It was easy to follow their guidelines; I wasn't the rebel of the family. My sister, on the other hand, dabbled in all of the above. My father grayed at his temples, my mother started getting Botox and I tried my best to be perfect so there was one less daughter to worry about. Then, when Torrence straightened up and married the right man, they'd been so relieved they'd showered her with a different type of attention. She'd put in three well-behaved years and they'd both forgotten the decade she spent snorting their money up her nose and fucking every dealer in town. Maybe all of that trying made me go crazy. Maybe the lack of attention from my parents pushed me toward Seth, my desperation to be accepted trapping me in a relationship any normal person would think bizarre.

I poke at my Jell-O. They love to feed you Jell-O in this place—wobbly and colorful, like our minds. Today is orange, yesterday was green. It's like they're trying to remind you that you're weak and unstable. I eat my Jell-O.

I have to get the fuck out of here. I have to find Hannah, make sure she's okay. Where once I slept, I am now awake. I saw Dr. Steinbridge today. I've realized that he is my keeper—not the electric doors with keycard access, nor the burly nurses who wrangle us like toddlers if we get out of hand. *Calm down, little Thursday, or we'll put you in the padded time-out room.*

Dr. Steinbridge has the power to say I'm well; he is God in this place of speckled sterile tile and fluorescent lights. One swipe of his pen (a Bic) and I am a free bird.

Hannah… Hannah. She's all I think about. I've become her savior in my own mind. If something has happened to her, I am responsible. If she is to be saved, I must get out of here. I married this man, gave my blessing for a third wife. When I saw that first bruise I should have spoken up, forced her to tell me what he did. For a moment, I doubt that she is real. That's how good they are—they can make you doubt your own mind in this place.

Eat your Jell-O!

I realize it is my duty to convince the good doctor that I have come to my senses, that my head is cleared of its delusional fog. That *I am whole and my husband is a one-woman man!* That Hannah and Regina are not real, but a sexual game my husband and I played. That's what they want to hear, isn't it? All I have to do is say I'm lying about Seth's penchant for plural pussy and I am a cured woman!

It can't happen too fast, my change, or Steinbridge will suspect that I am lying. During our daily sessions, I pretend to be confused. *Seth only has one wife? That wife is me?* Gradually, I become more myself, each session I am less confused, less insistent.

"What is wrong with me?" I ask the doctor. "Why don't I know what's real and what is not?"

I am diagnosed! The trauma of losing a child, never dealing with that loss in a healthy way, it put stress on my relationship with Seth. I blamed other women instead of focusing on my healing. When the good doctor asked what I thought triggered the mania that led to my mental demise, I thought of Debbie: chatty Debbie, nosy Debbie, Debbie with the big hair who suggested I snoop on the women who made me feel insecure. I don't blame Debbie for any of my actions; if anything, she woke me up. I wasn't the only one who suffered crippling insecurity, you could be any age. Hell, Lauren seemingly had a perfect life. I always thought she taped those anniversary cards to her locker to brag, to rub it in the rest of our faces that she had it better than us. But now I see the truth: women are stuck in a cycle of insecurity perpetuated by the way men treat them, and we are constantly fighting to prove to ourselves and everyone else that we are okay. Sure, women occasionally lose their minds over men, but does that mean we're all unstable, or that men made us unstable with their careless actions? I don't tell Dr. Steinbridge about Debbie or Lauren; he would say I was deferring responsibility. But that's not what I'm doing at all; I'm holding everyone accountable, because it takes a village to put someone in a mental institution.

My lack of dealing with issues is part of my unraveling, according to Dr. Steinbridge. I like the way that sounds: *my unraveling.*

But I'm not unraveling in the way they think I am; I'm unraveling out of my infatuation with my husband. I play the part of frail, painfully unaware woman. Stress has eaten at me, I have no coping mechanisms, my parents' lack of attention coddled me into a tight, naive little cocoon.

We take a tour of my daddy/mommy issues. My mother is a pleaser and my father is detached. As I watched my mother do more, more, more to earn my father's attention…well…I learned to express that love language. And when I do too much, I collapse under the weight of expectations. My empty womb has made me feel like I'm not a real woman, not worthy of my husband's love. They scraped all of my organs out, roped off my reproductive system: *closed for business.* Before my eyes, scenes from my miscarriage begin to flash in painful succession. I know I'm supposed to let them come, face them—as the doctor says. But they're memories I've never looked over, not even once, since it happened. It's easier to cope when you don't acknowledge what you're coping from.

Seth and I have just left our bed and breakfast, and we stop at a gas station to fill up and buy snacks for the road. We've just eaten but he insists the baby will need snacks, which makes me smile. He's so attentive: buying little gifts and kissing my swelling belly. One of my friends at the hospital told me that her husband is revolted by her pregnant stomach and refuses to touch it. I watch him through the car window, my heart swollen with pride. My husband, mine. And now we've made a baby together; my life couldn't be more perfect. He's so handsome as he walks toward the car, carrying two paper cups, a plastic bag hanging from his forearm. The cups hold tea; he says he asked for hot water inside and then used his mother's tea bags. It's bitter, but I've been drinking it for a week and the taste is growing on me. I dig in the bag while he finishes up with the gas. He's bought my favorite pregnancy snacks: unhealthy, processed garbage that normally make me blush with shame. But as I sip on my tea and pull things out of the bag, I feel only grateful for my thoughtful, observant husband. So sweet are the ranch-flavored chips and licorice sticks that resembled twisted, red plastic. The cramps start an hour and a half later. I don't want to say anything at first, remembering that my doctor said that some women experience Braxton Hicks contractions early in their pregnancies. The phantom pains a mere reflection of what is to come. I squirm uncomfortably in my seat, my open bag of chips falling to the car's floorboard, little speckled triangles spilling out around my shoes. It's not until I bend to retrieve the chip bag that I see the blood. It's pooling on the tan leather, staining my cream pants in a dark, ominous red. "Seth," is all I have to say. He looks over at me and pushes his foot down on the gas, his face pale at the sight of the blood. The nearest hospital: Queen County. When we pull up at the doors of the emergency room I already know my baby is dead, his life leaking out from between my legs.

Everything from there I could only recount in a sort of dizziness that was colored by fluorescent lights. The first time I had clarity of mind after the car ride to the hospital was five days later when they told me that my uterus had ruptured and in order to control the bleeding they'd had to remove it in an emergency surgery. I would never be able to become pregnant again. I'd let Seth hold me as I sobbed into his shirt, and then when he'd left to take a call from work, I'd gone to the tiny bathroom in my room and attempted to slit my wrists with a metal nail file. A nurse found me bleeding on the floor, staring at the blood, perfectly calm. It was a hack job, my wrists sawed open with something dull. The scars are thick and lumpy. I'd been calm until they tried to help me, then I scratched, and bit, and screamed that they'd killed my baby and were trying to kill me. That had been the start of my first stay at Queen County. The stay that had left me barren of womb and heart.

Dr. Steinbridge says that, in my grief, I created the delusion of three wives—women who were better suited for Seth, ones who could give him what I could not. God, it's depressing all the things that are wrong with me—even if only half of them are true.

I shuffle out of our sessions, my head ducked low, the scars on my wrists throbbing. I'm believably pathetic. He thinks I'm getting well. But in those bent-shoulder moments when I look my most humble, I am angry. Where is Seth? Why hasn't he come? He wasn't like this when I carried his baby—he was pandering, and catered to my every whim. Does he even feel guilty that he lied?

I've been jettisoned. I fume all the way back to my room, which is too cold despite the various complaints I've made with the nurses. My roommate is a woman in her late forties named Susan, who had a mental breakdown after she caught her husband having an affair. Weak Susan, I want to say. Try signing off on two extra marriages and being the forgotten middle wife.

Susan has no eyelashes or eyebrows. I've seen her searching for them when she's anxious, thin fingers reaching up like tweezers to pluck. She has a bald spot on top of her head, too, and a scattering of long brown hairs around her bed. I imagine by the time she gets out of here she'll be completely hairless, like one of those cats.

She's not in the room. I lie down on the bed, my arm thrown across my eyes to block out the light because we aren't allowed to turn off our lights during the day. I am drifting off into a semi-nap—which is the best you can do in this place—when a nurse comes in to tell me that I have a visitor.

My eyes snap open and my first thought is: I'm going to pretend *not* to be angry with him. That's right. I'll be docile and apologetic—the Suzy-homemaker type of wife he likes me to be. It won't be so hard, will it? I've been pretending for years, the anger bubbling under the surface, unexplored. *You're awake*, I think. *Do not lose grip of your awakeness.*

I stand up, alert and ready. There is no mirror to check my reflection in—mirrors are slit wrists waiting to happen—so I smooth my hair, wipe beneath my eyes. I have no idea what I look like, but I suppose the more pathetic, the better. When I run my hands down my abdomen, there is only a hollow and then two sharp knobs of hipbone that used to be buried underneath my bad habits of wine and cheesy pastas. I stick out my chest, which, thankfully, has not diminished. I have to get my husband on my side.

When I walk into the common area, it's not Seth I see, but Lauren. I feel a sense of disappointment. This is different than what was supposed to happen. I rearrange my face, hiding what I'm really feeling to smile at pain-in-the-ass Lauren. Lauren, whom I had drinks with, and told all my secrets to. Were we friends now?

I don't know if I'm happy to see her, but she's certainly happy to see me. She stands up from the table where she's been waiting and I see that she's wearing jeans and a Seahawks sweatshirt. Her face is contorted with concern as she makes her way over to me, dodging a woman who is doing interpretive dance in the center of the room. The place between her eyebrows is pinched.

"Thursday," she breathes, shaking her head. "What the hell?"

I like her so much in that moment that my little act of contrite humility I had ready for Seth drops away, and I latch on to her in a desperate hug. My moods, my thoughts, they're all over the place. I'm like a spider monkey, clinging in my relief to someone I know.

Lauren lets out a little yelp and I realize I'm strangling her, so I let go. She smiles at me in the way that old friends smile after something bad has happened to you. She already believes me, I can tell. I do have a friend.

"How did you find me?" I ask, breathless with anticipation.

"Your husband called the hospital—Seth, right?—and said that you'd be taking extended time off due to an illness. I tried to get in touch with him but we don't have a number. So, I called your mother—she's listed on your emergency contacts—and she told me where to find you."

I'm surprised that my mother admitted to a stranger that her daughter was in a mental hospital. Lauren had put in a lot of work to find me. I wonder if Anna's noticed that I've been missing, if she's reached out to my mother.

"Why are you here?" she says finally, once we've settled down in a spot by the window. The glass is streaked with water as an unusually hard rain leans east, slapping the glass and bending the trees. A woman's hair whips around her as she runs through the garden area below. As I lean into Lauren, a mother/son duo walk toward us, eyeing the empty chairs in our circle. I shoot them a vicious look and they scoot away somewhere else. Good. Go.

I tell her about going to see Hannah, and about finding Regina online. When I get to the part about Hannah's bruise, Lauren's eyes bug out. Another convoluted detail to add to this story. I tell her how Seth pushed me while we were arguing.

"I confronted him about all of it. He says I attacked him, that I fell and hit my head. When I woke up, I was here. Lauren..." I say, lowering my voice. "He's saying that I made it all up."

Her face is horrified. Her life is a mess, but mine is messier.

"That you made what up?"

"His polygamy. He has everyone convinced I'm crazy, including my own mother." I'm rubbing a piece of hair between my fingers and I abruptly stop, in case I look crazy.

Lauren doesn't seem to notice. Her eyes drop to the ground as she thinks.

"If everyone close to you is saying the same thing, they'll never believe you," she says. "You know how this stuff works."

I know.

"What about your friends? Is there someone I can call to come in here and back you up?" Her hands are splayed flat on her knees with just the pointer finger of her right hand moving up and down in quick succession. A nervous finger, I think.

"No," I say. "I've never told anyone aside from you. Not even my sister knows."

"Not a close family, huh? Sounds like mine."

"We're close without being close, if you know what I mean. We see each other often, but no one really knows what's happening behind everyone's eyes."

Lauren nods like she knows exactly what I'm talking about. Maybe all American families play the togetherness game—the one where you talk about sports and dine on casseroles (in the Pacific Northwest, it's gluten-free and organic), fight about politics and act like you have meaningful relationships when you're actually dying of loneliness.

"I don't know if she's okay," I say of Hannah. "She was off the last time I saw her. She called me the next day, but when I called her back, she didn't answer."

"Maybe I can contact her," Lauren suggests. "Does she have a Facebook or something?"

I give her all of Hannah's details. I remember her address off the top of my head but not her phone number.

"Do you know where he met this girl?" she asks me as I walk her to the doors.

I shake my head. In all my detective work, I hadn't asked Hannah where she met her husband, though I doubt she would have told me the truth.

"There's a photo," I say quickly. "On Regina's dating profile. I think Hannah and Regina know each other."

Lauren is startled; the plot has thickened. "Wait," she whispers. "Seth's other two wives know each other?"

I nod. "If you can find that photo we have proof. We can take it to Regina, make her talk…"

My plan is faulty. Thinking that Regina would come forward to back me up is far-fetched. Thinking that a photo could prove my claim that Seth is a polygamist is equally as far-fetched. But it's all I have. I could blackmail them.

Lauren promises to come back as soon as she has something, and I feel such immense relief that I hug her once more.

"Lauren," I say before she leaves. "You have no idea how much this means to me. I haven't even asked how you are..."

"Yeah, well, in light of your current situation, you get a free pass."

I smile at her gratefully before she turns in her visitor badge to the security desk and gives me a little wave. "I'll be back soon," she promises.

I walk back to my room, a renewed hope growing in my chest. I'm not alone. Seth wants me to believe that I am. He's taken my mother...my father. He wants me to be solely reliant on him. But I'm not sure why. I became a liability when I snooped after he told me not to. I know things that could ruin his business, his reputation. Of course he wants to shut me up, lock me up.

What if...? What if Hannah doesn't know about me? Maybe that's it. All along I've thought that all three of us were in cahoots, like some secret girl alliance. *Our man is so lovable he scored three women, and we're just so happy to be a part of it!* But Seth is going to great lengths to keep me locked away, sequestered. Perhaps to keep me from Hannah. To keep her from finding out. I think of the photo on Regina's dating profile, the blond in the corner of the photo who looked suspiciously like Hannah. What if Seth used the same story on Hannah that he used on me? The barren wife, the need to be with someone who would give him children… I could be removed from the equation altogether…so Seth could once again get what he wants.

TWENTY-TWO

Lauren comes back two days later, looking tired and wearing a puffy black jacket the color of garbage bags over her scrubs. She avoids looking at me as she handles a Starbucks cup, spinning it around and around between her fingers. Her fingernails aren't painted; I don't think I've ever seen her without her fingernails painted. I wonder if that's an upper-class cry for help, Lauren in distress. I'm too distracted to spend any time on niceties and small talk.

"I got you one, but they wouldn't let me bring it in."

Got me what? Oh! A latte—she's talking about a latte. I dismiss the coffee with a wave of my hand. "We're not allowed to have caffeine."

She nods, taking a deep breath before she begins, puffing out her cheeks and widening her eyes. I brace myself.

"She's not on Facebook, Thursday, there's nothing. I checked all of the social media sites—I even checked Pinterest and Shutterfly. She doesn't exist. God, I even tried changing her name around—you know people have all those cutesie handles nowadays…"

I nod, thinking of Regina, how I'd had to be clever with her name to find her.

"She's either deleted her profile or has extreme privacy settings," Lauren says. She picks at the cardboard sleeve around her cup. "I Googled her, too… Nothing. Are you sure that's her real name?"

"I don't know. That's the name I saw on the paper I found in Seth's pocket." I drop my head into my hands.

"What about the picture of Regina and Hannah? Did you find that?" She reaches into her purse and pulls out a folded piece of paper. Lauren's face is washed of color. She slides the paper across the table and I reach for it. My hands shake as I unfold it. It's a printout of the photo I'd found of Regina and the woman I suspect is Hannah. But when I look down at the grainy printout something is wrong. Regina is the same, her smile wide just as I remember it, but in the corner of the photo where I'd once seen Hannah there is a woman with dark hair.

"No," I say. *No, no, no…*

"Is that her?" Lauren asks. Her finger taps the photo, right where Hannah should be. "Is that Hannah, Thursday…?"

I shake my head, pushing the paper away. I'm cold all over. I rock slightly, shaking my head. Am I crazy?

If I think I'm crazy, maybe Lauren thinks so, too. I look up suddenly. "Do you believe me?"

"Yes…" But there's a catch in her voice. Her eyes dart

around the room like she's trying to find a loophole to my question. My heart does a little *squeeze, squeeze, squeeze.*

We sit in silence for a few minutes, looking out the window. Lauren, I notice, is slouching in her seat—another telling sign that all is not right. I don't know if she's bothered by my situation or if there's a burden of her own she's carrying.

"There's one more thing…" She's been holding on to this, saving it for last. Why won't she look at me?

I feel the figurative knots form in my belly and my knee starts to bounce under the table. I just want her to spit it out, get it over with. *Squeeze, squeeze, knot, knot…*

"Tell me…"

"Look, there's no easy way to say this. I made a few calls and…well…the house for the address you gave me… Ugh, Thursday! It's registered under your name." She covers her eyes with her palms.

My mind goes blank. I don't know what to say. I stare at Lauren like I misheard her until she finally repeats herself.

"What?"

She is looking at me differently. It's the way the doctors and nurses look at me, with cautious pity—*this poor girl, this broken thing.* I stand up and force myself to look her in the eyes.

"That is not my house. I don't know what's going on, but it's not mine. I don't even care if you don't believe me. I'm not crazy."

She holds up both hands as if to ward me off. "I didn't say you were crazy. I'm just telling you what I found."

I lick my lips as I back up. They don't give you Chap-Stick in this place; they try to soothe your mind but let your body fall to pieces. Everyone here is either dry or oily;

their hair plastered to their heads in stringy, wet-looking chunks, or decorated with tiny flakes of dandruff like they were just snowed on.

I'm trying not to do anything rash, like run off to my room without a goodbye, or yell—yelling would be bad. But it's taking all of my self-control. The way people perceive you is the really mentally thwarting thing in life. If everyone is against you, you start to question things about yourself, like now.

"Thank you for coming." I force the words out. "I appreciate you trying, anyway." I hear her calling my name as I walk briskly away—not running, not even trotting—just a quick exit so she can't see what I'm feeling.

In my room, I curl up on the thin mattress, my knees drawn to my chest, and press my cheek against the scratchy sheets. They smell of bleach and a little of vomit. Susan is staring at me from across the room; I glanced at her when I walked in the door, her lashless eyes alarmed, like she'd forgotten I live here, too.

I can feel her eyes boring into my back. This is usually the time when we're both in the room, between our group therapy sessions and dinner. *"A little downtime,"* they call it. Most of us use our downtime to reflect on how down we really are. It's a catch-22.

"How long have you been here, Susan?" My voice is muffled and I have to repeat my question when she squeaks back a mousy little response.

"A month," she says.

I sit up, leaning my back against the wall and hugging my pillow to my chest.

"Have you ever been in a place like this before?"

She glances up at me and when she sees me watching her, she looks away again. "Only once…when I was much younger. My father died and I didn't cope well." I like the way Susan sums everything up so you don't have to ask more questions. Her therapist must love her.

"And when did they decide you were ready to leave?"

Susan looks flustered. Two red spots appear on her cheeks and she begins knotting her fingers together.

"When I stopped being suicidal—or saying I was."

True that. At least I know I'm on the right track. I've stopped talking about it, all of it.

"I hope things get better for you, Susan. He wasn't deserving." I mean it, too. My thoughts for the last few days have been about women like me, and Lo, and Susan—women who give everything to the men who break their trust.

She looks up at me then, and without the support of her eyebrows, I can't tell if she's surprised or sad. She appears to be somewhat pleased by the time my words sink in. Like she's repeating them over and over in her head. *He wasn't deserving, he wasn't deserving.*

"Thank you," she says softly. "He really wasn't."

I nod, but I think, *Neither was Seth*. Not deserving. Not of the women who bow and cow and do everything to please him, nor of the life he's built on our backs. Why, he has a whole team behind him: legal, childbearing and money. I've never wanted to admit that part, that maybe he's with me for my money, for my trust fund. It's been a thing I don't think about.

I'm the money. I've never seen myself that way, never thought it played a factor in our relationship. But I'm rich by any sense of the word. My father has made sure my sister and I are well taken care of. My sister snorted most of her trust and then married a wealthy country club man named Michael Sprouce, Jr. That had been her saving grace in my parents' eyes. The money has never meant anything to me, only Seth has. And so I've always been generous...oblivious, even, handing over control to him.

But now...now everything feels different. *Is* different. He's sequestered me away and that isn't something you do to your wife, someone you love. It's what you do to someone you're trying to manage. But he's been managing all three of us all along.

Susan and I sit facing each other, our eyes glued to the ceiling as we wait for dinnertime.

I make a list in my head of things I must do when I get out: check the bank account, talk to the wives, contact Seth's parents and talk to his business partner, Alex, who doesn't know I exist. They can't keep me in here forever. I will get out, I will show everyone who he really is. He can't do this to me. This time I'm going to fight back.

TWENTY-THREE

I am released two days later. I say goodbye to Susan, who is in group, by leaving my little square of soap, an apple I'd stolen from breakfast and the hospital-issued bottles of shampoo on her bed. We were always complaining about not enough shampoo, like this was a hotel and not a mental health facility. Some of the complaining was just to feel normal; if you thought a lot about shampoo, you didn't think about anything important.

Seth is standing in the reception area, talking to one of the nurses, as the doctor walks me up with my paperwork.

"He's called every day to check on your progress," Dr. Steinbridge says softly. His breath smells like old man and onion bagel. "People deal with things differently, so don't be too hard on him."

I nod, gritting my teeth. What a little boys' club. Dr. Steinbridge wears a wedding band on his hairy finger but spends all of his time here. I wonder if Mrs. Steinbridge sits at home waiting for him or if she has a life of her own, and if there is someone in her life saying, *"He works hard, don't be too hard on him..."* Waiting...waiting...that's what women do. We wait for him to get home, we wait for him to pay attention to us, wait to be treated fairly—for our worth to be seen and acknowledged. Life is just a waiting game for women.

I'm still playing the docile game and I'll play it all the way off the property until I'm free. I set my face in an impassive mask as I put one foot in front of the other. Seth looks like a model of success and composure. He's wearing his Regina clothes: dark gray slacks and a forest green sweater over a button-down, his hair neatly gelled and combed, his face free of stubble. It's all a different style than he wears with me. I'm realizing that he's different with each of us, adopting different styles to match his wives. For Hannah it's the hoodies, baseball caps and band shirts: young clothes to match his young wife. The clean-shaven face and the work clothes are for Regina, so he can be the respectable businessman for his lawyer wife. I get the sexy Seth: the stubble, the suit jackets, the fitted T-shirts and expensive shoes. He's a chameleon and he gets to play house with variety. When we're a few feet away, Seth looks up from his conversation and smiles at me. Smiles at me! Like nothing is wrong and this is all normal and fine. Drop your wife off in a hospital for the mentally ill and disappear all this time without a word. I force my mouth into a weak return smile that doesn't reach my eyes. The nurse behind the desk glances over at me like I'm *soooo lucky*, and *what's a guy like him doing with a nut like you?* I want to pat her on the head and tell her he's the real nut in this relationship, but I ignore her and focus on Seth, my darling husband. I walk right into his arms like nothing is wrong, and stay there while he holds me. His cologne is overpowering, sharp...not the one he wears with me. I'm sure I look like a frightened, relieved wife, but as I'm pressed against his chest, smelling his Regina cologne, I am nothing but furious.

"Well, I'll leave you two to it," Dr. Steinbridge says. "Remember to call if you have any questions or concerns. My number is right on the paperwork there." He points to a spot on the sheet he's holding before setting it on the counter in front of Seth. We both thank him, our voices blending together as if we're a perfectly synchronized couple. We certainly have been in the past, mostly by my effort.

Seth has brought me a change of clothes: sweatpants and a long-sleeve T-shirt, and my Nikes.

"Your mother went to your condo and grabbed a few things," he says, handing them to me.

Your condo, I think. Why would he say *your* and not *ours*? I go to the bathroom to change and find that everything aside from the shoes is too big for me. I walk out, tugging self-consciously on my shirt, which is swallowing me up.

"You look great," Seth says when he sees me.

Skinny like Hannah! I think. On our way out, Seth grabs my hand and squeezes, and for a moment, I'm lost in remembering what it's like to be loved by him. *Wake up, Thursday!*

I wake up. I squeeze back and allow him to lead me to the car, but I am awake in every sense of the word. A month locked in a grimy place like Queen County has me staring around the parking lot in wonder. *Free!* I can run in any direction and I'm free. I climb into the passenger seat, adjusting the vents, as is my habit. Seth notices and smiles. It's all back to normal for him—predictable Thursday. *I'm awake!* When he walks around the front of the car I fume and practice hating him. It's not his car. What car is this? Everything is wrong: the smell is different, the seats...but I don't want to ask questions. He could accuse me of having delusions again. When he gets in, I smile, tucking both hands between my thighs to keep them warm. It's raining, gentle splashes on the windshield, not the violent rain of the past week. Seth reaches out and pats my knee. It's so paternal.

"Listen, Thursday..." he says, once we are on the highway. "I'm sorry about not coming to see you—"

That's what he's sorry for?

"You didn't call, either," I point out.

Seth glances at me. "I didn't call, either," he admits. Casual, like a husband admitting to forgetting an anniversary, not institutionalizing his wife. I could call him out for it right now, confront him about everything, but something is off; it's like the air is different between us, filled with tense static. As I look out the window, we pass a minivan and a little girl with red hair waves at me from her booster seat. I don't wave back and I feel guilty. I lift my hand too late and wave at the empty road. I feel crazy for the first time. I didn't feel crazy in Queen County, but I feel crazy now. Funny.

"I was...angry," Seth continues. He's choosing his words carefully. "I blame myself for what's happened to you. If I'd done better...been better... I didn't know what to say."

Angry? Does Seth even know what anger is? His life is crafted exactly the way he wants it, with three women to sate him; when one of us does something to upset him, he simply buries his cock and attention in someone else until his anger melts.

I think of all the things he could have said, things I want him to say. So many things…and then it hits me that he didn't say what he was angry about. Angry that I ratted him out to the psych ward? Angry that I accused him of hitting his young, pregnant, third wife? Angry that I'd been sneaking around to see said wife? Or perhaps angry about all of it. One accusatory word to Seth could cause him to turn the car around and take me back to Queen County, where Dr. Steinbridge would be waiting with a slew of new treatments that would leave me slack-jawed and drooling. I have to keep control, and that means pretending that I don't have any.

I'll give it to him—he looks genuinely wounded. My poor, victimized husband.

My body tenses.

"You lied to the doctors, made up stories…"

So even outside of the hospital Seth is holding to his theory that I'm lying. I can hardly believe it. My toes curl involuntarily in my shoes, and I stare straight ahead at the cars in front of us. I'm the only one who knows the truth other than Hannah and Regina. Seth has made sure that my friends and family see me as imbalanced and delusional. He could send me back to Queen County and no one would be on my side. I remember the look on Lauren's face the last time she came to see me, and bite the inside of my cheek. Hannah is out there, I know exactly where to find her. All I need to do is go talk to her. She reached out to me that last day, left a message asking for help. *Keep your mouth shut until you have proof*, I tell myself.

"I understand," I say softly.

Seth seems pleased enough with this that he doesn't feel the need to push the conversation further. He taps the steering wheel with an index finger. His body language is all different; I feel like I don't even know him.

"Are you hungry? Your mother restocked the fridge, but we can grab something, too, if you prefer that?"

I'm not hungry, but I nod and manage a half-assed smile. "I just want to be home. I'm sure I can find something there."

"Good," he says. "We can make something together— you've been promising to give me lessons for years..." His voice is overly cheerful. I don't know if there's anything worse than someone forcing cheerfulness down your throat when you don't feel a bit happy.

Giving Seth cooking lessons was one of those things we always spoke about but never truly intended to do. It's like saying you'd take ballroom dancing lessons, or go couples skydiving. *Imagine that!* and *Wouldn't that be fun!* Seth's about as interested in cooking as I am in building a house.

"Sure," I say, and to be more convincing, more pliable, I add, "That would be fun."

When we walk into our condo thirty minutes later I am prickly with nerves. The air smells fresh and I notice that he's left a window open in the living room. It's chilly inside and I go to close it. Seth is at my elbow, hovering, like I'm going to snap at any moment. I bump into him on my way back from the window and we apologize like strangers. I'm unsure if he wants to catch me if I fall, or return me to Queen County. This is what I wanted—to be home, yet I am coming home under completely different circumstances: my husband is not the man I thought he was, and I am not the woman I have been pretending to be. Everything looks the same and feels horribly, irrevocably different.

The first thing I do is take a shower: a long, hot, soapy shower. I lather the shampoo in my hair using double what I normally use, and I think of Susan. We hadn't exchanged information, but I'd like to find her one day, check on her. We could meet for coffee and pretend we didn't meet in a mental facility. When I step out onto my bath rug, my fingers are shriveled. I press the wrinkled pads together, chewing on my bottom lip. I'm anxious, but for the first time in a long time, I feel clean. I wrap myself in my furry robe, take a deep breath and step out of the bathroom, steam trailing behind me.

"I'm going to stay here with you for a while," Seth says.

A while? What does "a while" mean? If he'd said those words to me just a month ago, I'd be so thrilled I'd probably throw myself at him, but now I just stare. Two days? Three days? His presence already feels oppressive and it's only been a few hours. My home feels less private than the hospital I just left. Has he gone through my things? My drawers look rumpled, like someone with unpracticed hands has been shifting things about. Seth and I have always respected each other's privacy, but now that I know something about him, I'm sure he needs to know things about me.

"What about work?"

"You're more important than work. You're my priority, Thursday. Listen," he says, taking my hands. His hands feel wrong—awkward. Has it been so long that I don't recognize the feel of them anymore?

"I know I've failed you. I realize that I've put things before you. I want to make things right between us. Work on our relationship."

I nod like this is exactly what I want to hear. Forcing a smile, I twist my wet hair on top of my head. I'm as casual and compliant as the old Thursday. Skinnier, though! Seth's pretty little fuck doll.

"I'll make us something to eat. You hungry?" I need the distraction, I need to think without Seth watching me, but then he stands up, blocking my way to the kitchen. My heart leaps as adrenaline rushes through my body. If he tries anything, I'm ready, I'll fight him. I take a full breath, filling my lungs to capacity, and then I smile. It's the most genuine smile I've given anyone in weeks.

"No, let me," he says. "You rest."

I exhale, unclenching my fists beneath the sleeves of my robe. I extend my fingers straight out, trying to relax. Seth strolls into the kitchen, glancing around sheepishly. Even in my current situation I want to laugh at his uncertainty. Just like my father. He has no idea what he's doing. I stand frozen to the spot and then I call out, "I'm not sick, or tired, or broken."

He peeks his head around the doorway. "Maybe I should ask your mother to come..."

He says it in such a normal, cheerful way, except I don't want my mother here. And since when did my husband call my mother for backup? She'd fuss and cluck and look at me with disappointed eyes, judging my marriage. I walk into the kitchen, taking him in. He's standing in front of the open fridge, a package of chicken breasts in his hand. He has no idea what to do with it. I take it from him.

"Scoot," I say. I bob my head toward the kitchen door-way, indicating that he needs to leave.

He opens his mouth and I cut him off. "I don't mind. I want to keep busy."

That seems to appease him. He turns toward the living room, a weak shrug moving his shoulders. This is the es-sence of him; he makes a big show of effort. It's always given me the illusion that he's trying, working hard to please me; but in the end it's just an act and I'm the one who does the heavy lifting. I pull a pan from the cabinet, cut up an onion and fresh garlic and set them in the hot olive oil. I hate him. When the chicken is sizzling in the pan, I lean back against the counter, folding my arms across my chest. I can hear the television playing from the living room, the news. And then I realize what's happening: things are re-turning to normal. Seth is trying to make everything feel like it used to in hopes that I will slip into the role as seam-lessly as I always do.

I sink onto the floor, not sure what to do with myself. I have to get out of here.

TWENTY-FOUR

I'm not allowed to drink, not on my medication. It makes the next four days unbearable, as Seth and I sit on the couch and watch hour after hour of sitcoms, him on one side of the couch, me on the other. The space between us is widening every day. I fantasize about the sharp tang of vodka sliding down my throat, burning so good. The way it would first heat my belly and then roll slowly into my veins, settling somewhere in my head and making me feel light and flimsy. When did I start drinking so much? When Seth and I first met I didn't touch alcohol. Maybe it was seeing my sister consistently drunk and high that turned me off the stuff, but at some point I picked up the bottle and never put it down.

Seth doesn't drink—mercy sobriety. He gave up drinking when I was pregnant, too. It makes me wonder if he ever liked drinking or if he just reserved it for our time together. Sexy, dangerous Seth. He was playing a role with me, living out a fantasy.

The orange bottles that dictate my life sit next to my electric kettle in the kitchen, a line of sentries. It was Seth's idea to place them there.

"Why not in the bathroom?" I complained when I'd first seen them.

"So you won't forget," he'd replied.

But really, he put them there to remind me and anyone else who comes over that I'm sick. Every time I walk into the kitchen to get water or a snack, they catch my eye, their little white labels glaring.

My mother stops by with her minestrone soup. Soup— like I have a head cold. I could laugh, but I smile and take my "sick" soup. When she catches sight of the bottles, her face visibly pales and she turns away and pretends she hasn't seen them. People treat being sick in the body as fine, normal, empathy-worthy; they'll bring you soup and medicine, and press the back of their hand to your forehead. But if they think you're sick in the mind, it's different. It's mostly your fault—I say "mostly" because people have been told again and again that mental illness isn't a choice—it's chemical.

"I'm sorry I wasn't here when you got out of the hospital," she says. "Did Daddy tell you that I was visiting Aunt Kel in Florida?"

"Daddy? He doesn't talk to me. He's ashamed."

She stares at me oddly. "He's trying. Honestly, Thursday, sometimes you can be so selfish." *I'm the selfish one?* Where was my father? If he cared, where was he?

The medication makes me feel thick-limbed and sloppy. Seth disappears for a few days, presumably to go back to Portland to see the others. My mother stays with me, doling out pills each morning and each night. I get a sleeping pill at night—the only pill I'm grateful for. Sleep is the only time I rest from the reel of worrisome thoughts that run in a continuous stream through my mind. Planning, planning, planning…

The next time my mother comes, my father comes with her. I'm surprised to see him. In the years I've lived in the condo, my father has only been to visit a handful of times. *He's not the type to do the visiting*, my mother once said. *He's the type to be visited.* I chalked that up to my father's sense of self-importance; a king in his own mind, his subjects came to him. I stand aside as they shuffle in, wondering if Seth orchestrated their visit. He left not ten minutes ago, saying he needed to spend a few hours in the Seattle office. I'd barely gotten dressed when the doorbell rang.

"What are you doing here?" The words are out of my mouth before I can arrange them in a nicer way. My father frowns like he's not sure himself.

"Really, Thursday. What a way to show appreciation," my mother says. She marches toward the living room, her purse swinging on her arm like a little designer monkey. My father and I exchange an awkward smile before picking up the pace and following her. I'm acutely aware of his presence as we move through the hallway, made uncomfortable by it. He shouldn't be here and I shouldn't have been in the nuthouse, we both know this about each other. I have a sour taste in my mouth as I sit in the chair opposite them. Parents are emotional prison guards, always ready with their stern looks and Tasers.

"Your father has been worried sick."

She reaches into her purse and pulls out a tissue, which she dabs delicately to her nose while I look at my father, who is staring at me uncomfortably.

"I can see that," I say.

I'm eager to be rid of them. I have things I need to do. I decide to get down to business.

"Did Seth ask you to come?"

My mother looks affronted. "Of course not," she says. "Why would you think that?"

I open and close my mouth. I can't very well accuse him of keeping me prisoner—that would make me sound crazy. I arrange some bullshit about him being worried about me on the tip of my tongue but then my father beats me to it, speaking first.

"Thursday…" The expression he's wearing is the same one he used on my sister and me as children. I don't know whether to buckle down for the talking-to of a lifetime or to be offended that he still thinks I'm twelve. "Enough with this Seth business." He slices the air with his hand, palm down like he's chopping the "Seth business" in half. "All of that needs to be put behind you. You need to move forward."

"Definitely," I say.

"You should join a gym," my mother suggests.

"I will." I nod.

"Well, then…" My father sits up. His job is done. He is free to go home and watch the news, and eat the meals my mother serves him.

"I'm really tired," I offer.

My father looks relieved. "You go on to bed, then," he says. "We love you."

It's a lie. I hate him.

★ ★ ★

I see them to the door, already formulating what I'm going to do as soon as the lock latches behind them. Call Hannah…pack a bag…leave. Call Hannah…pack a bag… leave. But I don't even make it to the bedroom to look for my phone when Seth is walking through the door. He has that *Honey, I'm home!* look about him. Swooping in to rescue me from myself. I straighten up where I'm bent over the nightstand, silently cursing myself for not getting rid of my parents sooner.

"What are you up to?" It would be such a normal question if not for everything that's transpired the last few weeks. Now his tone frightens me.

"Looking for my cortisone cream." I smile. "I think the medication is giving me a rash." I scratch at my arm absently.

"Wouldn't it be in the medicine cabinet?"

"I had it next to the bed a few months ago, but maybe…" I look toward the bathroom, still scratching.

"I'll get it for you." His tone is bright but I see the barely perceptible shift in his eyes. He's walking differently: his steps stiffer, his shoulders held at a rigid angle. *What are you up to?* My shiver is delayed as I watch him step toward the bathroom, flicking on the light. He comes back with the cream a few seconds later. I paste a smile onto my face, like I'm grateful…relieved. It's a smile I would have worn months ago and meant it. I make a show of uncapping the tube and rubbing the cream on my arm. Seth leans in to examine the spot. I notice for the first time how much his hair is graying. The stress of three wives and the stress of keeping up with his lies must be taking a toll on him. He's put on weight, too. "I don't see anything," he says.

"It's itchy." My words sound flat even to my own ears.

221

He straightens up and meets my eyes. "I didn't say it wasn't."

We stand there like that for what seems like minutes but I know is only a few seconds, staring each other down.

"My mother—" I start to tell him that she was here with my father. Seth's eyes are on my arm again.

"She said she'd be back tomorrow. She will stay with you then," he says without looking up.

"I don't need a babysitter," I say. "I'm fine."

He turns away for the first time. "We care about you, Thursday. Until you're well again, someone will be here to stay with you."

I have to get out of here. I have to go.

We go to bed at the same time—couple's bedtime—but Seth doesn't sleep in the bed with me. He sleeps on the sofa, the television playing all night. It's the only time I'm alone and I'm grateful to have the bed to myself. It's all too much, this pretending. When I go to the bathroom he knocks on the door and asks if I'm all right. On my fifth day home, Seth gives me my phone back—*gives* my phone back like I'm a child who needs permission. There are texts from my boss wishing me a speedy recovery and telling me that my shifts have been covered, texts from Lauren before she found out where I was and texts from Anna from four days prior asking when we could chat next. I send a quick text to Anna apologizing for being busy and tell her I'll call soon.

When I look for the texts from Hannah, I find that they've been deleted, along with her number.

"My voice mails are empty," I say casually. "Did you delete them?"

He looks up from the book he's reading, a thriller he

chose from my collection. He's not turned a page in five minutes. He shakes his head, his mouth dipping at the corners as he glances up at me. "No."

That's it? No? He goes back to "reading" his book, but his eyes aren't moving. He's watching me. I set the phone down, humming as I move things around on my little desk, pretending to swipe at the dust. I am a happy wife. I feel safe and secure with my husband here. When he looks at me again, I smile as I straighten a stack of bills, making sure their corners are neat. *What are you up to, you fucking bastard?*

My fingers itch for my laptop, to search Hannah's name like I did that first time. It's been sitting on my desk, charging since the last time I used it. My laptop is password protected, so there's no way Seth could have guessed my password and wiped everything from there, too.

But the truth is I'm scared. I saw the look in his eyes the day I fell and knocked myself out in the kitchen. And Hannah—he hit Hannah. God, I don't even know if she's okay.

I bide my time. On the sixth night, I crush up one of my sleeping pills while I'm heating the soup on the stove. Seth is trying to find us something to watch on TV, since we've already worked our way through two seasons of some mindless reality show.

I ladle out the soup and stir the powder into his bowl of minestrone, then add hot sauce—just the way he likes it. We make it through one episode of *Friends* before he nods off on the couch, his mouth hanging open and his head thrown back as he snores. I say his name—"Seth…" and then, "Seth…?" a little louder. When he doesn't respond after a hard poke on the arm, I stand up carefully, my heart pounding. The carpet cushions my steps but still they sound like an elephant stampede. What would he do if he caught me? I've never gone through his phone before. There were no set rules about privacy other than in regard to the wives. I just never looked through his things and he never looked though mine. That is, until he went through it to delete Hannah's texts. It is a new age in our marriage.

His phone sits facedown on the coffee table. I try to remember if that is normal, if he's done this before. But no—his phone is always faceup, open and willingly exposed. A friend in college once told me about her cheating boyfriend, who she caught always putting his phone facedown. *I should have known*, she'd said. *That's such a clear indicator.* But Seth isn't exactly cheating, is he? He doesn't want me to see their names pop up on his screen. He's busy trying to convince me that they don't exist. I reach for his phone, never taking my eyes from his face. There is a commercial on TV about a woman with crocodile skin, when she uses their lotion she becomes magically smooth. She runs her fingers across her arm and smiles at me convincingly as I type in Seth's password.

His password has always been the same thing since we met, something horribly predictable I'd seen him type into his phone a hundred times. I'm surprised when his screen lights up and I'm given access to his home screen. Of course he hasn't changed it—he's in control of the situation, he's in control of me. His phone never leaves his side and I am, for the most part, supervised every minute of the day. Or he wants me to see. I go first to his contacts and search Hannah's and Regina's names. Nothing comes up, nothing. My husband does not know a single Hannah or Regina. But just a few weeks ago we'd been drinking cider at the market when Regina's name had popped up on his phone: a call about their dog. I hadn't imagined that. His text messages are void of anything interesting: my mother, my sister checking on how I am, work, clients, contractors…me. His voice mails are the same and so is his email.

I've not moved from the spot where I'm standing, but I'm breathing hard. He's cleared everything. He wanted me to find this and see…nothing. I set his phone back on the coffee table, careful to position it just the way he had it, then I creep over to my laptop. But it won't turn on. The power button stays stubbornly dark even when I hold it down. He's done something to it. I wipe my sweaty palms on my pants; my hands are shaking as I punch at the button one last time. I don't know if I'm angry or afraid. Why would he do this? Or maybe it wasn't him. Computers stop working all the time. *Two…three…four…*it doesn't turn on. No, I bought this computer just a year ago. It was fine before…before I told my husband that I'd found his other wife, that is.

I find my phone in a rush to text Lo and tell her what's happened. My thoughts come out in bursts as I glance over my shoulder to see if Seth has stirred in his sleep. I send one text after another until there are dozens of little blue bubbles on my screen. It looks manic and I immediately regret sending them. I delete each one in case Seth looks at my phone, and then wait for her to text me back, for the bubble to appear to acknowledge that she's seen what I've sent, but it doesn't come.

Seth has hidden my car keys and wallet. It's just past seven when I grab a change of clothes and dig out the spare car key fob I keep hidden in the junk drawer. I'll need cash. I bite hard on my lip as I slide the crisp hundred dollar bill from his wallet. He keeps another five hundred in the bread box for emergencies. My walk to the kitchen is a long one, and I agonize over what I'll do if the money is gone, but when I lift the lid, the first thing I see is the wad of cash, cello-wrapped in the corner and sitting next to one lonely raisin. I stuff an armful of necessitites into a bag and, with Seth still slumbering on the sofa, I head for the door. I freeze when the door chimes, the noise so loud in my own ears I'm convinced it has woken everyone in the building. My body tenses; Seth's hands would be on me at any moment, pulling me back. I whip my head around to see how close he is, ready to sprint away before he gets a grip, but when my eyes search the room, I see him still slumped across the sofa in sleep.

I don't really know how long I'll be gone. If I run out of cash I could call Anna, ask her for some money, but she'd insist on coming out here and then I'd have to explain everything. No…think…there has to be another way. And then it comes to me. I head to the elevator, my stomach in my throat. What if he woke up? What would he do to stop me? If he tried to restrain me, would I be able to get away? I could scream, and perhaps a neighbor would come to help. I jab at the elevator button, imagining every terrible thing that could go wrong. *Hurry, hurry…* It will take him a bit to figure out where I'm going. He'll check with my mother and Anna first, perhaps the hospital to see if anyone's heard from me. That will buy me a few hours. As a last resort, he'll assume I went to see Hannah, but by that time I'll already be there. As the elevator jars to life, it occurs to me that Seth may have placed a tracking device on my phone. I wouldn't put it past him, would I? There are apps for that. Phone locators. I hold the phone in my palm and stare down at it. Seth is a planner, Seth leaves no corner unswept. When the doors open, I hesitate only for a moment before I drop it on the floor of the elevator and step out.

TWENTY-FIVE

There are new planters in front of the house, great big ceramic things that look like they weigh a hundred pounds each. I wonder if Seth hauled them from the car to the path, positioned them for her as she stood a few feet away, calling out instructions. A happy family. She's planted bright orange and yellow calendulas in them. They sit neatly in the soil, new to the neighborhood and still tame in their growth.

I wonder what else has changed, if she'll be showing when she opens the door, holding her stomach while she talks to me. I had a habit of doing that even before I was showing, always conscientious of the life growing inside of me. I make my way past the planters and up the path that leads to the front door. I can hear the TV on inside, a show with a laugh track. Good, that means she's home.

I pause before ringing the bell. I left the house in a hurry and failed to even smooth my hair in the car before rushing out. Oh, well. Too late now. I ring the bell and stand back. A minute later, I hear footsteps and then the click of the lock. The door suctions open and the smell of cinnamon tangles with the night air.

Hannah is standing barefoot in the doorway looking very different than the last time I saw her. She's wearing pajama pants and a tank top, her hair pulled back in a low ponytail. I'm relieved to see her, and she looks well. Her eyebrows pull up when she sees me, her head tilting ever so slightly to the side. *Why that face?* I think. But then I'm suddenly self-conscious about my clothes, my hair. I probably look as unhinged as I feel. Hannah—ever so shiny and put together, like a beautiful china piece.

"I— You left a message—I didn't know if you were okay. You look great!" and then when she stares at me oddly, I add, "I haven't had my phone…"

My voice catches in my throat. Something isn't right. Hannah's face is polite, but stony. The only indication that she's heard me is the slight widening of her eyes, the whites flashing before her lids drop, sleepy and low, once again.

"I'm sorry," she says. "I'm not sure I understand. Who are you here for?"

"You…" I say softly. "I'm here for you." My voice is a wisp, unsure and quickly evaporated. I right my face, trying to look certain.

She lifts a hand and touches it lightly to the spot below her collarbone. She's confused, blinking hard. "I don't know you," she says. "Do you have the wrong house?" She looks past me to the street, as if to see if anyone is waiting for me, or if I am alone. "What house number are you looking for? I know most of the people on this street," she asks helpfully.

My mouth opens and closes and I feel a rush of cold prickling my skin from my neck to my heels. My breathing spikes and my eyelids grow warm.

"Hannah…?" I try one last time.

She shakes her head. "I'm sorry…" Her voice is firmer now; she wants to get back to her laugh track show.

"I—" I look around, up the street and down. There's no one outside, just the neat exteriors of the houses, windows lit by warm, yellow light. I feel locked out, isolated inside of myself. The warm, yellow light is not for me, it's for other people. I take a step back.

"It's me, Thursday," I say. "We're both… I'm married to Seth, too."

Her eyebrows draw together and she glances behind her into the house.

"I'm sorry, I think there's been a mistake. Let me get my husband, maybe he can help you…"

She's turning around, calling to someone inside. That's when I notice then that her hair isn't tied back in a low ponytail like I thought; rather, it's cropped short—a pixie cut.

"Your hair," I say. "Did you cut it recently?" I notice her belly, too, the flatness. I almost lift a hand to my own in confusion.

She looks afraid now, her eyes darting around for help. She lifts a hand to touch it, right at the nape of her neck.

"I hope you find who you're looking for," she says, and then shuts the door in my face. The smell of cinnamon is cut off and I'm left with the smell of damp earth and rotting leaves.

I stumble back, turning around halfway down the path

and running across the street to my parked car. As I fumble with the door, I turn back to look at the house, and see a shift of the drapes on the second floor, like someone is peeking out. Her—Hannah. But why is she claiming not to know me? What is happening? I climb into the car and rest my forehead against the steering wheel, my breath hissing from my lips in soundless heaves. This is crazy, I feel crazy. The thought is so uncomfortable that I quickly turn the car on and drive away from the house. I'm afraid she will call the police. How would I explain?

After pulling up an address on my car's GPS, I head for the freeway. Seth would check the larger hotels first—the hotels with robes and a minibar. He'd never consider anything else because he married a woman who prefers the finer things in life.

My head is aching and I realize I have nothing to ease it with; my travel tube of aspirin is in the purse Seth hid. For the first time in days my thoughts are sharp and clear— my headache is probably a result of my body coming down from the drugs I only pretended to take the last few days. I think of the orange bottles next to the kettle, the bitter taste of them as they melted to paste on my tongue. They were supposed to help, but they made me feel crazy, suffocating my thoughts, making me unsure of myself. Had that been what Seth wanted? To make me doubt myself and trust him instead?

Ten minutes later, the car's GPS takes me down a long dirt road. It's dark, but I know that to my left and through a heavy copse of trees is a lake. In the daytime, the lake is dotted with Jet Skis and paddleboarders—a weekend spot for college students and families. The road ends and I put the car in Park. The house in front of me is dark, large windows looming like hollow eyes. I grab my bag from the passenger seat and step out of the car. *Please, God, let this work*, I think as I head for the house. The house is two stories, surrounded by woods and down a long winding driveway. It's a boxy design that was popular in the sixties. There is still construction equipment lying about and I have to sidestep a large metal pipe when I get out of the car. I make my way across the curved driveway, my shoes crunching on the gravel. The lockbox hangs from the front door and I kneel in front of it, wishing I'd thought to bring a flashlight. The code is the same for all of Seth's houses; he'd told me that once when we were dating and he'd taken me to see a house he was building in Seattle. We'd wandered around the ten-thousand-square-foot mansion—me oohing and ahhing at everything inside—and then we'd had sex on the island in the kitchen.

I type the numbers into the lockbox, praying Seth hasn't changed the code. It opens with a satisfying click and I shake the key into my hand. I slide it into the keyhole, the door opens and I step inside. I stare around, feeling a deep sense of accomplishment. I'm hiding in plain sight. The air smells like cigarettes and damp towels, so I breathe through my mouth as I walk slowly into the house, my eyes darting around. The Cottonmouth house: source of endless headaches. It's on 66 Cottonmouth Road, which is why Seth nicknamed it the snake house. Four months ago, the owner of the house had a stroke and was hospitalized. His son, not knowing what the fate of his father would be and unwilling to foot the bill himself, put the project on hold indefinitely. Seth has been frustrated by the whole ordeal and has complained about it often, which is why I have all the details memorized. I open the drapes, letting dull yellow moonlight stream into the small entry space. The carpet is overworked, a once royal blue now faded to a patchy denim. It's rolled up in places where the contractors had started work on the floors. I gaze out of the window and up at the night sky. If the sun were out, the sky would be a goose gray, the clouds oppressively heavy. Time—this place has had so much time to crack, curl and fade. I walk over to the tiny entryway bathroom and risk turning on the light. I squat as I pee, scrunching my nose at the stale smell coming from the drain. There are rust stains in the outdated sink and a grating noise when I turn the tap off. When I lift my eyes to the mirror, I see pale, washed-out skin, dark moons in the scoops beneath my eyes. No wonder Hannah had looked so alarmed when she opened the door.

I wander upstairs and find a bedroom. There is floral paper on the walls, peeling at the corners, and an old bed is pushed against a wall. I sit on the corner of the bed, the mattress sloping beneath me. What am I doing here? Was I wrong in coming? The way Hannah looked at me, like she didn't know who I was. Had Seth warned her…? Threatened her…? Or… God. I run my hands through my hair, catch the snags and flinch at the pain it causes behind my eyes. Or—had she never seen me before? Could a person make an entire relationship up? In a different case, I'd call my doctor, ask him what he thinks, but I don't trust my doctor, or my husband, or myself. Seth has gotten to all of us.

My head still aches. I lower myself backward and roll onto my side, pulling my knees up to my chest. Just a short nap. Until the headache subsides and I can think clearly.

When I wake up, it's morning. I don't know what time it

is. Sleep has become a confusing thing in the last months—a mixture, I'm sure, of my changing locations and medications. I sit up and search the room for a clock, but the walls are bare except for the warped floral paper. Has Seth woken up yet? Has he started making calls to find me? I hadn't thought about a tracker on my car, but that seems extreme. Seth wouldn't…would he?

I take a shower in the master bathroom, listening to the clank of the pipes as they accommodate the lukewarm water that sprays through the showerhead. The towel I find is rough and scratchy, and I drop it before I'm fully dry and quickly pull my clothes over my damp skin. In my haste, I'd only brought jeans and a sweater. The once-clingy sweater now drapes loosely on me. Oh, well, it'll have to do. I shrug the insecurity away, pulling on my Converse and snatching up my keys before heading for the door.

It's time to talk to Regina.

TWENTY-SIX

Adele plays on the radio as I navigate through the early-morning traffic. I feel better today, more like myself. I turn up the volume and at the same time I slam on the breaks. The work truck I almost collided with surges forward another few feet and I follow more cautiously this time. Adele's voice is so melancholy that I suddenly feel the full loneliness of my situation. What am I doing here? Maybe I *am* crazy. I pull into the parking lot abruptly, cutting Adele off as I kill the ignition. No, Seth is a liar and I have to find a way to prove it. What happened with Hannah has been replaying in my mind all morning. I get a knot in my stomach remembering the vacancy in her eyes when she looked at me. Something is wrong and I need to get to the bottom of it. Reaching out to Regina is the only option I can think of. I think about the dating profile I set up for Will Moffit. It's been ages since I've checked it and I wonder if Regina thinks he's blown her off.

The offices of Markel & Abel are located in a three-story white stone building that faces a small lake. They share the building with a title company and a pediatrician's office. I peer into car windows as they drive by, heading into the underground garage beneath the building. One of them could be Regina. I consider cornering her in the garage, but that would accomplish little except making me appear unhinged. No, I need to do this the right way, the way I've planned. I tell myself this, but right before I get out of the car I start to cry. They're mostly numb tears; I can't pinpoint if I'm scared, or sad, or angry, but they won't stop coming. I catch them on the back of my hand, drying it on my jeans.

Something feels wrong, but I don't know what. I dry my eyes for the final time and swipe lip gloss over my lips, a poor attempt to look like a woman not falling apart. When I push open the doors of the building I can hear the squeal of a toddler and the pounding of little feet. A second later, a tiny blond human comes barreling around the corner, his exhausted-looking mother in fast pursuit.

"Sorry," she says, scooping him up as he knocks into me. He cuddles into her arms, looking pleased with himself, and dips his head to her shoulder. A pang of something in my chest—but I push it away, smiling at her as she adjusts him on her hip and carries him back toward the doctor's office.

I almost follow them just to see what will happen, then remember why I'm here. I climb the stairs to the second floor, slowing as I eye the glass doors. Behind them is a large sitting area flanked with brown leather couches, elegant and masculine. To the rear of the room, and directly in my line of sight, is the receptionist's desk. A woman with a topknot and glasses has a phone pressed to her ear as she types something into a computer. I feel overly conscious about my too-big sweater and scruffy jeans. I wish I'd brought something more appropriate.

Pushing through the doors, I walk directly to reception and greet her with a smile just as her call ends.

"Welcome," she says with practiced professionalism. "How can I help you?"

"I have an appointment," I say. "With Regina Coele." I pause, trying to recall the name I used when making the appointment. It feels like ages ago, not just weeks. "I'm Lauren Brian." I clasp my hands at my waist and try to look bored. She briefly glances up at me before typing something into the computer.

"I see that you missed your appointment last week, Mrs. Brian." She frowns. "We don't have anything scheduled for you today." She looks at me expectantly.

I lift a hand to my forehead and arrange my face into what I hope is a perplexed expression. "I… I…" I stutter. Tears fill my eyes as I lock my gaze with hers. I'd been locked away in Queen County, eating my Jell-O and staring at Susan's lack of eyelashes on the day of my appointment. I don't have to act flustered, since I already am. Lifting a hand to my face, I drop it abruptly.

"Things have just been so… I'm getting divorced," I say. "I must have mixed things up…"

I see her soften.

"Give me a minute." She stands and disappears down a corridor, presumably where the lawyers keep their offices. I look around the waiting area, still relatively empty this early in the day. An older woman sits in the far corner, a Starbucks cup in one hand and a copy of *Good Housekeeping* in the other. I perch on the edge of a chair closest to the reception desk, my fingers crossed and my leg bouncing in sync with my nerves.

She returns a few minutes later and slides into her seat. I can't read her expression.

"Mrs. Brian, Ms. Coele has offered to skip her lunch if you're willing to come back at twelve o'clock."

A good person, a nice person! I feel a leap in my chest as I stand and approach the desk. "I am," I say quickly. "Thank you for doing that for me." I mean it with all my heart, the gratitude thick in my voice.

She nods like it's nothing. The phone is ringing again; I'm getting in her way. I back away from the desk, glancing at the time on the wall. Four hours to kill.

I find a small clothing boutique in a shopping plaza nearby. *Pretty Missy.* I flinch at the name as I consider the window display. The ruffled knee socks and positive-vibe T-shirts are enough to turn me away, but I have time to kill and my options are limited. I catch sight of my reflection as I walk in the shop. My orange sweater reminds me of a prison jumpsuit. I riffle through the racks for thirty minutes before I find a brown suede jacket and white top to wear underneath it. Better, I think. I hand my cash over to the salesgirl and change in my car, dumping the sweater in the backseat before redressing. The new clothes are itchy and I scratch at my skin until it feels raw.

On my drive back to the white office building I see a bar, the Open sign flashing sporadically in the window. I check the time: three more hours. It's too early to drink, but I pull into the parking lot, anyway. There are only two other cars here. One of them probably belongs to the bartender, the other to the town drunk. I eye the older-model Mercedes as I head for the door, my shoes crunching on the gravel. I can already taste the liquor on the back of my throat. How long has it been since I had a drink?

When I push open the door, the smell of a dive bar greets me: a medley of stale air, spilled beer and body odor. I breathe in the smell as I slide onto a bar stool and order a vodka soda from a guy with tired eyes and a Van Halen T-shirt. I'm thankful he doesn't speak to me, just slides the drink across the counter without making eye contact and moves on to something else. This would be the time I'd pull out my phone, scroll through the updates my friends were posting on Facebook, maybe check the sales on my favorite shopping websites. I stare at my drink instead, the true body language of someone who's sitting in a bar before lunchtime, and plan what I'm going to say to Regina.

TWENTY-SEVEN

I'm buzzed. Three vodka sodas and I've had nothing to eat all morning. My vision teeter-totters and my limbs feel loose and undisciplined. I chide myself as I comb my fingers through my hair in the tiny bar bathroom, grimacing at my reflection. I look like a drunk: swollen face, red eyes and splotchy skin. At least I'd lost the orange sweater. I splash water on my face in the little sink before I head out.

I have exactly thirty minutes to pull myself together before I see my husband's first wife. What she thinks of me matters, which is why drinking was a bad idea. I am—was—technically her replacement. Despite the fluorescent green jealousy I feel toward her, I also feel a kinship. I want her to like me. She could help me. I'm like an eager puppy, abused and still wagging its tail for love. I stop at a gas station and buy eyedrops, gum and body spray. At the last minute I ask the guy behind the counter for one of the burner phones. The body spray is probably a bad idea— it's vanilla scented—but the bar was warm and I feel the dampness under my arms and on my lower back. I smell like a sweet, sweaty cupcake. I'm five minutes late when I run into the office. The secretary gives me an annoyed look when she sees me. *The least you can do, lady...*

"This way," she says, standing. I follow her down a hall of doors. It's all wrong, the way they've set it up. I'm reminded of high school, the long walk to the principal's office. I can smell vanilla and sweat coming off me in a mist.

Regina is seated behind her desk when the secretary knocks lightly and opens the door. She steps back without meeting my eyes and allows me to walk past her. Regina stands as soon as she sees me. She's tiny, as Seth said, but much prettier than in her photos. I'm staring; I realize this when it's only the two of us in the room, the secretary having taken her leave. This is surreal. She motions for me to sit in one of the two leather chairs that face her desk. Instead of reseating herself, she walks around the desk and sits in the empty chair next to me, crossing her legs. I smell her perfume right away, the sleepy scent of lavender. I wither in my chair, as if by doing so I could pull back the vanilla/sweat smell.

"Can I offer you water or coffee?" she asks. "Perhaps tea?"

"I'm fine, thank you." I push my hair behind my ears and straighten up in my chair. The principal mustn't know I'm afraid.

"I understand you're considering divorce." The cadence of her voice is mesmerizing—deep, yet feminine, like one of those old movie stars in black-and-white films. *Puuurrrr.*

"Not just considering," I say. "And by the way, thank you for giving up lunch to see me. I realize that I missed my appointment. It was very kind of you." My mother always said that confident people didn't overthank or overthink.

"It's business," Regina says. "Work now, food later, right?" She smiles. "So tell me about your situation."

I clear my throat. In the cuff on my sleeve I can feel the price tag I forgot to pull off. I thumb the cardboard, pushing it farther up my sleeve.

"My husband is a polygamist." It's a statement meant to jar an average person. I'd often thought about blurting it out at other times to strangers or my colleagues just to see the look on their faces.

Regina's face, however, remains the same. It's almost as if she hasn't heard me. She doesn't ask me to clarify or expound and it's not until she says, "Carry on," that I do.

"I am his legal wife. He has two others."

She stares at me, hard. "Are there children involved?"

I pause, thinking of Hannah, how she'd looked at me like she'd never seen me before when I rang her doorbell last night. The confusion and hurt in Seth's eyes when I told the doctor what he was. I feel a niggling doubt creep into my mind. *You are crazy, you are crazy, you are crazy.*

"His third wife is pregnant, not very far along."

"And these other wives, do they all share a home with your...husband?"

I shake my head. "Two live here, in Portland. I live in Seattle."

I search her face for any sign of recognition. Did she know as little about me as I had known about her?

"Do they know about you?" she asks.

I look long and hard at her face, the full lips lined and

colored in cherry, the splattering of freckles across her nose showing through her makeup. It's now or never, this is what I came for.

"Do you know, Regina? How much has he told you about me?"

Her expression never changes. She crosses her legs as she leans back in her chair, blank eyes drilling into mine. For the longest time we stay just like that, her watching me and me watching her. It feels like I'm about to fall off the edge of a precipice.

"Thursday," she says.

And I want to leap from the chair and scream, that one word validating everything I am here for. Regina knows my name, she knows who I am. Self-doubt is slime and glue, but Regina saying my name has washed me clean.

"Yes," I say, breathless...pathetic.

Her face is arranged in undisguised disgust. She sighs, uncrosses her legs and leans forward, forearms on thighs. She doesn't look so put together now, just tired. It's amazing what a facial expression can do to change someone's look.

"Seth contacted me. He said you might come by." She stares at the ground between her heels before straightening up.

So Seth already knows where I am. He knows me better than I realized. There is a sinking feeling in my stomach as I stare at her. While I've been imagining him scrambling to call my mother and Anna, he went straight to Regina. I blink hard, trying to disguise the shock that must be on my face. I thought I had been smart, but apparently my husband is smarter. Silly me. But that is the theme of my life for these last years: silly me. Seth had anticipated this, my breakaway from his plan. He'd thought about all of this, predicted my actions. Perhaps only in the last weeks, but maybe always.

"All right, Thursday, you came all this way, so tell me why you wanted to see me. I gather it's not about divorce." Her lips are tucked in at the corners—resolute and disgusted. She's very wrong about the divorce, but I don't tell her that. Let her think what she wants. All I want are answers about the man we both married.

I look around the office for the personal touches of the woman I'm speaking to: picture frames, rugs, anything that will tell me more about who she is. The decor is masculine, which could have very little to do with her; women don't opt for this much cherrywood. She has a penchant for ferns, as there are three in total: one sits on top of a bookshelf with its leaves spilling over the sides, the other is smaller and on her desk and the third rests on the windowsill— the healthiest of the three. They're well-tended, too, lush.

"I'm here because I don't know my husband. I was hoping you could give me some clarity." That's the nice way of putting it, really. My husband hits women and had me institutionalized for asking too many questions. As it turns out, I am a really stupid woman, and I need Regina to tell me that she was equally as stupid for trusting him, and then I can tell her about Hannah.

"*Your* husband?" Her face is amused, eyebrows raised.

I want to tell her that now's not the time to get into a pissing match about who Seth belongs to, but I stay quiet.

"I'm not sure I can help you—in fact, I'm not sure I want to." She smooths out her skirt and glances at her watch. It's subtle, but she meant for me to see it. I'm wasting her time. I suddenly don't feel as sure as I did a moment ago. The temperature has switched.

"You've been with Seth for eight years—" I begin.

"Five," she interrupts. "Seth and I were together for five years before the divorce, but of course you know that because you're the reason we got divorced."

I stare at her blankly. Of course I was, but she'd agreed to it. This isn't going the way I expected it to. Why is she being so sour about something she agreed to? Seth met and married Regina five years before me. I remember the jealousy at all the extra time they'd had together, how I'd never be able to catch up.

"And these last three...?"

"These last three, what?" She snaps that part, the poise falling away for the briefest of moments as something flashes in her eyes.

"That...you've been together. The plural marriage..."

Regina looks like I've slapped her. Her slender neck jerks back. I can see the starburst pattern of pink rising above her neckline. I've made her nervous. I don't know if that's good or bad, but it's something to be making her nervous.

"I'm sorry," she says, "I don't know what you mean."

I know that if I jump out of my seat and shake her while screaming, *Tell me the truth, you bitch!* the police will be called. At the very least, I'd be escorted out of the building and one more person would think I was crazy.

"Aside from the brief contact he made to tell me that you would be coming to see me, I have not seen or spoken to my ex-husband in years," she says.

Her words sever my next question. My mouth hangs open until I press my lips together, frowning.

I stare at Regina and then my hands. My thoughts are dumb, thick. I don't make sense and neither does Regina. I hear white noise and the pounding of my own heart.

"What do you mean?" I manage finally.

"I think you should leave." Her face is blanched as she stands up and heads for the door.

I follow her, not knowing what else to do. My thoughts are tangled between Regina and Hannah.

"You need help, Thursday," she says, looking squarely at my face. "You're delusional. Seth said you were sick, but—"

"I am not sick." I say it with such force that we both blink at each other for a few seconds. I repeat it in a calmer tone. "I'm not sick, despite what Seth has told you."

"Get out." She holds the door open and I stare past her, my thoughts spinning.

"Just tell me one thing," I say. "Please..."

Her lips pull into a tight line but she doesn't refuse.

"Seth's parents. Did you ever meet them?"

She looks confused. "Seth's parents are dead," she says, shaking her head. "They died years ago."

"Thank you," I breathe before walking out.

TWENTY-EIGHT

Hannah's car is parked in its usual spot along the curb. I walk toward it and briefly lay my hand on the hood as I pass, checking for heat. Cold. She hasn't driven it in a few hours. At least I know she's home. I move quickly up the path, past the planters to the front door.

I feel skittish, like someone is watching me, but in neighborhoods like this, there is always someone watching. It's specifically why Seth and I chose the anonymity of a condo instead of a neighborhood and a house: neighbors bearing casseroles in dishes they want you to return, walking their dogs past your house in the evening so they can peer into your windows. I look over my shoulder, scanning nearby windows suspiciously. "You really are crazy, Thursday,"

I say under my breath. New level of madness: talking to yourself in public.

The pressure on my chest is almost too much to bear as I near the front door. I feel like I can't get a good breath. My foot catches a pebble and I slide a little. *Take it easy, take it easy.* I stare down at my feet, the well-loved flats that are beginning to smell. If Hannah invites me in I don't want to take them off. Had she made me take my shoes off before? I can't remember. I ring the bell and step back to wait. What if it isn't Hannah who comes to the door? What if there is indeed a husband who is living with her? What will I say? My heart is racing as I wait, fingernails pressing into my palms. I've begun to sweat. I can feel myself grow clammy.

But then one minute turns into two, and two turns into three. I ring again and peer into the window. No lights are on, though that's not really telling since it's the middle of the day. But still, a dark day. The sun has been making short appearances every thirty minutes or so as it searches for holes in the clouds. I walk around the side of the house, past the large windows of the dining room and then through the gate, which is relatively easy to unlatch. If someone sees me they'll surely call the cops—a strange woman who looks nothing like Hannah circling a home in this upper-class neighborhood.

I've never been in the backyard, never even glanced at it when I was inside the house. It's pretty, Hannah's little secret garden. I can imagine in summer how the flowers must bloom, but for now the branches are bare, and the rose trellis is empty. There are two empress trees; one grows close to the back of the house, near a window.

I peer inside, scanning the house for any sign of life, and notice that the window is open, the screen the only thing that separates me from the inside. "Hannah…?" I call. "Are you okay? I'm coming in…" I wait, listening. Nothing— not even a shuffle. I consider the screen—it would be easy to pop out. I'd done it before in my childhood home when my mother accidentally locked us out while watering the garden. The fact that the window is open means she hasn't gone far. Perhaps she took a quick run to the grocery store or post office. Since her car is parked out front, was it Seth who picked her up? I have to move quickly if I really want to do this.

Before I can change my mind, I use my keys to pry the screen off and lower it gently to the grass. My hands are shaking as I pull myself over the ledge and lower myself into the living room. I wait for an alarm to sound, my whole body tense, but after a few seconds when nothing happens, I take a few cautious steps forward. I don't recall ever seeing Hannah mess with an alarm.

The house smells like someone's been cooking. I don't need to peek into the kitchen to know that Hannah was in the middle of something before she left. I take off running, around the corner and up the stairs, my feet pounding loudly on the wood floors. The first door at the top of the stairs is the master bedroom. I push it open, my eyes scanning the room for…what? I run to the nightstand closest to the door and yank open the drawer. A box of tissues, a few paperbacks, Tylenol—the normal junk. There has to be a photograph of Hannah and her husband somewhere.

I look in the dresser drawers, but they are sterile in their organization: underwear—squarely folded in tidy rows. Tank tops in various shades of neutral, socks, lingerie— nothing for men. Where are his drawers? I move to the closet, a tiny walk-in, and eye the gem-toned sweaters and row of jeans. No suits, no dress shirts, no brown loafers next to the line of pumps and flats. If a man shares this bedroom, one couldn't tell.

There is a small bathroom next to the closet, a single sink, a single toothbrush, peony-scented shower gel resting on the lip of the tub. The medicine cabinet: a diaphragm in its plastic case, various bottles of headache medicine, TUMS. No prenatal vitamins, no shaving cream. I scan the floor for Seth's dark hairs, so different than Hannah's blond. If he'd used this bathroom there would be hair—I was always sweeping it up in mine. *Nothing, nothing, nothing.* What is happening?

I move to the next room, an office. A desk sits against the far wall, so unlike Hannah. It's modern and square with hard lines—something cheap from IKEA. A cup of pens, a stapler... I search for a bill—something with her name on it or even his. It doesn't matter, I just need answers. One way or another, I have to know if I'm crazy or if Seth is crazy.

No bills, no mail. Everything is sterile, staged. Oh, God, why is everything so staged? The single closet in the room is empty except for a vacuum. No photos on the walls. Hadn't I noticed photos when she gave me the tour? A buffalo, perhaps—no, an alpaca! She'd had a large framed photograph of an alpaca. I'd thought it strange.

I run my hands over the space of wall where it had hung, searching for a hole in the paint where the nail had been. It's there, I find it, smoothed over and repainted to blend.

One more bedroom on this floor, and a bathroom. A floral comforter folded down on the bed, an antique lamp on the nightstand. Nothing personal, nothing as I remember.

What had I smelled downstairs when I climbed in the window? She'd been cooking something and left abruptly. I jog down the stairs and stop in the doorway to the kitchen. A plate of freshly baked cookies, plump, their chips still soft from the oven. I walk closer to the island; there's something else…a stack of papers…applications. I pick one up, my hand shaking as I lift it from the counter.

"Excuse me…" A voice behind me. Not Hannah. Clearly not Hannah.

"How did you get in here? Appointments don't start for another hour."

A woman stands in the doorway, her brows drawn in suspicion. She has the look of a Realtor or property manager: hair in a low ponytail, black slacks and a pink button-down. Positive but not overbearing. She's shoeless, her feet in panty hose. In her hands she holds the box of socks visitors are to place over their shoes when viewing the house.

"I'm sorry," I say quickly. "My mistake. I can come back, of course…let me get out of your way." My heart is hammering in my chest as I move toward the front door. But when I go to pass her, she doesn't step aside.

She frowns. "How did you get in here?" she repeats, folding her arms across her chest. She's one of those tough Sally types. Her kid gets shoved on the playground and she's taking it to the school board. The neighbor's dog keeps barking and she strong-arms the homeowner's association into fining them. I could tell her the truth, but chances are she'd call the cops. I eye the phone clipped to her belt. Such a professional.

"Look," I say. "I didn't mean to be a bother. I'll just let myself out."

"Oh, no, you don't." She takes up residence in the doorframe, reaching for her phone. I can see the open window behind me, the tree branches outside trembling in the wind.

If she turns her head to the left, she'll know. I get my shit together. Compose my face, square my shoulders.

"Move. Now."

She does, the military stance she took a minute ago melts away. Her face looks suddenly cautious as she watches me unlock the front door and step outside. I think about walking around back and replacing the screen, but that will only give her time to call the police.

Large strides get me to my car. I don't look back as I climb inside and turn on the ignition. I drive without purpose for several miles before I pull into the parking lot of a drugstore. I pull out the application tucked into the back of my pants and stare at the words. Hannah had never mentioned anything about moving. Where was she? Last night she'd been there, watching TV with someone, and today, the house is up for rent.

Without my phone, there's no one to call, nothing to search online. I could look for a library, use their computer. But no, there is still one person to follow, one story that isn't adding up. I don't know nearly enough about Seth's first wife. There is something about her that is nagging at me, something I can't place. I need to know more about Regina Coele. For now, Hannah and Seth can wait.

TWENTY-NINE

I am not crazy.

Seth is playing dumb, and Hannah has conveniently disappeared, which leaves me with one option: Regina Coele. She knows something. I'm convinced of it. She wouldn't have been so eager to get me out of her office if she didn't, claiming she hadn't seen or spoken to Seth in years. But I was there the night she texted him while we were at the market. I'd seen her name flash on his phone. She'd claim it was a courtesy call about their dog.

There was something about the careful way she worded everything. It was practiced, planned—they'd come up with it together to make me look crazy. But why? And what was Hannah's involvement in all of this? My stomach clenches at the thought of Hannah. I'd knowingly deceived her by not telling her who I really was. If Seth told her who I was after he found out what I'd done, I wouldn't blame her for being afraid of me. But would she really put the house up for rent because Seth's other wife had found her?

Maybe Seth made her pack up and put the house up for rent when he thought I would keep talking about his polygamy. But why? He isn't legally married to either of them, and in no danger with the law. Plenty of men have affairs; there's no punishment for fucking women outside of one's marriage. Has it been to protect his reputation? The business? Seth has never been the type of man who cared about what others thought of him, but then plural marriage struck up images of Warren Jeffs and dusty fundamentalist compounds in Utah—things no businessman in their right mind would want to be associated with. Would he go to these extremes just to protect his reputation? That's what I need to know. Before I can make my plans, I need to know what theirs is.

I'm strangely optimistic as I weave my car through end-of-the-day traffic toward the white stone building where Regina is wrapping up her day. I will not leave without answers. I imagine she's on the last of her clients, or second-to-last, since she works long hours.

"She stays later, works harder," Seth once told me.

The pride in his voice had confused me. Shouldn't he be complaining instead of making it sound like an admirable quality? I try to imagine what she will do when she leaves the office. Is she the type who grabs a drink with her friends after work? Or does she go home to heat up a TV dinner that she eats in front of the TV? I picture her office, the lack of anything personal to speak of who she is. No, she's not the type to waste hours drinking casually in a bar. She's the type who works at home. Every night she tucks cream folders under her arms, which she sets on the front seat for her drive home. She eats dinner at the end of a long table, the files open around her, glasses perched on her nose. That is the image Seth had given me, the one that caused me to dislike her. Too busy to meet our husband's needs. Perhaps he fed me that story so I would jump into action, overcompensating for what Regina didn't do. And I did, didn't I? Always wanting to be more than enough. When Seth first married Hannah, I'd been sick with jealousy. I felt so guilty about it, too; it was my fault we were unable to have a baby, my broken body that had failed my marriage. In an attempt to understand my role, I'd asked him what he got from each of us, how our roles were different. He'd told me to think of the sun.

"The sun provides light, warmth and energy."

"So you're…what…earth?" I'd quipped back. "Seems like we're the ones who revolve around you, not the other way around."

He'd tensed up at that, even as he moved his mouth into a smile. "Don't get too technical, Thursday. You asked me to explain."

I'd shriveled back, afraid my snark would make him love me less.

"So what am I?" I'd asked in a saccharine voice. His analogy had irritated me. I tried to hide it by bouncing my leg under the table. That's what I did—I hid things where he couldn't see. The three of us were there to primarily meet his needs, so what exactly did the sun get from the earth? My parents' marriage was far from perfect, but they needed each other mutually.

"You're my energy," he'd answered quickly. At the time

I'd liked that, being Seth's energy. I was temporarily sated in verbal orgasm. I was the one who filled him with motivation and drive, who kept him going. In my mind, I'd made it sound more important than the other two. Regina being light, and Hannah being warmth. I mean, how could you enjoy warmth and light if you didn't have energy?

Now, as I wait in the parking lot for Regina, I grimace at all the ways I justified what was happening. Hannah was Seth's warm, new pussy. Regina was his first love. A woman in love loses her sight first and then her courage. I tap on the steering wheel with my finger. I'm not crazy… or maybe I am…but there's really only one way to find out.

Regina walks out of the building an hour and forty minutes later. This is exactly the way Seth described her. She outstayed the secretary, who left over an hour ago, racing out of the parking lot in her Ford like she had a million better places to be. I watch as she walks briskly to an older-model Mercedes, her briefcase held stiffly in her hand. The car has seen better days; I note the wear on the paint and the dent in the bumper as she climbs into the front seat. It's the type of car that isn't old enough to be vintage, but it's too old to be considered "nice" by most people's standards. Since Regina is a private attorney, I expected her to drive a flashy new model. I turn on my ignition as she pulls out of the lot, following close behind.

My stomach drops when she pulls onto the freeway. I clutch the steering wheel tighter and focus on her bumper. It'll be hard keeping up with her in this traffic. I manage to stay a few cars behind, and when she veers off the highway, I'm right behind her, my heart beating hard, several people honking at me. Ten minutes later, after trailing her through a dull suburban neighborhood, she pulls into a dingy apartment complex called Marina Point. There is no marina in sight, just blocky buildings with hard edges painted prison gray. The measly plots of grass surrounding them are yellow and patchy. Everything looks jaundiced, and the few people who are milling about outside are congregated on a staircase, smoking. If I opened my window I'd know if it was pot or cigarettes, but I don't have time. Regina drives over the speed bumps like they're not even there. I wait for her to zip past the buildings, like maybe this is a shortcut, but she pulls into a numbered space—a resident.

I look around at the shabby disarray, my car idling in the road. This isn't right. A woman with a Louboutin collection doesn't drive that car, or live here. I decide she's visiting someone, a quick stop on her way home. Maybe she's dropping papers off to a client. But when she gets out of the car she takes her briefcase and folders with her, struggling to hold on to everything while she locks the car manually. I have to be able to see which unit she goes into. I quickly park across the street and wait until she's up the stairs before hopping out. Jogging, I reach the third floor just in time to see her door close. The sound of the dead bolt echoes in the concrete corridor as Regina locks herself inside. I glance around. There are no welcome mats, no plants decorating the doorsteps, just four empty doors, their numbers displayed beside them on cheap plastic plaques. A place of last resort. I stare solidly at her door for several minutes, 4L. And then I knock.

Her face is bare when she opens the door. In the few minutes she's been home she's already washed off her makeup. It's interesting that she's the type who immediately washes off her day while I fall asleep in mine.

She doesn't even try to hide her shock; she moves quickly, shoving the door closed. It swings toward me with force, but I am too fast. I wedge my foot in the gap and flinch when it squeezes painfully against my toes.

Regina yanks it open, glaring at me. Without her makeup, she looks like a child. An angry, insolent child who isn't getting her way.

"What? What do you want?" She holds the door trying to keep me out, red nails sharp against the peeling gray.

"You know what I want," I say. And then I do something I am even surprised by: I push past her and enter her home without invitation.

She turns her body to face me, her mouth slightly open. I see her eyes search around the room, looking for her phone. Who will she call—Seth or the police? I find it before she does, lunging toward it on the dining table. I pocket it before she can stop me and stare at her solemnly.

"I just want to talk," I say. "That's all I'm here for."

She considers the hallway outside for a moment. I can feel her decision in the air. If she screams for help who will come?

She must decide that her chances are better with me because she closes the door, all rigidness gone from her body. There is a feverish nervousness about her as she walks past me. It's smell and energy, a woman trapped in a room with someone she'd rather avoid. I'm contemptuous about the fact that she's not as interested in me as I am in her. Isn't it the mark of a woman to want to know things about other women? We abuse the information…compare ourselves rather than keeping it all separate. Even as I study her clean face and thick hair, I'm comparing.

"All right, Thursday," she says. "Let's talk."

THIRTY

There are expensive things in this inexpensive apartment. A leather sectional that once fit into a large living room, thick coffee table books stacked on top of a marble table. Everything is too big, which makes the room small and suffocating. I glance out of the window above the wrought iron dinette for escape, and see nothing but more rows of insipid gray buildings. It's really warm in her apartment, the heat turned all the way up to feel like summer. *She's in total life denial*, I think. Regina walks over to a section of the couch farthest from where I am standing, and sits down without inviting me to do the same. She curls up in the corner, a tiny ball of a woman. I take a seat, anyway, perching myself across from her on the edge of the leather so that I almost slide off. I try not to stare, but when you've wondered about a person for so long it's hard not to.

"Well?" she says. "What do you want to know?"

So different from the *How can I help you?* attitude earlier, surrounded by her ferns and wood and educational plaques. Here, in her living room, her things surround me.

"I want to be told the truth," I say.

"The truth?" she says, incredulous. "I don't think you ever wanted the truth, Thursday. You wanted Seth. I know about all of it…"

"What does that even mean? And why did you say that you and Seth were only together for five years?"

"Because we were," she says, exasperated. And then she adds, "Before you came along."

"You mean when it was just you two?"

"No! Oh my God, you really are crazy…" She shakes her head in disbelief. "Thursday, you had an affair with Seth. You're the reason we got divorced."

The silence that follows is deafening. A searing pain stabs through my head, running from temple to temple.

"That's not true," I say. "Why would you say that?"

She stares at me, a blank expression on her face. "Because it's the truth."

I shake my head. My mouth is dry. I want something to drink but I'm too proud to ask for water.

"No. He told me that—"

"Stop it," she says, cutting me off. Her eyes are wild. She closes them, suddenly shutting me out. "Just stop it."

Normally I'd back down, but not this time. I've been sitting in the dark for too long and I need answers.

"When was the last time you saw Seth?" Right away she makes a sour face, her lips puckered.

"I told you that—"

She looks down—at her lap, or her hands, or the pattern

on her pajama pants, but not at me. I see her shoulders lift and sink as she sighs.

"I saw Seth last week," she says. "Here at the apartment." When she sees the look on my face, she adds, "He owes me money."

"For what?"

"For losing everything," she snaps. "Do you think I actually belong in a place like this?"

Regina with the Louboutins? I want to laugh: no, probably not. I have the money to buy red-soled shoes, but I'm not the type. Regina, on the other hand, is used to lavishing luxury on herself. She wears designer and probably always used to drive the newest-model Mercedes rather than the beat-up junker parked in her spot downstairs.

"You're going to have to catch me up on this, Regina. I have no idea what you're talking about." I try to keep my voice patient, but it sounds like I'm talking through my teeth.

"His business. Things started going south a few years ago. Right before he married you," she says pointedly.

"Seth took a second mortgage on the house we bought together to keep the business floating, but then he still couldn't pay it. There was too much debt. Our house went into foreclosure. He promised to turn things around, make it right, but as you can see—" she lifts her eyes to the ceiling "—I'm here."

Why didn't I know any of this? Why hadn't he said something? I had enough money to contribute… I shake my head. I can't believe I'm thinking like this. Even now, sitting across from his other *wife*, after being institutionalized, I'm thinking about how I could have helped him.

"And did he give you money?" I ask.

I'm trying to imagine it all. Seth never spoke about his financial situation, especially with the others. We have separate accounts, though I'd given him a joint debit card to mine when we were first married. I'd always assumed it was the same for them.

She exhales, her cheeks puffing out. She looks like a child. How does anyone take her seriously?

"Yes, a little bit. Not enough. I have bill collectors knocking down my door. It's stressful."

"If you're not in a relationship, why didn't he just send you the money? Why did he have to come here?"

Her mouth tightens, a flesh-colored slash on her face. I realize then that she's a lonely, bitter woman, not the picture of power and grace that I'd imagined. *Oh, when our idols fall*, I think to myself. I prefer the version of her that I made up in my head, the one that made me feel insecure.

"Our dog died," she says. "And he wanted to tell me in person that he'd have more for me soon. A business transaction that's going to pay out in a few weeks."

So he wasn't lying about the dog. I wonder if he's lying about the business transaction. Seth closes on accounts all the time. His clients call him efficient and hardworking. He has one bad review on Yelp, which he stresses about weekly. His payouts on jobs are sufficient but not large enough to pay off big debts—or buy back big houses.

I test out the name of their dog. "Smidge?"

Regina looks at me in horror. "How did you know that?"

"Seth told me," I say, shrugging. *He told me things, too*, I think. I just never know what's true and what's not.

She blinks rapidly as she looks away, like she can't believe he'd do such a thing.

"I haven't been able to throw her things away yet." She

nods to a space between the TV stand and the kitchen where a basket of dog toys still sits. It's overflowing with bright balls and stuffed toys—a spoiled dog.

"Did you have sex when he came here?"

Regina's head snaps toward me, her face a mask of outrage. "How dare you," she says. But there's something there, concealed behind the anger...admission.

"You did." I swipe my hair behind my ears. I don't feel anything; of course I don't. I know Seth has been having sex with his other two wives this entire time. I just made sure the sex with me was better than anything they could offer. I was more waxed, more flexible, more responsive to his touch. Regina is back to just blinking.

"Why are you pretending with me? Seth is acting like I'm crazy, making up the entire story about his relationships with you and Hannah. I just want the truth."

"I don't know Hannah," Regina says. "And I've already told you that we've been over for a long time." Her legs are folded up underneath her, and I can't help but think it's to make her appear taller, like those heels she wears.

I shake my head. I'm not crazy. I'm not.

Her nostrils flare and I can see her chest rising and falling as she takes in short bursts of air. She's trying to keep control. But for what reason? She stands up and moves toward the door and I know she's about to tell me to leave. I have to do something, make her talk to me.

"I lost a baby..." The words tumble from my mouth and end with a dragging pain across my chest.

Regina freezes, her back to me.

It all started when I lost my baby. My life began to unravel, string by string. I may have been too consumed with grief to see the signs then, but I see them all now.

Seth's detachment, his wanting another woman, his pre-occupation with sex when we were together. I was no longer the woman he wanted to talk to, I was the woman he wanted to fuck. That's what my usefulness boiled down to in the end.

"I was five months pregnant. I had to…" I swallow the welling of emotion. I need to get this out. "I had to give birth to him."

Out of the corner of my eye I see her turn around to face me. I look up at her; her face is horrified, her mouth slack and her eyes large. He never told her. I bite the inside of my cheek and force myself to keep talking.

"He had red hair…just a little bit…but it was red. I don't even know where that came from. No one in my family has red hair…"

Talking about my baby validates his existence here, even if it was brief. He was so tiny and his red hair was more just a dusting of orange. The nurses had marveled at it, which only made me sadder. At the time I'd held on to that little detail, his body so small it was lost in the blanket they'd wrapped him in. I was allowed to hold him for a few minutes, my mind jumping between wonder and grief. *I made this. He's dead. I made this. He's dead.* I'd not named him, though Seth wanted to. Naming him made his death real and I'd wanted to forget.

Everything I keep so carefully guarded is welling up inside of me, my tear ducts burning.

"Seth's mother," Regina says softly.

I swallow hard. I'd never even seen a picture of his parents. Seth told me that they didn't care for having their photo taken.

"She did?" I want her to say more. I need her to.

"Yes. Long and beautiful."

I swallow the lump in my throat. "What happened to them? How did they die?"

Regina clasps her hands in her lap, shakes her head sadly.

"His father shot his mother, and then turned the gun on himself. It was tragic, a huge blow to the family."

My mouth falls open. "I don't understand. *When* did they die? What about the other wives? Their other children?"

She shrugs. "We were already married when it happened. His father wasn't well. He'd been diagnosed with schizophrenia when he was a boy, said God told him to do things. They were very...religious."

"Did you ever meet them?" I think about the cards, the ones that supposedly came from them, written in his mother's handwriting. No, Regina can't be right. Seth's parents had sent us a wedding present. Hadn't they? No, it was all Seth's perfectly constructed lie.

"I did. They were odd people. I was glad to move away. They didn't even come to our wedding."

I want to tell her that they missed ours, too, but she's on a roll and I don't want to interrupt her.

"Seth was somewhat obsessed with his father."

"In what way?"

She seems relieved to be talking about something other than her relationship with Seth.

"I don't know. I suppose in just the way boys are with their dads. They were close. His father was really unhappy when we left. Said Seth was abandoning his family."

"Did you ever try to have children?" I ask. A sudden change of subject.

Regina doesn't like this question.

"You know I didn't want children."

"Why?"

"Does a woman still have to explain herself when she doesn't want children?" she snaps.

"No… I mean…you married the son of a polygamist. He must have told you that he wanted a family."

She looks away. "He assumed I'd change my mind, and I assumed he loved me enough to drop it."

Something nags at the back of my mind, it's so familiar— a song you can almost hear the tune to but don't know the name of.

The defensiveness has returned in her voice, her guard up once again. "I've answered all of your questions, Thursday. Please." She glances at the door. "I'd like to be alone now." I take her phone from my pocket and set it gently on the table before walking away. Before I leave, I turn back to where she's standing staring out of the window, unseeing, and place a slip of paper on top of the magazines with the number to the burner phone I bought.

"Seth hit Hannah. You need to know that. When I found out and confronted him about it he got rough with me, too."

A muscle twitches in her temple, a tiny pulse.

"Goodbye, Regina."

THIRTY-ONE

When I leave Regina's apartment, my head is spinning. I pause at the top of the stairs, my hand on the railing. Someone has scratched the word *cunt* into the metal with their keys. Regina could be lying about everything. I can't actually trust my husband's other wife, can I? Could it be that Seth lied to her, too? Lied about me and our relationship? I thought that perhaps he was keeping things from his shiny new wife, Hannah, but maybe he kept Regina in the dark, too. Had he lied to us all? Who was this man? Had I loved him so unconditionally that I'd gouged out my own eyes? Seth, who told me that Regina didn't want children, and that's why he sought out a second wife. Seth, who never told Regina that I'd miscarried our baby. There are so many secrets, and I've been blind for too long.

It makes me feel sick that I've allowed all of this to happen. I need to speak to Hannah, make her tell me what's going on. Where has he hidden Hannah?

I drive back to the Cottonmouth house, feeling worse by the minute. My stomach makes a loud appeal for food. When was the last time I ate? I pull into a drive-through and order a sandwich and a soda, but when I unwrap the foil, the sight of it makes me feel ill. I throw it away, sipping delicately on the Coke. I'm feverish, my face clammy and warm. I stumble into the house, my head spinning. The empty walls swim around me, and the smell of paint and rot makes me gag. Suddenly, I don't want to be here. I'll sleep just a few minutes, enough to make me feel better. I duck into the room and lock the door behind me. It's only eight o'clock, but my body aches from exhaustion. I crawl into the stale-smelling bed, my eyes heavy, and I sleep.

"Thursday?"

I sit up in bed, groggy, and reach for my cell. It's not there. I can't find the time. I'm holding a phone to my ear and someone is saying my name. That's right. I'm in Portland. I left my cell phone in the corner of an elevator. This is a burner.

"Yeah…" I say, struggling to untangle the sheets and sit up. "Who's this?"

A woman says my name again. "Thursday—" And then, "It's Regina."

Suddenly, I'm wide awake, my senses on full alert. I throw my legs over the side of the bed and stand up.

"What's wrong? Has something happened?"

"No…" Her voice is uncertain.

I pace the tiny space to the window and back to the bed, the strange phone clumsy in my hand.

"Seth knows you're here. I told him you came to the firm. He's looking for you."

I sit down abruptly. I'm not surprised. But how long until he tracks me down?

"Why are you telling me?"

There's a long pause on her end. I can hear her breathing into the phone, clogged breath like she's been crying.

"Can we meet somewhere to talk?"

"When?"

"Now," she says. "There's an all-night diner two blocks from my apartment. It's called Larry's. I can be there in thirty minutes."

"All right," I say cautiously. "How do I know I can trust you?"

"I don't think you have any other choice." She hangs up. She's an attorney; she's used to getting the last word.

I hang up the phone and begin searching for my clothes. The only thing relatively clean is my orange sweater. I pull it on and slide into my jeans. My hair is a dirty mess. I brush it into a quick ponytail, splash water on my face, and I'm out the door five minutes after Regina's call ended. It's only when I turn on the ignition to my car that the dashboard lights up and I see that it's 4:30 in the morning. What would possess her to call in the middle of the night?

I'm seated in a booth in the nearly empty Larry's with a cup of coffee in front of me when Regina walks through the doors. She's wearing jeans and a sweatshirt, her hair in a knot on top of her head. She could be mistaken for a college student. She has a backpack slung over a shoulder—not the kind you run away with, just the kind you use as a purse. I watch as she surveys the diner, looking for me. My breath is jagged. I lift a hand as her head turns my way and she catches my eye. She takes her time working her way over to where I am, and I have the feeling she's questioning her decision to come here. She slides into the seat across from me, slipping her arms out of the backpack. I notice right away that her eyes are swollen and red. She takes a minute to settle in, fussing with nothing, before looking up. She is here, I realize, to unload a burden.

"Same as her," she barks when the server approaches our table.

I smile at him apologetically as he hurries off. It makes her angry to be honest. A hazard of her job. She reminds me a little of my sister, bossy and so sure of herself that she comes across as irritated with everyone else. My sister and I are so different; our relationship has always felt tepid, something we could both do without. So for the sake of our mother, we try to see each other at least once a month, which usually ends up being an awkward dinner. We document the night with an overly enthusiastic selfie that we then text to our mother. She gets so excited that we're hanging out that it makes the whole ritual more bearable.

I decide to keep the upper hand and be irritated with her for being irritated with me.

"Well?" I say, my voice terse. "Why am I here?"

She swipes her fingers under her eyes and then checks them for mascara. *You washed it all off this afternoon*, I want to remind her. Then she looks at me squarely and says, "The first year Seth and I were married, I had a miscarriage."

My heart sinks. I want to reach out and touch her hand, but there's something so stony about her face that I hold back. Regina doesn't seem like the type who wants comfort. I don't do the typical *I'm sorrys*, either. We aren't two girlfriends sharing heartache over coffee.

"Okay…" I say. My hands wrap around my empty mug for lack of anything better to do. The caffeine is already in my system and making me jittery.

Plenty of women have miscarriages, most of them early in the pregnancy. Maybe she's trying to find common ground.

"I was twenty-one weeks," she says. "I didn't know about…yours. Seth… He never told me."

I let go of my coffee mug and sit back. "Okay," I say again. "What did he tell you?"

She glances at me, unsure. "He said that you just hadn't gotten pregnant yet. That you were trying."

"You told me that you haven't spoken to Seth until recently, that you've been over for years, so why would he tell his ex-wife something like that?"

The server appears at our table with a fresh pot of coffee and a mug. She fills the empty mug without a word and sets it in front of Regina, then leans over to top mine off. When she's gone, Regina pulls her mug toward her, cradling it, but doesn't take a sip.

I stare at her without speaking, waiting for her to continue.

"What do you remember about your miscarriage?" she asks.

I bristle under her question. I don't remember much, I try not to; the details of my miscarriage are painful.

"Thursday…" Regina reaches out a hand to touch mine and I stare at it, shocked. "Please," she says. "This is important."

"All right…" I lick my lips and shut my eyes, trying to

remember the details of the most painful day of my life. "I remember a lot of pain…and blood. Being rushed to the hospital…"

"What about before that? Where were you?"

"I… We were away. A weekend trip north."

She leans forward, elbows on the table. Her eyebrows draw together, the slash between them deep. "What did you eat…drink…? Did he give you anything?"

I shake my head. "Of course we ate. Seth wasn't drinking alcohol because I couldn't. I had tea…"

"What type of tea?"

I don't miss the urgency in her voice. It looks like she wants to leap across the table and shake me.

"It was a tea he said his mother sent for me. To help with the nausea." The moment the words are out of my mouth I feel the blood drain from my face. I'm light-headed. I grip the edge of the table for support and close my eyes. Regina had said that Seth's parents were dead. Where did that tea really come from and why would he tell me his mother sent it?

"I had terrible sickness, all day…" I can feel myself swaying; I take a few deep breaths to calm myself.

"Herbal tea," Regina says softly. "In a little brown sack."

I nod. "Yes."

"Was it the first time he gave it to you?"

I think back. I'd been complaining about it; my doctor had prescribed something for the nausea but it hadn't worked, so Seth suggested I try his mother's tea.

"She's had quite a few pregnancies, Thursday," he'd said with a smile when I'd asked him if it was safe. *"All of my mothers used it."*

I'd laughed at that, and he'd winked at me. In the end,

he made me the tea, boiling water in the room's little kettle. It had tasted like licorice and coriander and once I added some sugar I hadn't minded it at all.

"You drank it all weekend?" Regina asked.

I nodded.

"All right," she says. "Okay…"

Her face is pale, her eyelashes fluttering. And then she opens her rosebud mouth and tells me a story. And I wish she could take it all back, swallow it into herself so that I can pretend it's not so. I'm not that stupid. I'm not that gullible. I'm not so easily used.

THIRTY-TWO

I leave the diner an hour later with nowhere to go. I don't want to go back to the Cottonmouth house with its peeling wallpaper and musty smell. After Regina told Seth I was in Portland, he'd waste no time driving here. To what— reason with me? Drag me back to Seattle? I'm not ready to see him. I could go home, drive the two hours and beat him to it. I'd have enough time to grab some of my things and go stay with my parents. But my mother had not believed me when I was in the hospital and I tried to tell her the truth. I have no idea what their communication has been like over the last few days. Most likely, Seth had told her a partial truth: that I disappeared in the middle of the night, and that they need to find me before I hurt myself. I'm on my own. The confrontation with Seth inevitable,

I'm going to have to face him soon, but Regina has asked for more time, and I'm going to give her more time. What she told me while sitting under the fluorescent lights of Larry's had given me chills, rolled my stomach, made me doubt myself. My coffee had grown cold, a film appearing over the top as I slouched in the booth and listened to the dry recounting of her experience.

I drive until I see a shopping plaza that houses a large chain grocery store. It doesn't open for another few hours. I park in the back of the building, out of sight of the street, where I don't feel exposed, and recline my seat all the way back so I can sleep. Just a few hours.

I wake with a start to someone pounding on my car window. I bolt upright, groggy and disoriented.

"You can't park here," a man barks, peering through the window.

He's wearing an orange and yellow vest, and while he pounds again he looks over his shoulder, distracted. I flinch as his fist hits the window close to my face. His fist is big and tan; it matches his shoulders, which are wide.

When he looks back at me, he says, "You're blocking the way."

I look behind him and see a garbage truck idling in the alley, waiting to get to the dumpster that my car is blocking. Without raising my seat, I turn on the ignition and hit the gas, driving around to the front of the store. I pull into another spot, thrown off by the sudden wake-up and the brute of a man who did it. Scrubbing the sleep from my eyes, I yawn. I need to go somewhere private, where I can think without garbage men screaming at me. I decide on the public library; they'll have computers I could use. I'd driven past it the last time I was in the city having dinner with Seth; the elegant brick-and-stone structure caught my eye with its old-school beauty.

I can't remember the street it's on or the name of the branch, I have to rely on my memory to find it. I have to rely on my instincts to find it. It takes me forty minutes of weaving up and down the busy Portland streets, trying to remember exactly where I'd seen it. When I finally catch sight of the building, a group of homeless men are packing up their belongings, getting ready to traverse the city for the day. Since it's still early, the lot used for parking is relatively empty, and I find a spot close to the building. The smell of urine hits me as soon as I step out of the car. Also, it's freezing without a jacket. I hurry toward the building and find the doors unlocked. Breathing a sigh of relief, I duck inside, shivering, clutching my orange sweater around my fingers like gloves. The interior of the library is all open space underneath a domed skylight. I walk quickly through the lobby and toward the computers.

"Two hours," she says. "No eating or drinking." Her voice is dry, brittle and unsympathetic. She's more recording than person. When I nod compliantly, she eyes me suspiciously, like I might be hiding my breakfast underneath my sweater, but I'm allowed into the room.

There is an elderly man already seated at one of the computers, wearing a fedora and jabbing intently at the keyboard with two pointer fingers. He doesn't look up when I pass him and so I have time to stare at his screen. A dating website. He's writing messages to a prospective partner. *Good for you!* I think. Seth would have called me nosy, made fun of my "all-seeing eye" as he called it. I have to remind myself that Seth's opinion no longer counts, and that if it weren't for my nosiness I'd still be in the dark, married to a man I only thought I knew.

I find a computer near the back and slide into the plastic chair. My mouth is gritty from the diner coffee and nap in the car, my hair a greasy mess. The librarian on this floor keeps shooting glances at me like I might run off at any minute with one of the outdated computers tucked underneath my arm. I tap my finger impatiently on the desk as I wait for the internet to load, glancing around every few minutes like Seth might walk in and catch me here. The screen finally pops up and I type in my first search, chin resting on my palm. There are three things I have come here to learn about, and Seth's parents are first up: Mama and Papa Polygamy! I type their names into the search bar, the names that Regina gave me: Perry and Phyllis Ellington, along with murder/suicide. There are no articles, no newspaper coverage. The only thing I can find is an obituary dating their births and deaths, their surviving child listed as Seth Arnold Ellington. According to Seth, there were other siblings from his other mothers, siblings much younger than him, since his father married his other wives when Seth was a teenager. But since Perry and Phyllis lived outside of the norms of society, there is little information on how to find Seth's half siblings, who are now barely teenagers themselves. Perry's legal marriage was to Seth's mother, who now shared a grave with him. The only people who knew what truly happened to Perry and Phyllis were the other wives...and my husband.

Abandoning that search, I think about the drug Regina had mentioned at the diner: misoprostol. A drug used to start labor, used in conjunction with mifepristone, it is said to be effective in bringing about abortion in the second trimester of pregnancy. Taken by mouth, it is safe to use until the forty-ninth day of pregnancy, after which it proves to bring on serious risks in the mother. My hands shake as I think back to the day my baby died. I move the mouse from link to link. I feel cold from the inside out, like my internal warmth has been snuffed out by the information in front of me. Used later in pregnancy it's more dangerous for the mother, causing low blood pressure, loss of consciousness and infections after the abortion has occurred. I let go of the mouse and lean back in my chair, covering my eyes with my palms. The day of my miscarriage, Seth had stopped at the gas station for snacks. I remember the paper cups of tea he carried out to the car, how grateful I'd been for such a caring husband. The tea, the tea he said was sent by his dead mother. *Oh my God.* If Regina was right, it was Seth who caused the miscarriage.

The pain I feel is almost unbearable. At the time of my miscarriage, I'd not seen the medical report from the hospital; I hadn't wanted to. Seth had been my protector during those days: grieving with me, sheltering me from the things I didn't want to hear. I wouldn't have managed to get through that time without him. He'd told me that his decision for a second wife came when Regina decided that she didn't want children. Why then would he end the life of his unborn child, endangering my life, too? Nothing makes sense. I want to pull at my own hair, scream from frustration. There can be no answers until Seth gives them to me. I want to see my medical files. I want to hear it all.

My last search is the most painful, prompted by Regina's last words before we parted ways outside of the diner:

"I think there's something wrong with him."

THIRTY-THREE

Despite how hard I try, I can't stop thinking about what Regina told me. Realization is a slow boil, but once you're there, the anger is hot and spitting. My husband is sick—not just controlling, but disgustingly sick. Why had I never pressed him about his home life? He hid his trauma, blowing off my questions about his childhood, redirecting everything to me. And now I'm horribly afraid for Hannah—for her unborn baby.

I hadn't always been so trusting, had I? There was a time when I wouldn't allow newcomers into my life, lest they distract me from my goals. What had it been about Seth that drew me in? Sure, he was handsome, but lots of men were. And he flirted with me, but that wasn't a first, ei-ther. There were men all around me who spoke, and offered, and prodded for my attention. I had received their interest with a detached politeness. Sometimes I went out to dinner with them, or grabbed a beer, or did the things that girls my age were supposed to do, but none of it ever felt good—the way I imagined it was supposed to feel. Not until Seth.

When I try to pinpoint why I'd been so drawn to him, wooed by his advances, it always boiled down to one thing: he'd been so interested in everything I was. He asked questions and seemed fascinated by my answers. I remember the way he raised his eyebrows when I said something witty, the soft, amused curl of his lips as he listened to me speak. It had seemed at the time that he didn't have any ulterior motive, he was just as drawn to me as I was to him: pure chemistry. He'd quizzed me for my exam on that very first night in the coffee shop, and asked me detailed questions about why I wanted to be a nurse. No one had ever asked me those questions before, not even my parents. But that was it, wasn't it? He'd had a carefully concealed plan, a strategy. A woman like me, detached from her family, devoted to her studies, was secretly longing for a connection. I don't think I cared who it would be: a man, a woman, a friend or a long-lost aunt. I was waiting for someone to see me. I don't know if I'm angrier with myself more for falling for it in the first place, or for not seeing it sooner. But I know that as humans we want to be heard, and so when someone does the hearing, we feel a connection to them. I was no different than any other woman who'd been made to feel special and then, over the course of time, abandoned by the man she'd given everything up for. Seth was a charlatan, a charmer. He used his personality to manipulate women's emotions. By the time he told me about Regina, I was already in love with him. I was willing to accept anything he had to offer just to be loved by him. I'm ashamed to think about it.

Right now Hannah is pressed somewhere under his thumb, blindly trusting, daydreaming of the life they'd have with their child. If what Regina had skirted around is correct, Seth is planning to do to her what he had done to us.

I sit on a random bench in the city, a line of food trucks in front of me. A man in a Dodgers hat stands close by, looking longingly at the taco truck across the street. I wonder why he doesn't just get a taco and make himself happy. It starts to drizzle but I don't move. There is something bothering me about all of this, something that isn't adding up. I close my eyes and try to fit all of the pieces together. Regina, Thursday, Hannah and Seth: what do we all have in common? What parts are we playing in Seth's game? Some people have moments of absolute clarity; my moment comes like a slouched lurker. I entertain it only for a few moments before deciding what to do. I stand up just as the man in the Dodgers hat jogs across the street. Instead of joining the taco line, he heads for a salad truck. I smile to myself as we both make our choices.

I've been home for a week. Home sweet home, which took the good part of three hours to tidy up after the way Seth left it. The night I got back, I found the condo a mess, like Seth had thought throwing all of the pillows and contents of my drawers on the floor would afford him answers to my whereabouts. The whole place smelled like rot, and upon inspection, I found the trash in the kitchen overflowing, the lid propped on empty containers of takeout and half-eaten fruit. My home felt strange…foreign. The first thing I did was find the 9mm my father had gifted me in my closet. Then I opened all of the windows and burned a candle for hours until the smell went away. Seth had found my phone where I dropped it in the elevator; it sat on the kitchen counter next to the bottles of medication I'd left behind, the screen smashed. I picked it up and turned it over in my hand. It felt like a warning, one I would be careful to heed. I'd left the phone where it was and carried the bottles of medicine to the bathroom, popping their caps one by one, dumping their contents into the toilet. The flush of water, the whirring of the tank refilling, were satisfying as I watched my prison disappear. My computer was gone, though he'd graciously left behind my wallet and keys. I called a locksmith, offering to pay them extra to come that afternoon, and while I waited I changed the alarm code.

After the locksmith changed both locks on the front door, I walked downtown, my shiny new keys in my pocket, to replace my phone and computer. Since I'd been gone for five days, the week ahead held appointments and phone calls. I needed to be able to check my emails and voice messages, my little burner phone useless except to make calls and send texts. As I waited to cross the street, the same street where I'd bumped into Lauren what seemed like a lifetime ago, I watched the faces of the people around me. When you removed yourself from your own thoughts and stopped to look at people—really look at them—you saw something surprising. Each of them—from the businessmen, phones pressed to their ears, loafers sidestepping puddles, to the tourists who lingered on street corners wondering which direction to walk—held a certain vulnerability about them. Did their parents love them? Did a man—a woman? And if the person who loved them left, how immense would their pain be? We busy ourselves trying not to be lonely, trying to find purpose in careers, and lovers, and children, but at any moment, those things we work so hard to possess could be taken from us. I feel better knowing I'm not alone, that the whole world is as fragile and lonely as I am.

With the lock and alarm code changed and the gun sitting on my nightstand, I manage to sleep that first night. But not without bad dreams.

Seth has not tried to contact me, though on the Monday after my return home, Regina calls my burner phone, which I've left on the charger, forgotten in the corner of my bedroom. At first, the noise startles me, the unfamiliar tinkling of the ringer. When I see it's her number I pick up right away, pressing the phone to my ear and using my free hand to block out the noise of the TV.

"Hello… Thursday?"

"Yes," I say.

"I found her. I know where he has Hannah."

I leave for Portland an hour later. The only things I take are my cell phone and the gun, which I drop into my purse right before walking out the door. I have to hurry. I replay Regina's words over and over in my head.

That day in the diner, Regina had told me a story of manipulation and abuse. Not the obvious kind; it was the type she didn't see coming. She'd married the charming and lively Seth, and their first year together had been magical. But soon after they moved to Seattle, he'd changed. She described him as sullen and moody. Most nights he'd not come to bed at all, and in the morning she'd get up and find him where she'd left him the night before: sitting in front of the TV with glassy eyes. He refused to bathe and only ate once a day. It began to scare her and she encouraged him to get help. Seth told her he was struggling with depression and promised that things would get better soon. He started working with Alex, building the company, and things did seem to get better for a while.

It was by accident that she saw the emails from his father. Seth had forgotten to close out the window and when Regina sat down at the computer she was able to see them all. She said the emails were sent before Seth's father had killed his wife and then himself. The emails were convoluted. His father raved about conspiracies the government had to kill him and his wives and take his children. He suspected Seth's mother of slipping medication into his food to make him tired and foggy. The very last email he'd sent Seth was the day before he died, where he'd outlined his plan to kill his wife and then himself. It would only be the two of them—he would spare his other wives. Regina had searched Seth's in-box for his replies, sure he'd tried to talk his father down, convince him to get help, but there was nothing of the sort. She'd confronted Seth about it and he'd gotten angry. It was the only time I'd seen Regina show any emotion other than her hard coldness. Her eyes had filled with tears as she told me how he'd smashed everything around him: vases, plates, he'd even tossed the television onto the floor. He accused her of snooping where she didn't belong. Then he'd threatened her. Grabbing her by the neck, he'd pushed her up against a wall until Regina had screamed out that she was pregnant.

Seth had dropped his hands immediately and smiled like the last ten minutes hadn't happened. And then he'd cried. Wrapping his arms around her waist, he'd sobbed uncontrollably, saying that he was sorry, and that talking about his parents' deaths had triggered something in him. As Regina stood numbly with his arms wrapped around her waist, Seth had promised to get help, saying things would change. They'd moved on from there and for the first months of her pregnancy, everything had been perfect: Seth, the doting father-to-be. She'd almost forgotten about the incident. And then, suddenly, she'd miscarried at twenty-one weeks along. She'd had a bump, and she'd already felt the baby move. She had to give birth to it—a girl. Seth had acted devastated, promising they could try again. But Regina refused. Frightened of experiencing the same thing, she got on birth control—the kind they insert into your arm—and focused on her career instead. He'd pleaded with her take it out and when she refused, they'd grown apart. Eventually, Seth suggested a plural marriage, because he wanted children. When Regina said no, he'd asked for a divorce and she'd given it to him, though he didn't stop coming around. He was paying half of her bills, as that had been the agreement when she'd given him the divorce. So when he came to Portland for work, he stayed at their old house, first in the guest room, and then back in their bed. I'd almost seen shame on her face when she told me they'd still have sex when he visited, even though he was married to another woman. She told me that she'd never known about Hannah, and I believed her.

"The week before my miscarriage, he'd started making me tea," she'd said. "I thought it was strange because he'd never been one to do much in the kitchen. He didn't even make coffee in the mornings, and then all of a sudden, he's boiling water and seeping leaves like an expert. It didn't occur to me until you mentioned it."

"It could be a coincidence," I'd said.

Regina had shaken her head. "He was the oldest of his siblings, and he resented them. Thought they took attention away from him. He told me that he hated having to share space with a bunch of toddlers…"

"What are you saying?"

She'd just stared at me like she expected me to get it and then she'd finally said, "I think he's going to do the same thing to this other girl, Hannah. We have to stop him. I need a few days to find out where she is."

THIRTY-FOUR

Regina sends me an address in the Pearl District and I punch it into my phone as I wait at the light to turn onto 5. I can feel my heart beating; it feels like it's lodged in my throat. I try to quell the panic rising in my chest. I have to hurry. I have to help Hannah. I'd only ever been to the Pearl District in passing, driving through what was once the warehouse district, now known for its art galleries and upscale residences. Seth and I had eaten lunch there at a restaurant that sat on the Willamette River, sucking oysters from their shells, and then held hands as we walked back to our car. It was a perfect day. Not long after, I'd found out I was pregnant, and wondered if our baby had been conceived that night under the crisp hotel sheets.

I make a few necessary calls as I drive, my voice calm

despite the level of mania I'm feeling on the inside. I'd tried calling Regina after she sent the text, but my call had gone straight to voice mail. *She will be there*, I tell myself. We're working as a team. Something lingers in the back of my mind but I push it away. She's all I have and I'm going to have to trust her. I'm jittery through the drive, leaning forward in my seat and talking to the cars that get in my way. Was Hannah all right or was Seth keeping her prisoner? Will she be relieved to see me or act like she doesn't know who I am?

It's all so unsettling, the type of wandering thoughts that could make you question your own sanity. I've certainly done enough of that in the last weeks. I push down on the accelerator and my car lurches forward, almost rear-ending a truck. I ride his bumper until he moves out of the fast lane. He gives me the finger as I speed by, yelling something into the wind. I ignore him and move on to the next car, almost slamming into the back of it, too. This continues for several miles until I see the flashing red and blue lights in my rearview mirror; the brief shrill of the siren sounds behind me, and I'm forced to move over two lanes to reach the shoulder. I wait for the officer to walk up to my window, my stomach clenching in knots.

"Ma'am, license and registration, please."

I'm ready. I pass them through the window, willing him to look into my eyes. He does, though I can't see his hidden behind reflective glasses—the type you see the police wear in movies. He disappears back to his cruiser, my paper held in his hand. After a few minutes he comes back.

"Do you know why I pulled you over?"

"I was speeding," I say without hesitation.

His face doesn't betray anything; he stares from behind his glasses, stony and expectant.

"I'm late. My fault, I totally deserve a ticket."

Still nothing. I tap my finger on the wheel, wishing he'd hurry up and get on with things. He hands me my papers.

"Be more careful next time."

That's all? I look at his badge: Officer Morales.

"Um...thank you," I say.

"You're all set," he says. "Have a good one."

It takes me ten minutes to merge back onto the highway, my heart still ringing in my chest. But once I am on my way I almost feel good—better than I had before. I ease up on the gas and follow behind a semi, keeping to the speed limit this time.

I cross the bridge into the city just as the sun is making its descent. Warm orange light illuminates the buildings, and for a moment, I get the impression that it's summer—a long time from now. This is all sorted out, a big misunderstanding, and my life is back to normal. The feeling is so powerful that I have to fight it back, push it away. A woman's greatest foe is sometimes her hope that she's imagined it all. That she herself is crazy rather than the circumstances of her life. Funny the emotional responsibility a woman is willing to take on just to maintain an illusion. I think about what it feels like outside: the air cold enough to show my breath. My life a twisted, frightening mess of deceit, my mind easily beguiled...that's my lesson as of late: things are not always what they seem. I shake off the last of the feeling, my resolve returning as I drive off the bridge and turn into the bustle of downtown Portland. Seth and his little harem. I'd checked my bank account before I left and found a pattern of cash withdrawals: two a week for the past six months. How had I not noticed before? Seth was syphoning money from my account to pay Regina back. I wonder if she knows where he's getting the money from, if it would have made a difference? He is going to answer for all of it. I push down on the gas pedal.

My GPS directs me to a building that is still under construction. Condominiums, four floors of them, brand new; there are signs along the street advertising their prices. Visit Our Sales Office! The west side is inhabited, while scaffolding still hangs on to the east side, plastic sheets covering the empty units that have yet to get their walls. I park and hesitantly step out. How could Seth afford this for Hannah while Regina lives in that dump? He was still trying to impress Hannah, I think. He'd have made a way to give his pregnant wife security. I call Regina as I stand next to my car, but it goes straight to her voice mail. I leave a message, my voice shaking.

"Regina… I'm here at Hannah's… I was hoping you'd be here… I'm going in. I just… I have to stop what's happening…" I hang up before I start to cry.

The doors into the building don't require a card for entry like mine does. The whole process of getting to Hannah's floor is relatively easy due to the lax rules surrounding the construction. I look at a laminated map of the building taped to the lobby wall and find that her unit is located on the second floor. As the elevator climbs upward, I reach behind me, lightly touching the cold metal of the 9mm. I'd moved it from my purse to the waistband of my pants before I got out of the car.

I have no idea what Seth's state of mind is, how he'll react to me being here. He's sick, a sort of serial baby abortionist, ending his own children's lives by endangering the lives of his multiple wives. God, what is wrong with me, getting caught up in all of this? What I do remember is the look on his face that afternoon I attacked him, the cruel coldness I saw right before I blacked out. And *blacked out* is too general of a description. I am sure he wrestled me to the ground, slammed my head against the kitchen floor, but my memory is shifty.

My heart is racing as I step off the elevator and onto Hannah's floor. Will Seth be with her or will she be alone? Her door is the farthest from the elevator. Will anyone hear me if something goes wrong? I pause halfway down the hallway, placing my hand on the wall, as I take a few deep breaths. Then I surge forward, walking faster than I normally would.

"Let's get this over with," I say quietly to myself. Then I'm in front of her door, palms sweating. I lift my hand and knock. My fist makes a loud *whamp-whamp* noise that echoes down the long hallway. The smell of fresh paint and newly laid carpet fills my nose as I glance behind me to see if any of the other doors will open. I hear a latch click and then the door swings wide. I've caught her by surprise. Hannah stands in the doorway with her mouth slightly ajar, a dish towel hanging limply from her hand.

"I need to talk to you," I say before she can say anything. "It's very important..." When she doesn't look convinced, I add, "It's about Seth."

Her lips press together and her forehead creases as she considers me. Her pretty face is twisted in worry as she glances into the apartment behind her and for the first time it hits me how young Hannah is. She's just a baby, I think. The same age as I was when I started nursing school. I'd fallen for Seth then, too, trusted him wholeheartedly. What would I have done if Regina had shown up at my home saying the same thing? It takes her a minute to decide what to do. I force myself not to look at her belly, to keep my eyes locked on her face. I don't want to know, do I? What if I'm too late? I wouldn't be able to live with myself.

She turns into the apartment, leaving the door open. I take that as my cue that I'm being permitted entry. Hannah walks over to the living room where the couch I'd seen in her former house sits. She crosses her arms over her chest as she stares at me. She looks uncomfortable. I close the door gently behind me and take a few steps toward her. There are boxes stacked against walls, unpacked and unmarked. She moved in a hurry. Through the bedroom door I can see an unmade bed, sheets heaped into a pile. I look for Seth, as is my habit: a pair of shoes, or the water glass he always sets on the bedside table. But I don't know his habits here, with Hannah, and for all I know, they could be very different from the ones I am familiar with. I move closer to her and she looks up, startled.

"How are you feeling?" I ask gently.

Her hand automatically moves to cup her belly. I remember that gesture so well, always conscious of the life your body was nurturing. Something loosens in my chest: relief. She's still pregnant.

"You told me he hit you, Hannah," I say. "Was that true?"

"No, you told me he hit me, Thursday," she says. "I tried to tell you it wasn't true and you wouldn't hear me."

"That's not true," I say. "I saw the bruises..."

Hannah looks stricken. She glances around the room like she's looking for an escape.

"He was angry that I found you and that I came to see you," I say. "When I got home after the last time you and I saw each other, I confronted him about you."

Her eyes go wide but her lips stay stubbornly closed, like she's afraid to say a word about it.

"We fought, it turned physical and the next thing I knew I was in the hospital."

Hannah shakes her head like she can't believe it.

"You know something is wrong with him. How he was raised...the way he's asked us to live..."

"Asked us to live?" she asks. "What are you talking about?"

There is the sound of a key in a lock and the front door swings open. My throat closes up and suddenly I feel like I can barely breathe in this tiny apartment. I claw at my neck. I don't know what I'm hoping to find there, a necklace, perhaps, something to hold on to and distract myself.

Seth walks through the door, plastic bags hooked on all his fingers. At first he doesn't see me. He walks toward Hannah, a relaxed smile on his face, and leans down to kiss her.

"I got the canned type of pears you like," he says, and then he stops abruptly when he sees the expression on her face. "What is it, Han?"

Her head swivels in my direction and Seth follows her gaze to where I'm standing. The look on his face is incredulous, like he can't believe I found them here. He sets the bags down and a can of pears rolls out and across the floor.

Hannah's pixie face is ashen, her lips a floury white as she stares between us.

"I'm here for Hannah," I say. "To warn her about you."

THIRTY-FIVE

Seth marches over to where I'm standing and grabs me by the arm before I can move away. The surprise he wore on his face just a moment ago is gone, replaced by something else. I'm afraid to look too carefully, so I keep my eyes on Hannah as he steers me toward the couch. He shoves me down and my knees buckle as I fall into the love seat. It's soft, the cushions wide and plush, and I sink into them. And then I'm struggling to straighten up, feeling clumsy and stupid. I grapple awkwardly with my body until I'm perched on the edge, pressing my knees together, ready to spring to my feet again. Hannah won't look at me. Her eyes are downcast as she stands near Seth. I wonder what he's told her, who she thinks I am.

"How did you find us?" he asks.

I clamp my mouth shut. I'm not about to tell him that Regina helped me.

"Thursday," Seth says, taking a step toward me.

I flinch back and I immediately feel ashamed. Surely he wouldn't do anything to me in front of his Hannah.

"I'm calling the police," he says, pulling his phone from his pocket. "You're stalking us. You're a danger to yourself and Hannah."

My mouth opens and closes in protest, but I'm too shocked to really say anything. Stalking? How could he act like I'm the danger to Hannah when he's the one who's been hitting her?

"You've gone too far," he continues. "It's over, it's been over for a while." He places an arm around Hannah's shoulders. Am I imagining that she's stiffened? "I've told Hannah everything. She knows about us."

Knows about us? Knows what? A pain shoots through my forehead and I narrow my eyes, blinking against it.

I don't look at Seth, I pretend he's not there; I look at Hannah, only her, the young girl whose life he's going to ruin. She looks tiny, so much younger than Seth; his arm around her almost seems paternal.

"Hannah," I say gently. "What has Seth told you about me?"

Her head snaps up as she meets my gaze, and Seth's shoulders go rigid. She glances at Seth, whose eyes are boring into me.

"I told her the truth," he says. "It's over, Thursday."

"I didn't ask you, I asked Hannah." I look over at her. "When I went to the house, you pretended not to know me…"

She bites her bottom lip, her eyes blinking furiously.

"You knew who I was," she says. "You came to our house, pretending to be someone else. You were stalking us..." Her voice rises in crescendo.

I need her to be calm and logical, to really listen to me. I nod. "You're right. I did come to your house. I was curious about who you were. I knew that Seth had relationships with two other women outside of our marriage and I wanted to see...you."

Her head jerks like I've slapped her. "What are you talking about?" She glances at Seth, then back at me.

"Seth and I are still married," I say.

"You're insane." Her voice shakes.

I look at Seth, straining my eyes so wide it feels like they're going to pop out of their sockets.

"This is what you told her?" I ask him. "She never knew anything about a plural marriage. So was that story just for me, then?"

A muscle jumps in his jaw. I can see by the look in his eyes that I'm right.

"We were living together as husband and wife, in every way," I say, turning to Hannah.

Hannah starts to cry. Seth reaches for her, but she pushes him away, her sobs filling the apartment.

"Look what you've done," she says to him. "Look what you brought into our lives."

I look at him for the first time. His mouth opening and closing. *Brought into their lives?* Seth brought Hannah into mine. I was here first.

For a minute I'm in shock. I picture him as my husband and not this monster. The man I loved, who would kiss me gently on the lips and rub my neck after a long day of work. I cooked him meals and he praised my ability; when something broke in the condo he'd get the toolbox and fix it with me standing over him, feeling pride at how good he was at everything. The hurt rushes through me and then all of a sudden it's gone, replaced by anger. How dare he. How dare he love me one minute and discard me the next.

Seth's attention isn't focused on me. It's focused on Hannah.

"She's not well," he says. "She just got out of a mental hospital. I'm sorry, Hannah… I love you, only you."

"Not well?" I say. "I was there because you put me there, because you were afraid of what I could say about you." I turn my attention back to his trembling girlfriend. "He was good to me—or so I thought—and I believed everything he told me. When I lost the baby, I became useless to him. Is that the type of man you want to be with, Hannah? Someone who lies to you, who hits you, who finds other women to meet his sick, insatiable needs. It wasn't only me," I say. "He's been with Regina, too."

"That's why you came here?" Seth hisses. "To accuse me of hitting the woman I love? Are you insane? You're the violent one. You attacked me when I tried to end things with you. We had to move to get away from you."

"There were bruises on her arms," I yell at him. "I saw them!"

"I told you what those bruises were from," Hannah interjects. "I bruise easily."

I shake my head. "Your eye…you had a black eye that day…"

She looks to Seth, uncertain, and for a moment I think I have her, that she's going to admit what happened. But then she says something that shocks me.

"We were having sex when it happened. I didn't want to

say that at the time. You and I had just met, and it was embarrassing to say. Seth accidentally elbowed me in the eye."

I stare at her in disbelief. Why is she still lying? "He shoved me once, when we were fighting. I hit my ear. Maybe he didn't directly hit you but—"

"Thursday, you came at me, pounding at my chest. I tried to hold you off...you fell..."

Seth's voice is exasperated, a deep line sliced between his eyebrows. *What an actor!* Hannah is looking from me to him like she doesn't know who to believe. I latch on to that, knowing getting her to believe me is the only way to get her away from him.

"No, that's not the way I remember it."

He laughs bitterly. "There seems to be quite a lot you're not remembering," he says through gritted teeth.

"Why is my name on your house?" I ask. I turn to Hannah. "The house you were living in belongs to me."

Hannah turns her face away, but Seth's eyes bug.

"Because it's your house, Thursday! Your grandmother left it to you."

"No!" I scream. But somewhere, deep in my mind, I know it's true. I'd already owned the condo when my grandmother passed away, and I'd offered Seth use of the house while he commuted back and forth from Portland to Seattle. He told me he'd do the renovations I wanted for free, in exchange for staying there while in Portland. A cry escapes my throat. I lift my hand to my neck. My breath is coming out in jagged gasps. How had I not known it was my house—my grandmother's? Hannah had given me a tour and I'd followed her around the rooms like a stranger.

"Your estate manager put it up for rent," he says.

I hate the way he's looking at me: pity and disgust mar his features.

"You're crazy," he says. It's dismissive, a shake of his head. He's glad to be done with me, he sees me as something to get rid of; he always has.

"No, I'm not." I'm shivering so hard I can hear my teeth rattle.

He laughs as I stare at him. "Of course you are. You've always been crazy. You were obsessed with my ex-wife, just like you're obsessed with Hannah. We were a mistake, Thursday, that's all. I liked fucking you, are you hearing me? That's all you were to me."

He turns to Hannah just as I grip the side of the sofa with one of my hands. The pain is frightening; I can feel it in my toes...my chest...my eyes.

"Baby," he says to her, "I made a mistake. Please..."

"Why didn't you tell me it was *her* house?" Hannah is backing away slowly, shaking her head.

"I was going to...after I ended it with Thursday. I didn't want to upset you. The baby... Please, Hannah, it was all a mistake. I'm so sorry." He's been caught in another lie. I take a hopeful step toward Hannah and Seth screams at me. "Don't you come near her!"

"A mistake with what?" I scream. "I'm your wife!"

The room goes quiet as both Seth and Hannah stare at me in horror.

"No, Thursday," I hear from behind me. "You're his mistress."

I freeze, my blood running cold. Turning around, I see Regina standing in the doorway, her purse slung over her shoulder as she looks around uncertainly. Our eyes meet for a second before she locates Hannah crying near the kitchen. She steps inside.

"You were his mistress and you offered to let him live in your house with his new wife."

"That's not true." But it is true. I remember now. When Seth married Hannah, my renters had just moved out; the house was open. I'd offered it to them. I thought it would buy me favor with Seth; I'd be the giving, selfless wife. I stare at Regina, tears filling my eyes.

"You were the reason our marriage ended," she says. "You had an affair with Seth."

I hear roaring in my ears. The tips of my fingers tingle.

"Regina told me everything, Thursday," Seth says. "That you came to her office pretending to be someone else, and that you forced your way into her home. Your crazy theories about how I caused your miscarriage, and how you insisted my parents are alive..."

"You told me your parents were alive! They didn't come to our wedding—you said it was because your father was in the hospital..."

"No," he says, shaking his head slowly. "That's why they didn't come to my wedding with *Regina*. I told you that story."

"No."

"Yes, Thursday. Oh my God, oh my God," he says.

When Regina looks at me there is nothing on her face; it's been wiped of expression. I stare at her and she stares back.

"Why would you do this?" I ask.

"Everyone all right?" she asks, looking from Seth to Hannah.

"Regina—" I say.

She cuts me off. "She left a message on my phone. Said she was coming here. I didn't know… I was worried."

A chill washes over me; it starts at the back of my neck and creeps down my body like an invisible hand. I try to catch her eye. What is she doing? Surely she came here to back me up. I want to ask her what's going on, why she won't look at me, but my tongue is glued to the roof of my mouth and my heart pounds steadily.

"I called the police," she says to me. "I told them you were coming here with the intent to harm Seth or Hannah, that you'd threatened to do so."

My whole body is trembling now. It's a setup, it was all a setup. When she'd told me she'd found out where Hannah was, I'd been too preoccupied to ask her how. She'd known all along where they were, and I'd played right into her hand.

I look at Hannah, who is crying fat tears. I think of Regina's dingy apartment, her bitterness, the things she told me about Seth. She wants to make me look crazy.

"You fucking bitch," I say, walking toward her. I don't know what I intend to do, but then she's in front of me and my hands are around her neck. It was a mistake; Seth is on me in a flash, grabbing my wrists and pulling me away. I struggle against him, kicking out, and feel my foot catch him in the knee. He grunts in pain and falls toward me, pushing me to the ground. I reach for the gun, the one I tucked into my waistband just in case. My hand is trapped, my fingers touching the cold metal; Seth's weight is on my upper body. I hear Hannah screaming, Regina is yelling my name. I can't let him hurt Hannah's baby. I struggle to pull the gun free, yanking it from the confines of my jeans. My finger finds the trigger. As Seth's knee comes down hard on my stomach I pull the trigger. I hear a loud pop and then Regina screaming out, telling Hannah to call 911. The air whooshes out of me at the same time I feel blood on my hands. Seth collapses on top of me, the gun trapped between us. His blood pools warm on my belly. I can barely breathe. And it's in that loss of breath that I remember. Seth approaching me at the coffee shop, him telling me that he was married, my initial anger, and then our affair, getting pregnant...and his wife, Regina, leaving him. I remember thinking he'd marry me now that Regina was out of the picture, that we'd be a family. But then I lost the baby... *Oh God, oh God.* Waking up in the hospital and the doctor telling me that I'd never be able to have another child. The look on Seth's face...

And then he'd left me. For Hannah. Some slut he met who was young enough and fertile enough to have his babies. They were both from Utah; she was ten years his junior. But I'd begged him to come back to me; I'd told him that I didn't care if he married Hannah, that I still wanted him. And so began our second affair.

THIRTY-SIX

It's different this time; I am more relaxed, less anxious. The staff knows me by name and I no longer feel like a faceless victim. Dr. Steinbridge sees me three times a week. He says we are making progress.

I wander the long, stale-smelling corridors, thinking about my choices, itemizing my weaknesses. There are so many moments in my life when I should have been awake and instead was in a sleepy, emotional trance. I allowed things to happen to me.

I take all of the classes and groups: my favorite is holistic yoga, where we all gather in a windowless room and perch fluidly on purple mats, breathing deeply and emptying our minds of our troubles. So many troubles we have, so many disorders. Lauren brings me dinner twice a week from my favorite take-out places, and my mother visits, wearing a guilty expression and bearing huge plastic containers of homemade cookies.

"Enough for everyone," she says.

I've never asked her what she thinks of the situation with Seth, or if she's in contact with him. I don't think I want to know. Once, when I said his name, a sour expression appeared on her face before it was quickly replaced by what I call her *everything is all right!* smile.

Anna has flown in twice to see me. The first time she came, she marched into Queen County with plenty to say about Seth, and loud enough for everyone in the vicinity to hear. Bless her. My father has not come. I don't expect him to. I am his broken child, an embarrassment. I lied to my parents about Seth and now they know the truth: I am a mistress, not worthy of marriage.

During my last week in Queen County, I sit alone at dinner near the window, my tray of shepherd's pie congealing in front of me. Jell-O, too, of course—always Jell-O. The water here tastes metallic and dirty, but I sip it slowly, staring out at the grassy lawn below. The window fogs from my breath and I breathe harder just to watch the patch of condensation grow and retract, grow and retract.

The therapy has been a breeze, really—helpful, even. After the police came to Hannah and Seth's temporary home and found Seth bleeding on top of me, I was taken to the hospital. I spent three days there recovering from minor wounds before they transferred me to jail to await my arraignment.

Regina had set me up, of course, getting me to believe and accuse Seth of causing both of our miscarriages. But this turned out to help my case. My lawyer got me off on insanity and they sent me back to Queen County, this time for a much longer stay. I was relieved actually, afraid they'd send me somewhere new.

During my first meeting with Dr. Steinbridge, just a day after I arrived, he told me that I'd been stalking Seth and his new wife for quite some time. He also told me that Seth's ex-wife, Regina, had corroborated the story by saying that I'd shown up at her work and her home, forcing myself inside and demanding information about them. Regina produced the voice mail I'd left her right before I'd charged into Seth and Hannah's condo. The doctor played it for me as I sat in the leather armchair across from him. I didn't move a limb as I listened, my body tense with anticipation. Even to my own ears, I sounded crazy. It was then that Dr. Steinbridge paused the voice mail, waiting for me to either deny or own these claims. I did neither. No point in denying the stalking part—that was true, regardless of how Regina had played me. I sat in silence, listening to him, the excuses dying on my tongue.

"You do not bear full responsibility for what happened," Dr. Steinbridge told me. "Seth is a troubled individual, the way he grew up, the abuse he claims he suffered. He cheated on both of his wives and emotionally manipulated you. He used you and played into your denial. But we aren't here to deal with Seth's issues, we're here to deal with yours. When you realized what was happening in your relationship with him, your mind created an alternate reality to deal with both the death of your unborn baby and the fact that Seth was moving on with someone else."

"But he never tried to end things with me," I said.

And then the good doctor produced half a dozen emails between Seth and me, all of which came directly from my email account. He let me read them. Seth, always logical, pleading with me to accept the fact that we were over and that he was sorry for cheating on Hannah. I had no memory of reading those emails, no memory of answering them. Dr. Steinbridge said that I deleted them in my desperation to pretend it wasn't happening.

"The police also found the account you created under the name Will Moffit, the one you used to get access to Regina…"

"Yes, but I only did that because I thought she was cheating on him…"

He'd looked at me sympathetically.

"What about Seth's parents? They sent me cards… I have them."

"The cards were part of your case. Your attorney presented them to the jury as evidence when you pleaded guilty by reason of insanity. You wrote them. They brought in a handwriting analyst to prove it."

I saw myself in line at the grocery store, a stack of cards on the conveyor belt. I'd whimpered, pressing the heels of my hands to my eyes.

"It's right there, Thursday, right in front of you," he'd said, tapping the papers with a finger. His fingers were gloriously bent, like knobby tree branches. I watched them poke at the printed pages in fascination. "You and Seth were never married. He had an affair with you when he was married to his first wife, Regina. Regina left him when she found out that he got you pregnant." He'd paused to let that sink in. "But you lost the baby, and that caused you to enter a psychotic episode."

Seth had not caused our miscarriages, but Regina made me believe that he had. Why? Regina had lost a baby—that all came out in the trial—but much earlier than mine, at eight weeks. She testified that she caught Seth tampering with her birth control. I'd looked back at Regina at that very moment, as she sat on the other side of the courtroom, remembering her confession in the diner that day, and I'd seen her face pale.

Once I made Seth the enemy in my mind, it was so easy to believe what Regina fed me. My baby had been healthy one day, moving and kicking, and then he'd just stopped. There was no medical reason found. Sometimes those things just happen, babies stop living.

"Dr. Steinbridge," I say during one session. "Isn't it funny that Seth never mentioned any of this the last time I was here?"

"He never claimed to be your husband, Thursday. When you came in last time it's because Seth tried to end things with you. He admitted as much to me when I spoke to him privately, that he was married to someone else, and that you were his mistress. His wife, Hannah, figured out who you were on the last night you saw her. Do you remember?"

I remember having dinner with her, going to the bathroom and coming out to find her gone. I tell the doctor this.

"Seth figured out where you were and texted her. He told her to leave right away."

"But when I got back to my apartment, he was there. His hand was beat up..."

"Yes, well, he claims he punched a wall when he found out you were stalking his wife. You attacked him when he told you it was over. I imagine he felt a sense of duty in visiting you here after that."

"But he came to pick me up, take me home."

"No," the doctor says. "Your father picked you up and took you home."

I laugh at that. "Are you kidding me? My father came to see me once after I got out of here. He doesn't care about me."

"Thursday," Dr. Steinbridge says. "I was there. Your father came, brought you clothes, stayed with you for a week until you crushed Ambien into his dinner and snuck out to drive to Portland."

"No," I say. My limbs feel odd, like they're not a part of me. The doctor has it wrong, or he's lying. Maybe Seth got to him, paid him off to keep quiet...

"You were on heavy medication and still suffering from delusions."

I want to laugh. How crazy do they think I am, mistaking my father for Seth?

I stand up suddenly, my movement so abrupt my chair falls backward and hits the ground with a metallic smack. Dr. Steinbridge stares up at me from where he's sitting, his hands folded calmly on the desk. His eyes, shaded by those caterpillar eyebrows of his, look sad. I feel as if I'm evaporating, slowly being sucked away into oblivion.

"Close your eyes, Thursday. See it again as it really was."

I don't have to, I don't have to close my eyes—because it's playing out like a reel in my mind.

I see those days in my condo, except this time I see it the right way: my father hovering and handing me my pills, my father reading thrillers from my bookshelf, my father watching *Friends* with me on the couch.

"No," I say again, my eyes filling with tears.

Seth hadn't come to get me because he told me our affair was over and he'd gone back to his wife. Seth had abandoned me for the second time. *I wasn't enough. I wasn't enough.* I deserved to be alone. My wail is a siren, loud and shrill. I claw at my face, my arms, anything I can reach. I want to scrape off all of my skin, scrape until there is nothing left but muscle and blood, until I am merely a thing and not a human being. There is warmth on my fingertips when they charge in and grab me; my blood leaves stains on their scrubs.

In my first year as a nurse, a man came into the ER two weeks before Christmas with a crushed skull. His name was Robbie Clemmins and I swore I'd never forget his name, so tragic was his accident. A roofer who volunteered in his spare time at a nursing home, he'd been hanging Christmas lights on the outside of the building when he'd fallen two stories and landed on his back, smacking his head on the pavement. When someone found him, he was conscious, lying on his back and speaking in a calm, normal voice. He was reciting an oral report he'd given in the fifth grade about how to properly skin a squirrel. When they wheeled him into the ER he was sobbing, muttering something about his wife, though he wasn't married. I remember seeing the concave in his head and wanting to throw up, and then later the X-rays in which his skull looked like a cracked egg. The impact had jarred his brain; chips of his skull entered the brain tissue and had to be removed during a surgery that lasted eight hours. Though we saved his life, we were unable to save who he was before the accident. I remember thinking how fragile we were as humans, souls covered in tender flesh and brittle bone; one wrong step and we became someone else entirely.

My brain is intact in the traditional way; I did not fall from a roof, though it seems I fell at some height from reality. Dr. Steinbridge has diagnosed me with a list of things I'd be embarrassed to repeat; the bottom line is that I have an unhealthy brain. I often sit in my room and picture my brain enflamed and oozing with my various diagnoses. There are days where I want to crack my own head open and remove my brain, and I find myself fantasizing about all the ways I can do it. I want to get better, but sometimes I can't even remember what's wrong with me. I am in my room one afternoon when I look up and see Dr. Steinbridge standing in the doorway. The serious look on his face tells me he has news.

"Regina Coele has requested a visit with you," he tells me. "You don't have to see her if you don't want to."

I'm touched; his interest in my case has become more tender than the stiff, formal way our relationship started.

"I want to talk to her," I say. And it's true—I've been waiting for this for a year, wading through the days until I could come face-to-face with the answers Seth's first wife holds.

"I'll put in the approval form. I think this may really help you, Thursday. To put things into perspective and to move forward."

It's two weeks before a nurse comes to tell me that Regina is here to see me. My heart pounds as I walk to the rec room, wearing sweats and a tank top, my hair piled on top of my head in a messy knot. When I glanced at myself in the mirror before leaving my room I looked relaxed...pretty, even.

Regina is dressed smartly in a button-down shirt and dress pants, her hair pulled away from her face in a chignon. I make my way over to where she sits, smiling at some of the nurses as I pass them.

"Hello, Thursday," she says.

She eyes me up and down, a look of surprise on her face. She was expecting a mess. I am not a mess. I do yoga every day, and I eat my fruits and veggies—I've even been sleeping well. My body is healthy even if my mind is not. I slide into the seat opposite her and offer a smile. I imagine it's a peaceful smile because I'm no longer twisting and turning with apprehension.

"Hi," I say.

I've thought about Regina almost every day since coming back to Queen County. The thoughts aren't angry or mean; it's more of a distant curiosity. I am too medicated to be angry at this point.

Her nostrils flare as she watches me, both of us so carefully waiting for the other to speak.

"How have you been?" Icebreaker words!

I divert. "Why are you here?"

"I don't really know," she says. "I guess I wanted to see how you were."

"To make yourself feel better or worse?"

Her pale skin flushes, strawberry-red patches appearing on her cheeks and chin. Regina's game had a steep price; she may have meant to punish me, but Seth and Hannah will be paying for the rest of their lives.

"Both, I suppose. I never intended for things to go as far as they did…"

"Then why?" I ask.

"You ruined my life. I wanted you to pay for that."

My thoughts run ahead, spiral back and then sink into a mire of remorse and guilt. I hadn't known I was ruining her life…or had I? The reality I made up ruined everyone's lives, but Regina wasn't as innocent as Hannah had been. She'd used my weakness against me; she'd set me up.

"Well, you got what you wanted, didn't you?"

"Yes," she says finally. "I suppose I did."

I'd been so eager to blame someone for the death of my baby that I'd never questioned her story, and Regina, so eager to punish me, had never imagined the outcome it would have.

"I knew you had issues with mental health, but I had no idea the stories you made up in your own head—about the polygamy."

I look away, ashamed. Shame is a powerful reality check. Dr. Steinbridge said that it was shame that caused me to create my alternate state of reality. I was good enough for Seth to fuck, his mistress for both of his marriages, but not good enough to love.

The doctor is teaching me to cope with my shame, to deal with it. *"Make decisions you can live with…"* he says to me.

"I wanted to make you look crazy. I didn't know you *were* crazy."

I bristle at that. "You think you're not?" I shoot back. "You think it's normal to do what you did? I may be the one in here, but at least I can admit what I did. You told me he scared you to get me to further believe he was abusing Hannah. You made me believe he'd caused your miscarriage and mine. All to get me to go there that night."

She stares at me, her mouth thinning into a straight line of denial. Of course she didn't want to think she was as bad as me. I didn't want to think of myself as the other woman; denial is a twisted, perverted soul-thinner.

"You're the one who brought the gun. You shot Seth," she hisses. "I wanted you punished for ruining my life—I didn't want Seth to get hurt."

I'm enraged by the disgust I hear in her voice. I close

my eyes, willing myself not to be angry. I hear Dr. Stein-bridge's words: *"You are only responsible for yourself."*

"Yes. But you could have helped me and you chose to use me instead. You handed me the delusion."

Regina's face is a mask of self-righteousness. My in-sides ignite, fingertips tingling. Seth and Hannah did not deserve what happened to them. Seth was a cheater; he'd had an affair with me when he was married to Regina, and then, when I couldn't have his children, he'd moved on to someone else: Hannah. But he'd continued his af-fair with me even after he'd married Hannah. The rejec-tion had caused me to lose touch with reality. Seth would never walk again; my bullet passed through his spine. He would never chase their child across a park, walk her down the aisle... I am responsible for that. The pain of realiza-tion hurts my stomach.

"Were you lying when you told me that Seth was vio-lent with you? You said he pushed you against a wall..."

"No, that wasn't a lie," she says. "Seth has a temper."

My ear stings; it always stings when I think of Seth. I think of Hannah and her bruises, once again wondering if she was lying to protect him. I suppose I'll never know the truth. There's comfort in knowing he's in a wheelchair. He'd not be able to hurt a woman physically again, and his days of cheating are over.

"I'm glad we both got away from him," I say.

"No, no, no," Regina says. "This isn't a little club. I'm not like you." She laughs. "You're crazy."

And that's when I think of Robbie Clemmins and his broken brain, his skull smashed to pieces, his life altered forever. He was a different kind of broken than I am, just like Regina. Except I have been sent here to pay and she is still lying. Her laughter hurts my ears. I cover them with my palms, pressing hard, trying to block out the sound. It's the same as that day in my kitchen, Seth calling me crazy, looking at me with disgust in his eyes. I'm shaking when I rear back, slamming my head into Regina's nose. The force slams my jaw together. I bite through my bottom lip and feel the shards of a broken tooth. She screams, a hand reaching out to touch the spray of blood rushing from her nose. I jump over the table, knocking her to her back. Her head hits the floor and I see the shock and panic in her eyes— eyes wide with fear. Robbie didn't know what was happening to him when he lay on his back, his brain dying, but Regina will. I cradle her head between my hands and slam it into the floor. I can hear shouting, so much shouting.

"Help!" someone screams. *"She's going to kill her!"*

I *am* helping. I'm helping myself.

★ ★ ★ ★ ★

ACKNOWLEDGMENTS

Gratitude to my editor, Brittany Lavery, and all of her colleagues at HarperCollins. My agent, Jane, you're a soul saver. I was feeling very deflated before you found me. Miriam, your direction in helping me shine up this book was invaluable.

Rhonda Reynolds, you've called me many things over the years: wild child and creative genius. But my favorite thing you've called me is daughter-in-law. Thank you for answering all of my questions about nursing and hospitals and psych wards. I love you.

Traci Finlay, this journey started with you. Thank you for always being willing to read, help and fix a plot hole. Your direction and thoughts on this story were what pushed me to finish it. You're cooler than me, but not one to rub it in my face.

Cait Norman, the other nurse in my life. I know some of my questions scare you. You're a good sister.

The PLNs! The best girl gang.

Colleen Hoover, Lori Sabin, Serena Knautz, Erica Rusikoff, Amy Holloway, Alessandra Torre, Christine Estevez and Jaime Iwatsuru. Cindy and Jeff Capshaw. Scarlet, Ryder Atticus and Avett Rowling King—Mama loves you. Joshua, for carrying me out of every bad place and never complaining about it. You're the best human I've ever known.

THE
WIVES

TARRYN FISHER

Reader's Guide

GRAYDON
HOUSE

1. Thursday has a complicated marital situation, one that differs from typical plural marriages. Do you think you could ever share your spouse with two other partners this way?

2. How tempted would you be to find out about the other spouses, even if you'd promised not to? Would you break that promise?

3. What kinds of things does Thursday sacrifice in order to be with Seth?

4. Discuss this story in light of current news stories about women's rights and the current feminist moment.

5. How much of Thursday's online snooping do you think is justified?

6. How much sympathy did you have for Seth? Why? Did your feelings change as the story developed?

7. What did you make of the relationships between the women in this story—not just the wives, particularly Thursday and Hannah, but between Thursday and her

friends Lo and Anna? Why do you think Thursday doesn't have more female friends?

8. How do you think Thursday's relationship with her parents informed her own marriage? What do you think about Seth's relationship with his parents?

9. What did you make of the ending?

Authors often get asked about their inspiration for their books, but this is such a unique thriller! How *did* you come up with the idea for it?

My husband and I used to watch this show on Netflix about a man whose wife comes back to life five years after dying of cancer. Except she comes back to find out that he's married to her best friend, and her best friend is nine months' pregnant. I just have to tell you how stressful this show was to watch. I found myself rewriting the story in my mind, asking myself what I would do. And so for weeks I'd pound my husband relentlessly with questions. What would he do if I died and came back to life, and he was remarried? Who would he love more? Would he leave her for me? And you know what he said? "I'd just stay married to you both." Wrong answer. I wanted him to choose me, but what if he couldn't? What if it was more complicated than that? When I get that obsessed about an idea I know I have to find a way to write about it. That's all I need: a scenario, and a rush of emotion, and I have a book idea.

Thursday has a singular voice. What was it like to develop that?

It's always been my priority to listen very closely to what women have to say. For Thursday I assembled their stories into one voice. We suffer similarly.

You've published a lot of romance in the indie space, but this is your first thriller! How was it different to construct this kind of story? Did you find it easier? More difficult?

I am a character-centered writer, so I create a personality and then I drop that personality into a situation. It doesn't really matter if you're writing about how love kills people, or how other people kill people; a well-developed character will drive the plot.

Speaking of the indie space, you've had quite a lot of success in that sphere. What made you go with a traditional publisher this time, and how do these two experiences differ?

I think as an artist I'm unhinged, and so I write about unhinged people. Seven years ago "chick lit" was a thing. Women wanted to read "light" books and that's what publishers were looking for. As a result my rejection letters all said the same thing: your protagonist is too villainous, women won't relate. I laughed and then I self-published to prove them wrong. In the indie world women embraced my morally corrupt characters; they leaned in to the unreliable narrator. Meanwhile Gillian Flynn, Paula Hawkins, Caroline Kepnes and a handful of other female writers were starting the trend in traditional publishing. There wasn't space for a writer like me ten years ago, and now there is. So here I am.

What or who are some of your influences as a writer?

Stephen King. The literary majesty. The thing about Stephen King is that he could write in any genre. Any. He's an intellect; he has a hawk's eye for human nature. If he wanted to write a Pulitzer Prize—winning novel he could. He writes about the things we don't want to acknowledge in ourselves: the raw ugly *things. He writes about it with such ease it's exciting. You can't sit at better knees when learning how to write. All hail.*

How did your feminism inform the writing of this story?

There's definite allegory in Thursday's story. I'm showing you a woman breastfed into the patriarchal model. That's all of us, isn't it? Just now we're starting to make noise about it. But in order to collectively gather our female voices we had to be pushed to a breaking point. I wanted to write about a woman who was pushed too far, because we've been pushed too far.

That ending is such a shock! Did that come to you right away, or was it something that developed organically as you wrote the story?

It developed with Thursday. She was one thing at the start of the book and another by the end. Situations change us, push us into uncomfortable realities. The more I pushed Thursday, the more reckless she became.

***The Wives* is set in Seattle and Portland. You also live in the Pacific Northwest, though you grew up in Florida. What drew you to such a different climate?**

Heat and sunlight make me miserable. I'm my best in moody weather. Washington State is very expressive: the people, the landscape, the weather. I'm always inspired here.

What books are on your nightstand?

All the Ugly *and* Wonderful Things *by Bryn Greenwood,* Followers *by Megan Angelo,* Angela's Ashes *by Frank McCourt.*

What are you working on next?

It's called Crawlspace, and I'll leave it at that!